Walking Into Love

Book One: A Willow Creek Romance

Tess Merkt

THE WORSHIP WALKING CO

For Marqua.

You taught me that Jesus was real, that tulips were worth planting,

and that every person who came to your door deserved a warm welcome

and something fresh from the oven.

You loved fiercely. You loved joyfully.

You made everyone who sat on your back porch feel like they belonged there.

Chapter Twenty-Six is yours and Dad's.

So is everything in me that knows how to love well.

I am who I am because of you.

And The Overflow Cafe...the welcome, the warmth, the table always open...

that is you too.

Until we sit on that porch again.

With all my love,

your daughter

Contents

CHAPTER ONE

Coming Home

The city apartment had been too quiet for how loud her mind was.

January. Right after the holidays. The kind of week that existed only in performance. Strategy decks and revenue targets and the exhaustion of being excellent at something you had stopped believing in.

Elle had spent eleven days running from meeting to meeting, carrying a version of herself that smiled at the right moments and asked the right questions. She had not prayed anything more than a quick, functional, Lord help me, since sometime in November.

She was still carrying everything. Just not for the same reasons anymore.

Her laptop still glowed open on the coffee table, presentation decks and emails stacked like demands that never slept. The city lights blinked through the window. Outside, the world kept moving...efficient, relentless, indifferent, the way cities did.

Inside, Elle sat on her couch and stared at nothing.

On paper, she was thriving.

Account executive.

High-level meetings.

Revenue she'd learned not to think about too long, because thinking about it made her feel hollowed out in ways she couldn't explain to anyone who hadn't been there.

Leading teams.

Being the Christian woman in the room who tried to speak with integrity, to represent Jesus with her whole career.

She had believed that would be enough. For years, she had believed that. Then one January night she sat on her couch and stared at nothing and understood, very quietly, that it hadn't been.

Corporate life had a way of shrinking people into performance. The company had spoken about community and values, but over the years Elle had watched the priorities bend: profit first, people second, always a new goal, always a new reason to run faster. And Elle, who had once believed she could change the world with kindness and courage, had begun to feel like something was changing her instead.

Not into someone immoral.

Just into someone numb.

She didn't stop loving Jesus.

She just stopped making space for Him.

Her prayers had become quick and methodical. Like messages sent into heaven the way she sent emails.

"God, help me get through this."

"God, give me wisdom."

"God, please make this week lighter."

And then there was Daniel.

She didn't let herself stay on that thought long. She never did.

But tonight it surfaced anyway. The hollow that wasn't just burnout. The way she had softened herself over a year, letting his priorities quietly replace hers. Staying quieter about her faith to keep the peace. Believing that proximity to someone who used the right words was close enough to the real thing.

It hadn't been.

She hadn't lost herself all at once.

That was the part no one told you about. It didn't happen in a single dramatic moment you could point to and say, that's where it went wrong. It happened in a hundred small choices, each one so reasonable that she had made them without hesitating.

Like the dinner with his colleagues.

One of them had asked her, almost in passing, what she did on Sundays. She had said she went to church. She had watched the temperature in the room shift the way it did sometimes, that particular kind of polite silence that wasn't hostile, just done.

Daniel hadn't said anything.

And neither had she.

After, in the car, she had told herself it wasn't the right moment. That she was still getting to know his people. That there would be other opportunities.

There had been other opportunities.

She hadn't taken them either.

One dinner at a time, one quiet choice at a time, she had learned to leave that part of herself in the car. It wasn't that she stopped believing.

She still prayed.

She still read her Bible in the mornings.

She just, stopped letting it be visible. Started treating her faith the way you treated something fragile when you weren't sure the other person would handle it carefully.

It had felt like wisdom at the time.

It had felt like love.

Now, sitting alone in her apartment with the city lights blinking outside, she understood what it had actually been.

She had made herself smaller so someone else could feel larger.

And he had left anyway.

Not because she'd hidden that part of herself.

She wasn't sure that was even why.

She just knew that when he walked out, she had stood in the middle of this apartment and thought, with a clarity that was almost worse than the grief: I don't know where I went.

When he left, cleanly, for someone more aligned with his actual ambitions, Elle wasn't only heartbroken. She was ashamed of who she'd been becoming.

She pressed her fingers against her eyes.

Not tonight. She couldn't carry that tonight too.

The weight in her chest had become heavier than her whole career combined when she finally reached for her Bible. Not because she felt strong. Because she felt desperate. Like someone reaching for air.

When she opened it, it fell to Psalm 23.

As if God had placed it there Himself.

The Lord is my shepherd; I shall not want.

Elle read the line and started crying so hard she had to cover her mouth.

Because she wanted so many things.

Rest. Peace. Purpose. Clarity. Joy again. Herself again.

Jesus.

"I want," she whispered into her empty apartment, voice breaking. "I want You. I don't want to live like this anymore."

Her eyes blurred as she read on.

He makes me lie down in green pastures. He leads me beside still waters. He restores my soul.

That line, He restores my soul, undid her completely.

She pressed the Bible to her chest, tears soaking into the cover.

"Restore me," she begged. "Please. I don't know how to lead myself anymore."

And then, quietly, steadily, the truth of the Psalm reached deeper than her panic.

He leads me in paths of righteousness for His name's sake.
Paths.

Not ladders. Not hustle. Not striving.
Paths.

Something in her spirit whispered what she hadn't wanted to admit: she didn't need another promotion. She needed a new path. She needed to come home to Jesus first, and maybe home to Willow Creek too.

Not in defeat.

In obedience.

Elle wiped her face, took a trembling breath, and whispered the most honest prayer she had prayed in months:

"Okay, Lord. Lead me."

And in the stillness of her apartment, peace settled, gentle and sure, as if God had answered without words:

Come home. Walk with Me again.

** * **

Three months later, the first thing Elle noticed when she crossed the Willow Creek city limits was the color.

Not the painted kind, though there were fresh porch swings and bright front doors and spring wreaths already hanging like hope. It was the living kind. Green returning to branches. Bright dots of daffodils blooming in yards like little declarations. Tulips lining walkways in reds and pinks and yellows, their faces lifted toward a sky that couldn't decide whether to be blue or gray.

April.

Early spring in the foothills of Mount Rainier meant the mountain still wore snow like a crown, even while the town below it began to wake up.

Elle rolled down her window as she drove, letting the air pour in.

It smelled like damp earth and pine and something clean, like rain had rinsed the world overnight. Her hair lifted against her cheek. The coolness met her skin and made her breathe deeper than she had in months.

Home.

The thought landed softly. Not dramatic, not loud.

Just true.

Her hands tightened around the steering wheel, not because the road was difficult, but because her heart was full in a way she didn't know how to organize. This was supposed to feel like relief.

It did.

It also felt like stepping into a story she hadn't expected to revisit, the one where Elle Whitaker was a girl who loved Jesus simply, who sang worship without self-consciousness, who believed God's voice was something you could hear if you stayed close enough.

She swallowed, throat tightening, and whispered as if the Lord were sitting quietly beside her.

"Okay, Jesus," she said softly. "I'm here."

A pause.

Her breath fogged faintly against the inside of the window.

"Show me my purpose again."

The words hung in the air. Not as a demand.

As surrender.

And something deep in her spirit...tired, tender, but alive, shifted like it recognized the sound of a prayer it had been trying to pray for a long time.

* * *

Obedience hadn't been dramatic.

It had been deliberate.

Three months of finishing projects, handing off accounts and closing chapters she'd once thought were her whole story. Three months of wrapping up leases, boxing up life and letting go of the identity she'd built in the city.

Three months of learning to trust that God wasn't taking something from her.

He was leading her into something.

Her phone buzzed on the passenger seat. A message from her mom:

Mom: *The flowers are blooming and your dad has checked the driveway four times. We're ready when you are. Call when you're close.*

Elle smiled, warmth spilling through her chest.

She typed quickly at the next red light.

Elle: *Five minutes out. Tell Dad to stop pacing. Love you.*

She paused, then added:

Elle: *And yes, I brought coffee.*

Because some parts of her still felt like home too.

* * *

Her parents' house sat at the end of a quiet cul-de-sac, blue shutters bright against spring light. The yard looked exactly like her mother's heart... cared for and welcoming. Daffodils clustered near the walkway, and flowers lined the porch steps in tidy rows like someone had planted joy on purpose.

Elle parked.

She didn't even have time to unbuckle before the front door swung open.

Her dad appeared first. Still tall. Still strong. Still carrying that gentle pastoral steadiness even in jeans and a flannel. He didn't wave. He just walked down the steps like he couldn't wait another second.

Elle stepped out of the car and shut the door quietly.

And then her dad was there, pulling her into an embrace so firm she felt the tension in her body finally release.

For a moment, she couldn't speak.

She just held on.

His arms felt like safety. Like answered prayers she hadn't known he'd prayed.

"Hi, sweetheart," he murmured into her hair.

Elle's throat tightened. "Hi, Dad."

He pulled back, hands still on her shoulders, eyes scanning her face like he was searching for the parts she hadn't said out loud. "You okay?" he asked softly.

A layered question.

Elle nodded, then laughed, because the laugh was the only thing keeping tears from spilling in the driveway. "I'm... I'm here," she said.

Her dad's expression softened like that was the answer he'd been waiting for. "Good," he said quietly. "That's a good start."

Her mom appeared next, apron on, hands already open, moving quickly like she intended to hug the places in Elle that had been worn thin.

"Oh, Elle," she whispered.

Elle closed her eyes.

Let herself be held.

Let herself be daughter, not achiever.

Let herself be loved without earning it.

* * *

Inside, the house smelled like spring and home.

Coffee was poured. Warm rolls appeared. Her dad asked questions softly, not interrogating, just gathering pieces of her life with gentle care. Elle answered what she could. Smiled when she could. But some things still lived too deep in her chest to say out loud.

Not because she didn't trust them.

Because she was still processing them with God.

After a while, her mom pointed toward the hallway. "Your room's ready. Fresh sheets. And I..." She hesitated, then smiled. "I left your Bible on the nightstand. I thought you might want it close."

Elle's eyes stung. "Thank you," she whispered.

Upstairs, her childhood bedroom waited like time had folded itself carefully. The bed was made. A mason jar of tulips sat on the dresser, bright and alive. The bulletin board on the wall held updated photos: weddings, babies, holidays. Proof that life had moved forward while she'd been away.

Elle set her bag down slowly and stood in the middle of the room, breathing in the quiet.

Then she sat on the edge of the bed and pulled her Bible into her lap.

She rested her hands on the cover for a moment.

"I'm listening," she whispered.

When she opened it, it fell to Psalm 23 again.

As if the Lord were smiling. As if He were saying: I'm still your Shepherd. I didn't stop.

Elle read quietly, her voice barely more than breath.

He restores my soul...

Her eyes filled.

"Restore me," she whispered, not as desperation now, but as trust. "Keep restoring me."

Outside her window, a breeze stirred the flowers on the porch below, their petals nodding like agreement.

Elle exhaled slowly.

* * *

Dinner was the way Whitaker dinners had always been, unhurried and warm. Her mom moving between the kitchen and the table with the efficiency of a woman who fed people as a love language. The conversation easy and layered the way family conversation was when you had been apart long enough to have things to say.

Elle ate and listened and let herself be in it. Fully in it. Not managing the moment or performing gratitude but simply receiving the ordinary holiness of her parents' table after a long time away from it.

She had almost made it through the whole meal.

Her dad refilled her coffee, he always remembered, always without asking, and settled back into his chair with the ease of a man who had nowhere else to be.

"You know the old Daily Bread building has been sitting empty," he said. Offhandedly. "Word around town is someone signed the lease. Local, apparently. No one seems to know much yet."

Elle looked down at her mug.

Her mom looked up from her plate. "Hmm. I wonder who."

"Eli Carter's been asked to do the renovation," her dad continued. "Good man. He serves at The Gathering Place." He took a sip of his coffee. "You'll probably run into him."

She had been inside the Daily Bread building once, years ago, before it closed. She remembered the floors. Old wood, worn smooth in the paths people had walked most. The kind of floor that told you everything about how a place had been used. She had not thought much about the foundation then. You never thought about foundations. You only knew they were there by whether the thing above them held.

The table was quiet for a moment.

Elle set down her fork.

She reached into the pocket of her cardigan.

And placed a key on the table.

Just that. Just the key, worn brass and small and entirely ordinary-looking for something that had cost her months of prayer and the last remnant of the safe plan she'd had for her life.

Her mom looked at it.

Her dad looked at it.

Then they both looked at her.

"It's mine," Elle said quietly. "The lease. The Daily Bread building." She paused. "I'm going to open a coffee shop."

The silence that followed was not empty.

It was the kind of silence that a room held when something true had just been said in it, something that required space before any words could follow.

Her mom's hand moved to her mouth.

Her dad did not move at all. He looked at the key on the table between them and then at his daughter, and something moved through his expression that she recognized: not surprise, exactly. Something closer to recognition. As if a prayer he had been praying quietly in a back room of his heart had just walked through the front door.

"I've been planning it for three months," Elle said. The words came more steadily now that they were out. "I didn't want to say anything until I was sure. Until it felt less like a dream and more like a beginning." She looked at the key. "I think it's a beginning."

"Oh, sweetheart," her mom whispered.

"The whole town will be in there," her dad said quietly. Not a question. A recognition.

"That's the idea," Elle said. "A place where people can come and stay as long as they need to. Good coffee. The right atmosphere." She paused. "Community."

Her mom reached across the table and covered Elle's hand with both of hers. She didn't say anything else. She didn't need to. It was the Whitaker way, words for what needed words, touch for what words couldn't carry.

Her dad was quiet for another moment. He looked at the key. He looked at Elle. Then he pushed back his chair, reached across the table, and picked up the key, not to examine it, but the way you picked something up when you wanted to hold it with intention.

He folded it into his hand.

And then he bowed his head.

"Lord," he said, voice low and certain, the voice he used when he meant every word completely. "You know my girl. You have known her since before she knew herself. You brought her home on paths she couldn't see from where she was standing." A pause. The kitchen clock ticked softly. "We ask You to go before her into that building. To make it everything You see when You look at it. To fill it with the people who need to walk through that door." His voice thickened slightly, the way it did when he was moved and choosing not to hide it. "And Lord, thank You. For leading her. For not letting her stay lost. Thank You that she listened."

The amen settled over the table like a warm hand.

Elle's eyes were full.

She had not cried when she signed the lease. She had not cried when she gave notice at her job or turned in her parking pass or boxed up ten years of her corporate life into the back of her car.

She cried now.

Because her father had prayed over her the way he had prayed over her whole life.

Specifically, quietly, without requiring credit. Some prayers landed differently when you had been away long enough to understand what it had cost the person to keep praying them.

Her dad reached across and set the key back in front of her.

"Nobody outside this table needs to know yet," he said simply. "Not until you're ready."

Elle nodded. She wrapped her hand around the key and held it.

"Thank you," she managed.

Her dad smiled, the smile he had for moments when God had done something he had been praying about and he was choosing not to make a production of it. "Don't thank me," he said. "You did the hard part."

"Obedience is the hard part," her mom said softly. "And you did it."

They sat together at the table for a long time after that, the three of them, the key between them and the spring evening settling outside the windows and the coffee growing cold in a way that nobody minded.

* * *

That night, as the spring sky dimmed and the house settled into quiet, Elle lay beneath the familiar quilt and listened to the sounds of home: her mother moving around downstairs, her father's low voice in the living room, the creak of the house that held so many memories.

She folded her hands over her chest.

The key was on the nightstand beside her Bible.

She looked at them together for a moment, the Word that had led her here and the small brass promise of what here was becoming.

"Jesus," she whispered into the dark, "thank You for bringing me home."

A pause.

Then: "Show me my purpose again."

Peace settled over her like a promise.

The key was real.

And that, just that, was enough to begin.

Chapter Two

The Gathering Place

Sunday morning in Willow Creek felt like a fresh start you could breathe in.

The air was cool but not sharp. Early April had a chill that carried the promise of warmth later. Somewhere nearby, birds argued cheerfully in the trees. A thin layer of clouds softened the sunlight, and beyond the rooftops, Mount Rainier stood steady, watching over the town like it always had.

Elle stepped out onto her parents' porch with her travel mug in hand, her Bible tucked under her arm, and a feeling of renewed hope.

She paused at the top step.

Across the yard, daffodils nodded in the breeze like they'd been planted on purpose as a reminder: new things come back to life.

Elle breathed in slowly.

Then she whispered, as if she and Jesus were sharing a secret in the spring air, "First Sunday back."

Her heart beat a little faster. Not out of fear, but out of tenderness. Worship had once been her language. Church had once been her rhythm. And yet returning felt like walking into a place she loved after too much time away, unsure if she still belonged.

She held her mug with both hands, letting the warmth steady her fingers.

"Meet me there," she prayed quietly. "I need You."

Not because she had it all together. Because she didn't.

A peace settled over her. Not fireworks, not a voice. Just the gentle certainty that God wasn't waiting with crossed arms.

He was waiting with open hands.

Elle stepped off the porch and began walking.

* * *

The Gathering Place sat on the edge of downtown Willow Creek, simple and welcoming. Its white exterior looked brighter against the gray spring sky, and the wooden doors were propped open like an invitation instead of an entrance.

A chalkboard sign near the steps read:

WELCOME HOME. COME AS YOU ARE.

Elle stopped for a second, her throat tightening.

Welcome home.

She hadn't realized how badly she needed those words until she saw them.

She climbed the steps and stepped inside.

Warmth met her immediately, heat and laughter and the scent of coffee drifting through the lobby. People stood in small circles, talking easily. Someone hugged someone like it was normal. Children wove between legs like they belonged everywhere at once.

Elle stood just inside the doorway and let it wash over her.

This wasn't polished.

It was alive.

A few faces turned toward her. Curious, friendly. Then someone's expression shifted from polite recognition to surprise.

"Elle?"

Elle turned.

Mara stood a few feet away, eyes wide with joy like she couldn't believe what she was seeing.

For a heartbeat, they simply stared.

Then Mara crossed the space quickly and pulled Elle into a hug that felt like a door opening.

"You're really here," Mara said, voice thick.

Elle laughed softly into her shoulder. "I'm really here."

Mara pulled back, hands still holding Elle's arms like she needed proof. "Why didn't you tell me this was happening?"

Elle smiled. "I think I needed to walk in quietly."

Mara's expression softened, understanding settling into her eyes. "Yeah," she said gently. "I get that."

Then she smiled again, brighter. "Well. You're not invisible here. Come on."

Elle followed as Mara guided her toward the sanctuary doors.

"You picked a good Sunday," Mara said. "Pastor Nathan's message last week... I don't know. It's been sitting heavy on people, in a good way."

Elle nodded, her heart already feeling raw in the safest way.

As they moved through the lobby, Mara greeted people easily. Introductions happened quickly. Names and smiles and "So good to meet you!" But it wasn't overwhelming. It was warmth without pressure.

Then, before Elle could take another step.

"ELLE!"

Grace barreled toward her like a small joyful hurricane.

Elle braced instinctively and laughed as her younger sister wrapped her in a hug that nearly lifted her off the floor.

"You're here," Grace said, breathless. "You're really here. I told Mom if this was a prank I would need therapy and pancakes."

Elle hugged her back tightly. "I'm here for real."

Grace pulled back, eyes already glossy. "Okay, I'm not crying. I'm just having a normal human reaction to my sister returning from corporate captivity."

Elle blinked. "Corporate captivity?"

Grace nodded solemnly. "It's a thing."

Mara snorted softly.

Elle laughed, and the laughter felt like air returning to her lungs.

Grace grabbed Elle's hand like she might vanish if she let go. "Come on. Sit with us. I saved you a spot. Dad and mom saved you a spot. Apparently, God saved you a spot."

Elle swallowed hard.

"Okay," she whispered.

They stepped into the sanctuary.

* * *

The room glowed softly, lights dimmed just enough to feel peaceful. Tall windows lined the side walls, and outside them the spring sky sat pale and bright. On stage, the worship team prepared quietly, checking instruments, adjusting microphones.

A low ambient hum filled the room like a gentle invitation.

Elle slid into the seat between Mara and Grace, her heart beating fast and slow at the same time. People around them chatted in warm murmurs, but the room held an underlying expectation. Like everyone came believing God could meet them.

Then the worship leader stepped forward.

"Good morning, church," she said warmly. "If you walked in today carrying anything heavy... you don't have to carry it alone."

Elle's throat tightened immediately.

The first chord rang out. Soft keys, gentle guitar.

Worship began like a river starting small.

Then it rose.

Voices joined. Hands lifted. The room shifted, not emotionally manipulated, not forced. Just surrendered.

Elle closed her eyes.

At first, she didn't sing.

She listened.

The sound of a congregation worshiping together did something to her spirit that she couldn't explain to people who hadn't experienced it. It wasn't performance.

It was hunger.

It was faith.

It was a room full of people saying with their voices what their hearts sometimes struggled to believe:

God is here.

Elle's eyes stung.

She let the first tear fall without fighting it.

She sang quietly on the second verse, her voice soft but steady.

And the moment her voice joined the room, something inside her cracked open. Not in pain, but in relief.

Like she'd been holding her breath for three months.

Like she'd been trying to be strong alone.

Like her soul recognized home.

Her hands lifted slightly, palms open in front of her. Not high, not dramatic. Just honest.

Jesus, she prayed between lyrics, *I'm here. I'm back. I don't even know how to explain what You rescued me from but thank You.*

The music grew, the room filling with harmony. The worship leader's voice rose, pure, strong, anchored in Scripture and presence.

Elle felt goosebumps lift on her arms.

Not because of volume.

Because of God.

The next song slowed, quieter, more intimate. The kind of song that asked you not to sing loudly but to surrender deeply.

Elle's tears came freely now.

She didn't care who saw.

Grace's hand touched her back gently, a sisterly reminder: you're safe.

Mara leaned closer, whispering, "Let Him meet you."

And He did.

In the stillness, Elle felt something settle. A peace that didn't come from circumstances changing, but from Christ drawing near.

Her mind flashed to Psalm 23.

He restores my soul...

Her breath shook.

"Restore me," she whispered again, almost without thinking. "Restore me."

And it was as if the Lord answered. Not with words, but with presence.

I'm here.

Elle exhaled, her shoulders lowering for the first time in what felt like years.

* * *

Near the back of the sanctuary, Eli Carter stood at the sound booth.

He'd arrived early, like he always did. Checked the cables. Balanced the monitors. Made sure the microphones were clean and the transitions smooth. It was quiet work. Invisible work. He'd chosen it for that reason, though he didn't examine that reason too often.

There were things about himself he kept at the sound booth level, functional, steady, not on display.

As worship filled the room, he scanned the congregation the way he always did, watching levels, reading the room with the kind of attention that looked detached but wasn't.

That's when he noticed her.

Three rows back. Left side. Sitting beside Mara.

He didn't recognize her. But something made him pause.

Not because she was drawing attention. Because she wasn't. She was worshiping like the room had emptied out and it was just her and God left standing in it. Eyes closed. Tears slipping down her cheeks quietly. Hands lifted slightly, palms open. Not for show. Like someone releasing weight they'd carried too long in silence.

Her lips moved between lyrics, too quiet to hear from here.

Eli felt something tighten in his chest. Not attraction. Not quite curiosity.

Something older and harder to name. The kind of recognition that came from having stood in a similar place once, surrender that looked like defeat from the outside and felt like the first honest breath in months from the inside.

He'd been there.

He adjusted the fade, steady and careful.

When he glanced back up, she was still worshiping. Still present. Still not performing.

A thought passed through him, quiet as a whisper:

Someone just came home.

He didn't know who she was. He didn't need to. The moment belonged to her and to God.

But he didn't forget her face.

He wasn't sure he was supposed to.

* * *

After worship, Pastor Nathan stepped forward and opened his Bible.

His voice was warm and steady. The kind that didn't entertain so much as shepherd.

He spoke about foundations. About building on Christ. About the difference between a life constructed on achievement and a life constructed on obedience. He paused at one point and said something that landed quietly in Elle's chest like a stone dropped in still water:

"The strongest foundations aren't built in the good seasons. They're built in the ones where you had no choice but to trust."

Elle stared at her hands.

She thought of January. Of the apartment. Of the Bible falling open.

Of Daniel, and who she'd let herself become.

Of the lease with her name on it, sitting in a building she hadn't walked into for years.

The Lord wasn't accusing her.

He was inviting her.

She exhaled slowly and let the sermon continue washing over her.

When the service ended, people lingered again...talking, laughing, hugging. Grace grabbed Elle's arm immediately. "You're not leaving," she said. "You're going to say hi to people. You are going to let yourself be known."

Elle laughed softly. "Okay."

Mara's smile warmed. "Welcome back to Willow Creek."

Elle breathed in slowly, looking around the lobby at the faces, the warmth, the ordinary holy joy.

And she felt it again.

Peace.

But underneath the peace, something else had stirred too. Something quieter, more specific. Like a corner of her heart that had been boarded up for a long time had just let a little light in.

She wasn't sure what to do with that yet.

She tucked it away carefully, the way you carry something fragile when you're still learning to trust your own hands.

CHAPTER THREE

Hidden In Plain Site

Church never emptied quickly in Willow Creek.

People lingered in the lobby long after the final amen, as if leaving too fast might undo whatever God had just done.

Elle stood near the coffee table with Grace on one side and Mara on the other, holding a paper cup she hadn't actually sipped. She kept taking in the room. Faces, laughter, gentle conversations about sermon notes and lunch plans.

The daffodils planted outside the church windows were visible through the glass, bright yellow against green grass. April sunlight pushed its way through thin clouds, lighting everything in that soft Northwest way that felt hopeful without being loud.

"You cannot disappear upstairs to your childhood bedroom," Grace announced firmly, breaking into Elle's thoughts. "It's illegal. I checked."

Elle smiled. "You checked?"

"Yes. It's in the Willow Creek Sister Code. Article four. 'Returning siblings must participate in public reentry.'"

Mara laughed softly. "Translation: we're going to lunch."

Grace pointed toward downtown. "Diner. Immediately."

Elle hesitated for only a second.

Three months ago, before that Psalm 23 night, she wouldn't have said yes so easily. She would have calculated her calendar. Checked her phone. Mentally prepared for what she might need to accomplish afterward.

Now?

She just nodded. "Okay."

Grace grinned triumphantly.

As they gathered their things, Elle noticed her father near the sanctuary doors, talking quietly with a man she didn't recognize. Tall, broad-shouldered, listening more than speaking. Her dad placed a hand briefly on the man's shoulder the way he did when a conversation mattered.

Elle almost asked Grace who it was.

But Grace was already pulling her toward the exit, and the moment passed.

* * *

Downtown Willow Creek in April looked like the town had decided to stretch after a long winter.

Tulips lined storefront windows. Hanging baskets were just beginning to show signs of life. The air carried that clean scent of damp pavement and budding trees.

They walked slowly.

Not because they had to.

Because no one was in a hurry.

Grace waved at someone across the street. Mara stopped briefly to ask a woman about her mom's knee surgery. Conversations happened naturally, spilling into sidewalks and doorways like they'd always belonged there.

Elle felt something loosen in her chest.

This was what she'd missed.

Not noise.

Connection.

Community.

They reached the diner, a corner building with wide windows and a bell that chimed when the door opened. The hostess smiled immediately.

"Same booth?" she asked Mara.

Mara nodded. "If it's free."

"It's free for you," the hostess replied warmly.

Grace leaned toward Elle as they followed her. "See? Celebrity status."

They slid into the booth near the window. Sunlight filtered in gently, warming the table.

Menus were barely glanced at.

* * *

"So," Grace said, elbows on the table, chin in her hands. "Start talking."

Elle laughed. "That's vague."

Grace narrowed her eyes. "You know what I mean."

Mara's voice was softer. "Only what you're ready to share."

That word again.

Ready.

Elle traced her fingertip along the edge of her water glass.

"I was doing well," she began slowly. "Career-wise."

Grace nodded. "Obviously."

Elle exhaled. "But I started to realize something. The company kept saying it was about people. But the longer I was there, the more it became about profit. Growth. Performance. And I kept trying to be the person who held the line. Who led with integrity. Who showed that you could love Jesus and still thrive in corporate America."

Grace leaned back slightly. "That sounds like you."

"It was," Elle admitted. "But it started to cost more than I realized."

Her voice lowered.

"I was exhausted. Not physically. Spiritually."

Silence settled across the table.

"I didn't stop believing," Elle added quickly. "I didn't walk away from God. I just drifted. I got busy enough that I stopped listening."

Mara reached across the table and rested her hand gently over Elle's. "That happens."

Elle swallowed.

"It wasn't one big breakdown," she said. "It was a thousand small compromises with rest. With prayer. With abiding."

Grace didn't joke this time.

She simply listened.

"And then January hit," Elle continued quietly. "Post-holiday. The busiest season. I was carrying everything."

She paused, the memory surfacing with more texture than she expected.

It wasn't just the work she'd been carrying. She knew that now. She'd been carrying the weight of a version of herself she didn't recognize anymore. Someone who had gone quiet in all the wrong ways to keep a peace that was never real.

She didn't say that part out loud.

Not yet.

"I went home one night and sat on my couch and stared at nothing," she continued. "And I reached for my Bible. When I opened it, it fell to Psalm 23."

Grace blinked. "Psalm 23?"

Elle nodded. "'He restores my soul.'" Her voice trembled just slightly. "I didn't even realize how much I needed restoration until I read that."

Mara's eyes glistened.

Grace reached across and squeezed Elle's hand. "And He did."

Elle nodded slowly. "He did."

The waitress interrupted gently to take their orders: pancakes, coffee, eggs. And when she left, the table felt lighter somehow.

Not because the story was small.

Because it had been spoken.

* * *

After breakfast, they wandered again, stepping back into the spring air.

They walked without aim until Grace slowed suddenly.

"Wait."

Elle followed her gaze.

A storefront stood ahead with paper covering the windows. A simple sign taped to the door read:

THE OVERFLOW CAFE

Coming Soon.

Nothing else.

No details.

No explanation.

Just possibility.

Grace tilted her head. "I've heard people talking about this place."

Mara nodded. "Nobody knows much. It's been quiet."

Grace stepped closer to the door, trying to peek through the paper. "Well, I love the name."

Elle stood still.

The words landed somewhere deep.

Overflow.

Her hand slipped into her coat pocket almost unconsciously. Her fingers wrapped around her keys. Cold metal. Solid. Real.

She studied the sign for a moment, her thumb pressing against the edge of the key in her pocket.

Grace tried the door handle. Locked.

"Figures," Grace said, stepping back with a grin. "Very mysterious."

Mara smiled. "Willow Creek could use something new."

Elle lifted her eyes to the sign one more time.

Coming Soon.

A warmth spread through her chest, but underneath it something else flickered too. Not fear exactly. More like the feeling of standing at the edge of something wide and not being able to see the other side.

She thought of what her father had said over dinner. Eli Carter. Good man. Solid faith. She'd nodded and looked down at her coffee cup and said nothing.

Not yet, she told herself. Not today.

She turned back toward her sister and friend as they resumed walking, their laughter filling the street.

She would have to go in eventually.

She would have to introduce herself to the man her father trusted.

She would have to let someone else's hands touch the thing she'd only held in prayer.

The thought made her chest pull in a way she didn't entirely understand.

She fell into step beside Grace and Mara and let the spring air carry the afternoon forward.

One day at a time.

That was enough.

CHAPTER FOUR

New Circles

By Wednesday morning, Willow Creek had already begun to feel less like a place Elle was visiting and more like a place she was slowly stepping back into.

Spring sunlight slipped through the kitchen windows as she stood at the counter, wrapping both hands around a warm mug of coffee. Outside, the last traces of morning chill clung to the air, but the promise of a brighter afternoon lingered in the soft light stretching across the yard.

Her mother moved around the kitchen humming quietly, packing a lunch for Elle's dad the way she had for decades. The simple rhythm of it settled something in Elle's chest.

No conference calls.

No urgent emails.

No performance metrics waiting to be hit before noon.

Just morning.

"Any plans today?" her mom asked gently.

Elle took a slow sip of coffee and leaned against the counter, letting the warmth settle into her hands. "Nothing urgent," she said with a small smile. "I think I'm still figuring out what normal looks like here again."

Her mom's expression softened. "That's allowed, you know. You don't have to have everything mapped out this week."

Elle let out a quiet breath. "That's going to take some getting used to."

Her mom set down the lunch container she was packing and stepped closer. "This season doesn't have to be rushed," she said gently. "You just got here."

Elle nodded slowly, letting the words land.

Before she could respond, footsteps sounded on the stairs and Grace appeared, already dressed, already energetic, already mid-thought.

"Okay," Grace announced, grabbing an apple from the counter. "You're coming tonight."

Elle blinked. "Where?"

"Midweek women's group," Grace said, like this had already been decided. "Mara's leading discussion. Paisley's bringing snacks. Janelle's bringing something healthy that none of us will eat but we'll all pretend to appreciate."

Their mom gave her a look. "Grace."

Grace shrugged. "What? I'm being honest."

Elle laughed softly, the sound lighter than it had been in days.

Grace turned back to her. "You need people, Elle. And they're really good people. Also, they already know you exist and are excited."

That tugged gently at Elle's heart. Not pressure. Just invitation.

"I'd like that," she said quietly.

Grace grinned. "Perfect. Wear something comfortable. And by comfortable I mean emotionally prepared to be loved."

Elle shook her head, smiling.

Maybe she was ready for that.

* * *

Her dad came in from the garage just before noon, setting his keys on the hook by the door with the quiet ease of a man completely at home in his own life.

Elle was still at the kitchen table, her notebook open, her coffee long cold.

He glanced at the notebook, then at her. "Working?"

"Thinking," she said. "Same thing, lately."

He smiled and pulled out the chair across from her. This was how her dad operated. He didn't force conversations. He simply made himself available and waited for the door to open on its own.

Elle closed her notebook.

"I've been thinking about the cafe," she said. "The timeline. What needs to happen first."

Her dad nodded slowly. "Eli stopped by the church office this morning, actually. We talked through a few things."

Elle looked up. "You talked to him about the cafe?"

"Just logistics," her dad said, his tone easy. "He wanted to know if I had any of the original building records. The old Daily Bread space has had a few owners over the years. He likes to know what he's working with before he starts. Says it's how his dad taught him." He paused. "His father was a carpenter too. Built things all over eastern Washington. Eli grew up working beside him."

Something about that settled quietly in Elle's chest.

Built things beside his father.

She thought of the old building on Main Street, brick and weathered, windows papered from the inside. The way old things held stories in their grain.

"Is he good?" she asked. "I mean, really good. Not just reliable. Does he care about the work?"

Her dad considered that with the seriousness it deserved. "He doesn't cut corners," he said finally. "I've watched him. He builds things to last. And he understands that some spaces carry more weight than just square footage."

Elle was quiet for a moment.

"He's going to want to meet with you soon," her dad continued. "Go over the vision before he draws up plans. He won't build something without understanding the why behind it."

Elle nodded.

"He won't build something without understanding the why."

She wrote that in her notebook after her dad stood and moved toward the kitchen.

She wasn't sure if she was writing about Eli or about herself.

* * *

The Gathering Place felt different midweek.

Quieter. Softer. The sanctuary lights were dim, but smaller rooms off the main hall glowed warmly. The air held the faint scent of coffee and whatever candle someone had lit near the welcome table.

Elle followed Grace down a short hallway toward a cozy living-room-style space where a few women already sat in a loose circle. Bibles open, drinks in hand, conversation flowing easily.

Mara looked up first.

Her face lit instantly. "Elle!"

She stood and crossed the room, pulling Elle into a hug that felt like she'd been expecting her all day.

"I'm so glad you came," Mara said warmly.

"Me too," Elle admitted.

Grace stepped aside with a satisfied nod, like her mission had been accomplished.

"Everyone," Mara said gently, turning back to the group, "this is Elle. She just moved back home."

A woman with bright eyes and a warm smile leaned forward immediately. "Finally," she said. "We've heard about you for years."

Elle laughed softly. "I hope only good things."

"Oh, all good," the woman assured her. "I'm Paisley."

Paisley's energy felt like sunshine. Open, welcoming, effortless. She reached out and squeezed Elle's hand like they were already friends.

Next to her sat a quieter woman with kind eyes and a calm presence that seemed to settle the room without effort.

"I'm Janelle," she said gently. "It's really good to meet you."

There was something deeply peaceful about her voice, like someone who prayed often and listened even more.

Elle felt her shoulders lower without realizing they'd been tight.

They made space for her easily, shifting chairs and passing her a warm mug of tea someone had brought extra.

No interrogation.

No spotlight.

Just welcome.

Mara opened their study with a simple prayer, her words unpolished and sincere. "Lord, thank You for bringing us together tonight. Thank You for new seasons and old friendships and the way You always know what we need before we ask."

Elle closed her eyes.

New seasons.

The phrase landed softly.

As the discussion unfolded, Scripture and reflections and gentle laughter woven between honest moments, Elle found herself speaking more than she expected. Not everything. Not all at once. But enough.

Enough to feel seen.

Paisley shared a story about her work at the children's hospital that made everyone laugh and tear up in the same breath. Janelle spoke quietly about trusting God in waiting seasons. Mara guided the conversation with steady wisdom that felt grounded in lived experience, not just knowledge.

And Grace kept everyone balanced with humor and heart.

At one point, as conversation shifted toward prayer requests, Mara glanced at Elle gently. "Anything we can be praying for as you settle back in?"

The room didn't lean forward. No one stared.

They just waited.

Elle swallowed.

"I think..." She paused, choosing honesty without oversharing. "I think I'm in a rebuilding season. Spiritually. Personally. I just want to follow where God leads next."

"I know that season," Janelle said quietly.

Mara reached over and squeezed Elle's hand once. "We'll pray for clarity. And peace while you're waiting."

Something in Elle's chest loosened.

Not because answers had come.

Because she wasn't carrying the questions alone anymore.

* * *

Later, as chairs shifted and people gathered their things, Paisley turned to Elle with an easy smile. "A few of us usually grab coffee or walk the trail on Saturdays. You should come."

Grace nodded enthusiastically. "Yes. She should."

Elle smiled, warmth spreading through her chest. "I'd like that."

They said their goodbyes slowly, the way people do when leaving feels less like an ending and more like continuation.

Outside, the evening air held that early-spring coolness again, soft and fresh. The sky lingered in dusky blue, and the first stars were beginning to show faintly above the outline of the mountain.

Grace nudged her as they walked to the car. "Told you."

Elle glanced over. "Told me what?"

"That you needed people."

Elle looked back at the church building for a moment. The warm lights glowing through windows. The sense of quiet life inside.

"Yeah," she said softly. "You were right."

They drove home mostly in comfortable silence, the kind that didn't need filling.

Elle rested her forehead lightly against the cool window and watched the dark shapes of trees pass by.

She thought about what her dad had said.

He won't build something without understanding the why.

She thought about Eli Carter, a man she hadn't met yet, who had grown up building things beside his father, who checked the bones of old spaces before he touched them, who wanted to know the why.

She thought about the key still sitting on her dresser.

Tomorrow, she would call him.

She would set up a meeting.

She would walk into the old bakery and say out loud, to another person, what she had only said so far to God and her parents.

The thought sent a small, nervous flutter through her chest.

Not because she doubted the calling.

Because saying it out loud to a stranger would make it real in a new way.

And the last time she'd let someone into something that mattered deeply to her, she had walked away smaller than when she started.

She pressed her fingers against the cold window glass.

That was then, she told herself.

This is different.

She almost believed it.

CHAPTER FIVE

Daily Bread

I t began with rain.

Not a light mist or a passing drizzle, but steady, soaking spring rain that washed the streets of Willow Creek clean and turned the sidewalks slick with reflection.

Elle sat in her car for a moment, windshield wipers sweeping rhythmically back and forth, watching water gather in thin rivers along the curb.

April in Washington had a way of doing this. Rinsing the world before it fully bloomed.

She wrapped her fingers around the small brass key resting in her palm and let her forehead fall gently against the steering wheel.

"Okay, Lord," she whispered. "If this is from You...let it be more than a business."

Rain tapped against the roof like a quiet amen.

She had called Eli's number that morning. No answer. She'd left a brief message, her voice steadier than she felt, asking him to meet her at the building when he had a chance. He hadn't called back yet.

She told herself that was fine.

She came anyway.

She stepped out of the car and pulled her coat tighter around her shoulders, the scent of wet pavement and fresh earth rising around her. Across the street, the mountain was barely visible through the gray, but it stood there all the same. Steady, unseen but sure.

The building waited.

Brick.

Weathered.

Windows papered from the inside.

And above the doorway, faint but unmistakable beneath years of wear, painted directly onto the brick in faded cream letters:

Daily Bread Bakery

Est. 1952

Elle stopped in the rain.

Her breath caught.

Daily Bread.

The words felt almost too perfect.

She stepped closer, rain dampening her hair as she traced the old lettering with her eyes.

"Give us this day our daily bread," she murmured softly.

Provision.

Faithfulness.

Enough.

For decades, this place had fed the town. Families had walked through these doors. Children had pressed their hands to these windows. Generations had carried warm loaves home from this very sidewalk.

And now...

Her fingers tightened around the key.

Overflow.

She closed her eyes briefly.

"You don't waste history, Lord," she whispered. "You build on it."

Rain slid down her cheeks, cool and cleansing, and she laughed softly at the realization that she couldn't tell if the moisture on her face was rain or tears.

Maybe both.

She stepped under the small awning, unlocked the door, and paused.

This was it.

The first step into something she had only seen in prayer.

"Use it," she whispered, hand resting on the door handle. "Use me."

Then she turned the key.

* * *

She had been here once before, years ago. She remembered the floors. But memory hadn't prepared her for what it felt like to be here now, with the key in her hand and the calling in her chest.

The door opened with a soft groan.

Air rushed past her. Cool, dusty, carrying the faint scent of flour long settled into wood.

The sound of rain shifted as she stepped inside, now muffled against brick and glass.

The space was empty.

But not lifeless.

Light filtered through the tall front windows, softened by gray skies. Dust floated in the air like suspended memory. The wooden floors were worn smooth in places, slightly uneven with age.

Elle stepped further in, her footsteps echoing gently.

At the back of the room stood the remains of what must have been the main counter. Old wood scarred but sturdy. Behind it, shelves still lined the wall.

She walked slowly, reverently, like she'd stepped into something sacred.

Her throat tightened.

This wasn't just square footage.

It was a story.

Her hand brushed the top of the old counter, and a faint trace of flour dust lifted into the air.

"I wonder how many loaves of bread were shaped here," she whispered.

Rain drummed softly against the windows.

Near the far wall, something caught her eye.

A wooden bread board leaned against the base of a cabinet, worn smooth from years of use. Beside it, a small brass bell rested on the shelf above the counter. And tucked behind it, almost forgotten, hung a faded wooden sign:

Fresh Every Morning

Elle reached for the bread board first.

It was heavier than she expected. Solid. Scarred with knife marks and years of kneading.

She ran her fingers across its surface and felt tears rise again.

Daily bread.

Fresh every morning.

Provision.

Faithfulness.

And suddenly, standing alone in the quiet echo of the old bakery while rain washed the world outside, Elle felt the weight of the calling settle fully into her chest.

She set the bread board gently on the counter and stepped into the center of the room.

Then she did the only thing that felt right.

She knelt.

Right there on the old wooden floor, knees pressing into history.

"Jesus," she whispered, hands resting open on her thighs. "This space has fed people for seventy years. Let it feed them again."

Her voice trembled, but she didn't stop.

"Not just coffee. Not just conversation. Let it feed their souls. Let this place be safe. Let it be full of prayer. Let it be full of worship. Let weary people walk in and feel You before they understand why."

Rain thundered briefly against the windows, louder for a moment.

She smiled through tears.

* * *

She had thought about the name for weeks before it came.

Not in a brainstorm session. Not on a whiteboard. It had come the way the most important things came to her lately, in stillness, in surrender, in the middle of a psalm she'd read on the worst night of her year.

My cup overflows.

She had laughed softly through tears when she read it that January night, Bible pressed against her chest.

"I don't feel like I'm overflowing," she had whispered.

But maybe that was the point.

God restores.

Then He fills.

Then He overflows.

The name hadn't come as a brand. It had come as a promise.

Standing now inside the Daily Bread Bakery, rain washing the world clean outside, Elle let the vision rise without forcing it.

Long tables filled with conversation. Handwritten prayers covering a wall, some of them tearstained, some of them triumphant, all of them honest. Worship music playing softly in the background, low enough that you could think but present enough that you couldn't ignore it.

Students studying. Mothers gathering. Strangers becoming friends.

And in one corner, half-hidden by a window, a woman sitting alone with her coat still on and her hands wrapped around a cup she wasn't drinking. Looking like she'd come in out of more than just the rain.

That image stopped Elle cold.

She hadn't conjured it consciously. It had simply appeared, specific and quiet, like a face she recognized without knowing why.

That woman needed to be here.

Whatever it cost to build this place, whatever it required, it needed to exist for her.

The thought came clearly and she opened her eyes, heart pounding softly.

"Yes," she breathed.

She sat back on her heels and reached for her Bible, which she'd set on the old counter when she first walked in. She hadn't planned to open it here. She'd brought it the way she brought it everywhere now, less as a habit and more as a lifeline.

It fell open near the middle of John.

She almost turned past it. Her eyes were still blurry.

Then a line caught her.

Jesus speaking.

"I am the bread of life. Whoever comes to me will never go hungry, and whoever believes in me will never be thirsty."

Elle went completely still.

She read it again.

Slower.

The bread of life.

Daily Bread Bakery.

The Overflow Cafe.

She pressed her hand flat over the page as if she needed to hold it down.

For years, this building had fed people bread. Good bread. Faithful bread. Fresh every morning, just like the sign said. And it had mattered, of course it had mattered, every loaf carried home, every family fed, every child who pressed their face against that window.

But Jesus had said it first.

He was the bread.

The thing people had always been hungry for without knowing it.

Not the coffee. Not the warm room. Not even the community, as beautiful as that was.

Him.

She felt her breath go shallow.

This place hadn't just held a bakery.

She sat with her hand flat on the page for a long time.

"You planned this," she whispered, half laughing, half undone. "You planned this before I did."

Rain hit the windows.

She bowed her head over the open Bible and stayed there for a long moment, not praying in words, just breathing, just present, just held.

When she finally lifted her head, something had shifted.

The name wasn't just hopeful anymore.

It was from Him, from His Word.

The Overflow Cafe wasn't just a place where cups would be filled.

It was a place where the Bread of Life would be present.

That changed what she was building.

It changed who she needed to be while she built it.

She stood slowly, wiping her cheeks.

"Overflow," she whispered. "Not just enough. More than enough."

* * *

Then reality returned gently.

The contractor.

She checked her phone.

No messages.

No call.

She glanced at the time.

Ten minutes passed.

Then twenty.

Rain continued to fall, steady and cleansing.

Elle felt the flicker of disappointment rise. Not anger, not panic. Just that familiar tightening she'd known in corporate life when something didn't go according to plan. The old instinct to fire off an email, to follow up, to manage.

She noticed it the way she was learning to notice things now.

Named it.

Set it down.

She exhaled slowly.

She picked up the small brass bell from the shelf and tapped it lightly.

It gave a soft, clear chime. The sound echoed gently through the empty space.

Fresh every morning.

She smiled.

Maybe he had a reason. Maybe the timing wasn't hers to manage.

Her dad had told her Eli didn't cut corners and didn't rush. A man like that probably didn't operate on someone else's urgency either.

She placed the bread board carefully against the wall and set the bell back on the shelf.

Then she locked the door behind her and stepped back into the rain.

Water soaked through her coat almost instantly, but she didn't rush to her car.

Instead, she lifted her face toward the gray sky and let the rain wash over her.

Old things washed away.

New things beginning.

"Lead me," she whispered.

* * *

Eli Carter had listened to the voicemail twice.

Standing in the parking lot of the hardware store, rain coming down steady on his shoulders, he had played it again just to be sure.

Her voice was calm. Professional. The kind of voice that had learned to sound steady even when something underneath it wasn't.

He recognized that.

He called back immediately. No answer.

He drove to the building anyway, pulling up just as a woman in a dark coat was stepping back into the rain from under the awning. She lifted her face toward the sky for a moment, eyes closed, rain running down her cheeks, and she looked, he thought, less like someone who was disappointed and more like someone practicing something.

He almost called out.

But she turned and walked to her car before he could, and something about the moment felt too complete to interrupt.

He sat in his truck and watched her drive away.

Then he got out, walked to the door, and tried the handle.

Locked.

He stood under the awning and looked up at the faded lettering above the door.

Daily Bread Bakery.

He'd passed this building a hundred times. Known it was sitting empty. Known someone had finally signed the lease.

He had done a walk-through recently, just to read the bones of the place before committing to a plan. He hadn't touched anything. Hadn't moved a single piece of what was left inside. That wasn't how his father had taught him to approach old buildings.

You looked first. You listened. Then you decided what needed to stay and what needed to go.

He hadn't known until his conversation with Pastor Whitaker that the someone was the pastor's daughter.

He hadn't known until he heard her voicemail that her voice would sound like that.

Her number was still on his screen from the missed call.

He pulled out his phone and typed a short message.

Eli: *I came by. Must have just missed you. I'll be there Tuesday morning, 9am, if that works. Sorry for the delay today.*

He sent it before he second-guessed the wording.

Then he stood in the rain for another moment, looking at the old brick building with its papered windows and its worn lettering and its decades of story held inside its walls.

His dad had always said the same thing when they approached a new job together.

Find out what it was built for first. Then you'll know how to honor it.

Eli nodded once to himself, the way he did when something settled into place.

Tuesday.

CHAPTER SIX

The Path

The rain had washed everything clean overnight.

By morning, Willow Creek looked like it had taken a deep breath. The sidewalks glistened faintly, the air smelled like pine and damp earth, and the sky stretched soft and pale above the outline of Mount Rainier.

Elle stepped onto the walking trail just after sunrise, pulling her light jacket closer around her as a cool breeze moved through the trees. Drops of water still clung to the branches overhead, occasionally falling in quiet, gentle taps onto the path below.

She inhaled deeply.

Fresh.

Renewed.

Like the whole world had been rinsed while she slept.

Her sneakers moved in a steady rhythm along the familiar trail just outside town, the gravel crunching softly beneath each step. This had always been her place growing up. Where she talked to God, sorted through thoughts, and let worship music carry what she couldn't always say out loud.

Some habits didn't fade.

They waited.

She reached into her pocket and pulled out her phone, tapping her playlist without much thought. Music filled the quiet instantly. Brandon Lake's voice rising through the morning air, unfiltered and honest.

She smiled.

"I guess it's just You and me out here," she murmured.

No one else was usually on the trail this early. Not on a weekday. Not after rain.

So, she didn't bother with earbuds.

She let the music play freely, lifting her face slightly as the first chorus swelled.

Gratitude...

Her steps slowed.

Her heart softened.

"Thank You," she whispered quietly, not even sure what part of her life she was thanking Him for in that moment. Just that she could.

The path curved gently ahead, framed by tall evergreens still dripping from the night's storm. Sunlight began pushing through the branches in thin, golden lines.

Elle closed her eyes briefly as she walked.

Not enough to be careless.

Just enough to pray.

"Lead me," she whispered. The now-familiar prayer resting easily on her tongue. "I don't need the whole plan. Just today."

She rounded the bend.

And collided directly into someone solid.

* * *

"Oh...!"

The impact was gentle but unexpected. Her foot slipped slightly on the damp gravel, and for a split second she felt herself tipping backward.

A hand reached out instantly.

Strong.

Steady.

Warm.

It caught her elbow and then her hand in one smooth motion, grounding her before she could lose balance.

"I've got you."

The voice was calm. Low. Assured.

Elle's eyes flew open.

She found herself inches from a stranger. Tall, broad-shouldered, rain-damp hair still slightly tousled as if he'd walked through the same early morning mist. His grip was firm but respectful, steadying rather than holding. There was a small scar near the edge of his jaw, pale against his skin, the kind that came from working with your hands rather than from being careless with them.

For a moment, neither of them moved.

Brandon Lake's voice carried clearly between them from her phone speaker, still playing at full volume somewhere near her side.

Elle blinked.

"Oh, my goodness," she said quickly, breath catching as awareness rushed in. "I am so sorry. I thought I was the only one out here."

His mouth lifted slightly at one corner. Not quite a full smile, but something warm lived there.

"So did I," he said.

He released her hand slowly once he was sure she was steady. The absence of contact left a faint, unexpected awareness in its wake. Not dramatic. Just noticeable.

Elle reached quickly for her phone and lowered the volume, her cheeks warming. "I usually have headphones," she admitted. "I just didn't think anyone else would be walking this early."

His gaze flicked briefly toward the phone, where the last notes of the worship song faded softly into the quiet morning air.

Recognition crossed his expression.

Not surprise.

Understanding.

"Good choice," he said simply. "I love that song."

Elle felt her shoulders relax slightly at his tone. No judgment. No awkwardness. Just quiet acknowledgment.

They stood facing each other for a moment, the world around them still dripping from rain, the air fresh and cool between them.

Up close, she noticed the steadiness in his posture. The kind of presence that felt grounded, not in a showy way. Just in a way that suggested he knew who he was.

His hands, she noticed, were a working man's hands. Calloused at the palm, sure in how they held themselves even at rest.

"I really am sorry," she said again, offering a small smile. "I promise I don't usually tackle strangers on walking paths."

That earned a fuller smile, brief but genuine.

"I'll recover," he said.

A pause settled between them.

Not uncomfortable.

Just present.

He shifted slightly, gesturing down the path behind him. "Trail's a little slick past the bend."

"Thank you," she said softly.

He gave a small nod, the kind that felt polite but sincere, and stepped aside to let her pass.

Elle hesitated half a heartbeat.

Then she stepped forward, offering one last quick smile. "Have a good morning."

"You too."

She continued down the path, heart beating just a little faster than before. Not from embarrassment. Not from anything she wanted to examine too closely.

Just from the unexpectedness of it.

After a few steps, she let the music rise again, softer this time, and lifted her face toward the filtered morning light.

"Okay, Lord," she whispered, a hint of a smile touching her lips. "That was unexpected."

Behind her, the sound of footsteps faded in the opposite direction.

Neither of them looked back.

* * *

Eli walked for another half mile before he slowed.

He wasn't sure why.

The trail opened into a clearing where the mountain came fully into view, snow-capped and unhurried above the tree line. He stopped there the way he sometimes did, hands in his pockets, just looking.

His dad had always said the mountains were God's way of reminding you that some things didn't need your help to stand.

Eli had thought about that a lot over the years. In eastern Washington, working beside his father on jobs that stretched from before sunrise to after dark. In the years after, he'd moved from town to town, taking what work he could find, carrying the trade his father had given him like a set of tools he knew how to use even when everything else was uncertain.

He hadn't thought about Sarah in a while.

He thought about her now, briefly. Not with bitterness. Just with the clarity that came sometimes on quiet mornings, when you were far enough from the old pain to see its shape without flinching.

She had wanted him to be someone arriving somewhere. Someone whose ambitions moved in a straight line toward something visible and impressive. He had loved her and tried, for a time, to want what she wanted.

But you couldn't build a life on someone else's blueprint.

Eli exhaled slowly, watching his breath fog faintly in the cool air.

He thought about the woman on the trail.

The worship music playing openly, no earbuds, no apology for it. The way she had prayed out loud without seeming to realize she was doing it. The steadiness behind her embarrassment when she'd found her footing.

He thought about the voicemail he'd listened to twice.

Her voice had sounded like that too. Steadier than the situation required.

He pulled out his phone and checked the time.

Tuesday was two days away.

He put the phone back in his pocket and looked at the mountain for another moment.

Then he turned and headed back down the trail, his boots finding the familiar rhythm of the path, his mind already moving toward the work ahead.

He had a building to understand before he could begin.

CHAPTER SEVEN

The Reveal

By Sunday, the rain had passed completely.

Sunlight stretched warm and golden across the steps of The Gathering Place as people lingered after service, talking in clusters beneath budding trees. The air carried that unmistakable early-spring blend of cool shade and warm light, the kind of day that made you want to stay outside longer than necessary.

Elle stood with Grace, Mara, Paisley, and Janelle near the edge of the courtyard, her Bible tucked under her arm, heart still tender from worship.

She had spent most of the week replaying the rain-soaked moment inside the old bakery. The worn bread board. The faded Daily Bread sign. The prayer on her knees.

* * *

"Did you hear?" Paisley was saying now, eyes bright. "Whoever is opening that new cafe must be close to announcing something. I saw someone unlocking the door this week."

Grace nodded immediately. "Yes! Mara and I walked past it the other day. We were trying to spy through the windows like normal citizens."

"Normal citizens?" Mara raised an eyebrow.

"Highly invested normal citizens," Grace corrected.

They all laughed.

Elle's stomach fluttered.

This was it.

She could keep listening.

Or she could step into it.

"The name is so good," Janelle added gently. "The Overflow Cafe."

Paisley nodded. "I love that. It sounds hopeful."

Grace turned back to Elle. "You should see it. It's in the old bakery building. Daily Bread. It's kind of poetic."

Elle felt her throat tighten.

Yes.

Poetic.

Provision to abundance.

Her hands grew slightly damp against the spine of her Bible.

This was no longer about secrecy.

It was about timing.

And something in her spirit whispered: now.

She inhaled slowly.

"It's me."

The words came softly.

Almost swallowed by a breeze.

Grace blinked. "What?"

Elle lifted her eyes, heart pounding but steady.

"I'm the one opening it."

Silence.

Four faces stared at her.

Then...

"YOU'RE WHAT?" Grace practically shouted.

A few people turned their heads.

Grace didn't care.

"You're opening The Overflow Cafe?" she continued, hands flying to her chest. "You're kidding. You are absolutely kidding."

Elle shook her head, a small, tremulous smile forming. "I signed the lease before I left the city."

Mara's eyes widened slowly, understanding dawning. "Elle."

Elle nodded, emotion rising gently into her throat. "I wanted to be sure," she said quietly. "I didn't want to announce it before I felt peace. I've been praying through it. I wanted it to be His, not just mine."

Grace stared at her for a full second.

Then she squealed, full, unapologetic joy, and pulled Elle into a hug so sudden it nearly knocked her backward.

"Why didn't you tell us when we walked past it?" Grace demanded into her shoulder. "We were literally standing in front of it!"

Elle laughed through forming tears. "I know. I just... I was waiting."

Paisley opened her mouth. Then closed it. Some answers didn't need the question.

Mara stepped forward, her voice warm but thick with emotion. "Elle, this is beautiful."

Tears slipped down Elle's cheeks now, but they weren't heavy.

They were grateful.

"It's in the old Daily Bread Bakery," she said softly. "I went inside this week for the first time as the owner. I knelt on those floors and asked God to let it feed people again. Not just physically. Spiritually."

Janelle's eyes glistened. "That's holy."

Grace pulled back just enough to look at her. "Do you realize what you're doing? This town is going to live in that place."

Elle exhaled slowly, overwhelmed but anchored. "I just want it to be a place where someone can walk in exhausted," she said. "And leave feeling like they're not alone."

Mara squeezed her hand. "You're going to need help."

Elle laughed softly through tears. "That's actually why I was going to say something today. I have a contractor coming Tuesday."

Grace's eyes went wide. "Wait, who?"

"Eli Carter," Elle said, keeping her voice even.

* * *

Something shifted in Grace's expression. Not dramatically. Just a small, knowing flicker that Elle didn't entirely trust.

"Eli Carter," Grace repeated, drawing the name out slightly.

"Grace," Mara said, a gentle warning in her tone.

"What?" Grace said innocently. "I'm just repeating the name."

"Dad said he doesn't cut corners," Elle said firmly. "That's what matters."

"Of course," Grace agreed, nodding with exaggerated sincerity.

Paisley pressed her lips together to keep from smiling.

Janelle looked quietly skyward.

Before Elle could redirect the conversation, a voice came from the direction of the church steps.

"Grace."

They all turned.

A tall man was making his way across the courtyard toward them, moving with easy, unhurried confidence. He had the kind of steady presence that didn't announce itself but somehow arrived before he did.

Grace's expression changed entirely.

It was subtle. A fraction of a second where something softened behind her eyes before she pulled her usual brightness back into place.

Elle noticed.

She filed it away.

"Luke," Grace said, her voice perfectly casual in the specific way that meant it wasn't casual at all. "You actually came to the second service for once."

"I had a reason," he said simply. He nodded to the group with a warm, unhurried smile. "Morning." Then his gaze settled on Elle. "You must be the sister."

"Elle," she said, shaking his hand. His grip was firm and genuine.

"Luke Callahan," he said. "I've heard a lot about you from your dad."

"Good things, I hope."

"All good," he said. Then his attention moved briefly to Grace with an ease that looked practiced and felt anything but. "You eating after this?"

Grace blinked. "That depends. Are you asking the group or are you asking me?"

"The group," he said.

"Then yes," Grace said. "We're eating."

Mara made a small sound that she quickly converted into a cough.

Elle looked between them and understood, without needing it explained, that this particular dynamic had a history she hadn't been present for.

She stored that away too.

* * *

Her father found her near the end of the courtyard as the crowd thinned, the way he always did, appearing quietly at her side without making an entrance.

"I heard a celebration happening over here," he said.

Elle smiled. "Word travels fast."

"Grace is not known for her indoor voice."

They walked a few steps together, unhurried.

"Eli texted me," her dad said after a moment. "Said he's looking forward to Tuesday."

Elle kept her eyes on the path ahead. "That's good to know," she said.

"He's a good man," her dad said. Not pushing. Just placing the words down gently the way he placed everything.

"You keep saying that," Elle said.

"Because it keeps being true."

She was quiet for a moment.

She thought of what her dad had said about Eli. That he wanted to understand the why before he drew a single plan. That his father had built that into him.

She thought, almost without meaning to, of the trail earlier that week. The stranger who had caught her. Who had heard the worship song playing from her phone and said simply: good choice, I love that song.

She had not connected those two things yet.

But something about them sat side by side in her chest in a way she did not quite know what to do with.

"Tuesday," she said, more to herself than to her dad.

"Tuesday," he agreed, smiling at something she hadn't said.

Sunlight filtered through the budding trees above them.

Elle looked up at it for a moment, feeling the warmth on her face.

She had told four people today.

Four people who loved her now knew what she was building.

And the man who would help her build it was already thinking about the why.

She exhaled slowly.

Tuesday couldn't come fast enough.

CHAPTER EIGHT

You

The old bakery didn't feel empty anymore.

Not after Sunday.

Not after the reveal.

Not after the way her friends had wrapped around her calling, like it belonged to all of them.

Elle unlocked the door to The Overflow Cafe on Tuesday morning, heart lighter than it had been in months. The sun streamed boldly through the tall windows, no rain in sight, the world outside bright and rinsed.

She stepped inside.

The air still carried faint traces of flour and old wood. Dust glimmered in beams of light stretching across the room like quiet invitation.

She set her bag down on the old counter and stood still for a moment.

"Okay, Lord," she whispered. "We're building something."

She reached into her pocket and pulled out her phone.

If she was going to measure, plan, and dream, she needed worship.

She tapped her playlist without hesitation.

The room filled instantly.

Not softly.

Not politely.

Cody Carnes' voice rose full and unfiltered into the high ceilings of the old bakery, echoing off brick and wood and history.

Elle smiled.

She moved toward the center of the room, arms folding loosely around herself as the music swelled.

The sound transformed the space.

What had been empty now felt alive.

Hope reverberated against brick walls. Lyrics climbed the tall windows. The old bread board leaning against the counter felt less like relic and more like foundation.

She closed her eyes and let it wash over her.

This wasn't performance.

This wasn't a stage.

It was surrender.

"I don't want this to be about me," she whispered over the music. "If You're not in it, I don't want it."

Her voice caught.

"Fill this place. Let it overflow."

The chorus built.

Her hands lifted slowly. Not high, not dramatic. Just open.

"Thank You," she breathed. "For bringing me home. For not giving up on me. For restoring my soul."

The music swelled higher.

And she didn't hear the door open.

* * *

Eli paused just inside the threshold.

The sound hit him first.

Worship music, full volume, filling the old bakery like it had been waiting decades to hold something sacred instead of flour dust.

He hadn't expected that.

He set his tool bag down quietly just inside the door and looked up at the high ceilings, listening for a moment the way he did when he first entered any old space. Reading the room. Taking stock.

Don't rush in with your tools. Stand still and listen to what the building has been carrying.

Then he saw her.

Standing near the center of the space.

Eyes closed.

Hands lifted slightly.

Face tilted toward light streaming through tall windows.

Worshiping.

Not aware she wasn't alone.

His mouth curved slowly.

Small knowing smile.

Of course.

He leaned one shoulder lightly against the doorframe, giving the moment its space instead of interrupting it. He recognized the song. He recognized the posture. He recognized the quality of someone not performing faith but living inside it.

He had seen that kind of surrender before.

Not often.

He waited until the song softened slightly before clearing his throat, gentle and respectful.

"Am I interrupting?"

Elle's eyes flew open.

She turned quickly, heartbeat spiking.

And froze.

He stood near the door, tool bag at his feet, sunlight cutting across his shoulders.

Recognition hit instantly.

Warm.

Calm.

Unmistakable.

"You."

The word left both of them at the same time.

Then they both laughed softly.

His smile deepened just slightly, a quiet chuckle escaping him.

"I had a feeling," he said.

Elle pressed a hand lightly to her chest, shaking her head in disbelief. "You're the contractor."

"And you're the cafe owner."

There was no awkwardness.

No scrambling.

Just timing.

She lowered the music quickly, cheeks warming slightly. "I really need to stop assuming I'm alone when I play worship at full volume."

He adjusted his grip on the strap of his tool bag. "I don't mind it."

The words were simple.

Honest.

Something about the way he said them made her stomach flutter just slightly.

Professional, she reminded herself.

Stay professional.

"I'm glad you came," she said, steadying her voice. "My dad said you would."

He nodded once. "He speaks highly of you."

She blinked. "He does?"

"He doesn't waste words."

That made her smile.

* * *

He stepped fully into the space now, looking around with assessing eyes. Not critical. Just attentive.

He moved through the room unhurried and deliberate. He crouched near the base of the old counter, ran his palm flat along the floor, then pressed two fingers against the wall as if taking a pulse.

Elle watched him work without speaking. This way of listening before acting. Of treating old things with the same seriousness you'd give new ones.

Maybe more.

"Good bones," he said quietly, standing. "Old buildings like this, they last."

"Daily Bread Bakery," she said, gesturing toward the faded lettering on the brick outside.

His gaze lifted.

He read it slowly.

A faint shift crossed his expression. Appreciation, maybe. The particular recognition of someone who understood what it meant to build something that outlived you.

"Fits," he murmured.

"For what it was," she said.

"And what it's becoming," he replied.

Their eyes met again.

Not intense.

Not dramatic.

Just steady.

She exhaled softly. "I want it to be a place where people can breathe. Pray. Sit without pressure."

He nodded slowly, taking that in.

"That's worth taking the time to build it right," he said.

The words settled between them like promise.

He pulled his measuring tape from his back pocket and walked toward the entry, crouching to check the threshold. His movements were practiced and sure, the motions of someone who had done this long enough that the work had become a kind of language.

Elle found herself studying the way he held the tape. The steadiness of his hands. The small scar near his jaw catching the light when he tilted his head.

She looked away.

She crossed to the counter and opened her notebook instead, focusing on the sketches she'd made. The layout she'd imagined. The long tables, the prayer wall, the corner by the window where the light would be best in the mornings.

"Tell me about the corner," he said without looking up from the threshold.

She blinked. "What?"

He stood and nodded toward the far-left window. "You keep looking at it. What do you see there?"

Elle hesitated.

This was the part she hadn't said out loud to anyone except God. The specific vision. The woman with her coat still on. The cup she wasn't drinking.

She had learned to be careful about the things she shared with people before she knew whether they were safe to share them with.

She knew that lesson more deeply than she wished she did.

But something about the way he asked, without pressure, without performance, just a straight and genuine question from a man trying to understand what he was building, made her answer.

"I keep seeing someone sitting there alone," she said quietly. "Someone who came in out of more than just the rain. Someone who needed a place to exist for a minute without having to explain herself."

She stopped, slightly surprised she'd said that much.

Eli was quiet for a moment.

Then he nodded once, slowly, like something had just been confirmed.

"That changes how I think about the entry," he said simply.

Elle stared at him.

"It does?"

"If that's who you're building it for," he said, turning back to the threshold, "then the first thing she feels when she walks in matters more than anything else. The light. The width of the door. Whether the floor feels solid under her feet."

He crouched again, pressing his palm flat against the old boards. Eli was quiet for a moment, still looking at the threshold. "People feel safe spaces before they understand why."

Elle's throat tightened.

Those were almost exactly the words she had prayed on her knees in this room.

Let weary people walk in and feel You before they understand why.

She didn't say that.

She just looked at him for a moment, this man crouching over old floorboards with his father's hands and his father's patience and felt something in her chest shift in a way she didn't entirely have words for.

"Try not to tackle me again while I'm working," he said, glancing up with that quiet half-smile. "Insurance paperwork gets complicated."

Elle laughed. Real, unguarded.

"I'll do my best."

Sunlight poured through the windows.

Worship music still hummed softly in the background.

And inside the old Daily Bread Bakery, now becoming The Overflow Cafe, two paths that had crossed in rain were beginning to build something.

CHAPTER NINE

Miles of Joy

Saturday arrived like a celebration.

Willow Creek woke early under a bright, clear sky, the kind of morning that made the snow on Mount Rainier look sharper and the greens along the foothills look newly painted. The air still held a spring crispness, but there was warmth underneath it now, the first hint that summer was coming.

Elle stood at the edge of the town park with her ponytail damp from a quick shower and her running shoes tied tight, feeling the buzz of people gathering like a living current.

A 5K in Willow Creek wasn't just a race.

It was a reunion.

Kids darted between legs holding balloons. Couples stretched and laughed. A few older women wore matching shirts and walked like they were on a mission. A cluster of teenagers posed for pictures near a banner that read:

WILLOW CREEK COMMUNITY 5K

Strong Bodies. Strong Hearts.

Someone had set up a table with water bottles and snacks. Another table held sign-up sheets for volunteer opportunities and local outreach programs. A worship playlist played softly from a speaker near the registration tent, not loud enough to overpower conversation, but present enough to remind everyone what kind of town this was.

Elle pressed her hand briefly to her chest.

This was what she'd missed.

Not the noise.

The togetherness, the community.

Grace appeared beside her in a bright yellow windbreaker, practically vibrating. "Okay," she said, scanning the crowd like a coach. "We're going to win."

Elle laughed. "Grace, it's a community 5K."

Grace nodded solemnly. "Exactly. And I plan to dominate the community."

Mara joined them, smiling, her hair pulled back neatly and her sweatshirt sleeves pushed up. "I'm just hoping to finish without regretting every life choice I've ever made."

Paisley came bouncing up next, already sweaty like she'd done a warm-up lap around the entire park. "Oh my gosh, this is the best day ever. Look at all these people! Look at that stroller brigade. Those moms are warriors."

Janelle arrived last, calm and steady, holding an extra bottle of water as if she'd known someone would forget. "Good morning," she said softly. Then she looked at Elle and smiled. "You look happy."

Elle blinked at the simplicity of the statement, and at how true it was.

"I am," Elle admitted quietly.

Grace leaned in. "And you're going to be even happier because after this, we're getting coffee."

Mara raised an eyebrow. "From where?"

Grace looked at Elle with dramatic significance. "From her future empire."

Elle laughed, cheeks warming. "It's not an empire."

"It's a ministry disguised as caffeine," Grace corrected. "Don't be humble at me."

"We're not open yet." Elle said, "so we'll have to settle for a diet coke from the market."

"Done," Grace agreed instantly.

The announcer's voice came through a microphone, cheerful and loud. "All right, Willow Creek! Before we start, let's take a moment to pray."

The crowd quieted.

It wasn't forced. It wasn't performative.

It was just normal.

Pastor Nathan stepped forward and prayed a simple blessing over the runners and walkers, over health and community and protection. He prayed for strong bodies and strong hearts, for families, for unity, for purpose.

Elle closed her eyes, letting the prayer settle into her spirit.

When the amen came, the crowd's energy returned instantly. Laughter, cheering, people shuffling toward the start line.

Grace stretched dramatically, as if preparing for the Olympics. "No mercy."

Mara pointed at her. "If you sprint off the line like a lunatic, I'm not chasing you."

Grace grinned. "You don't have to chase me. Just admire me from afar."

Paisley snorted. "I'll admire you when you're crying at mile two."

Grace gasped. "Betrayal."

Janelle's eyes twinkled quietly. "We're all just glad you're here."

That statement landed softly in Elle's chest.

Me too, she thought.

The countdown began.

Five. Four. Three.

Elle took a breath.

Two. One.

And they were off.

* * *

Elle didn't run to prove anything.

She walked because walking had always been where she met God.

Her pace was steady, her breathing easy as she fell into rhythm alongside her friends. The trail looped through the park and out toward a shaded path lined with evergreens and early spring blossoms. Sunlight filtered through branches overhead in soft, shifting patterns.

Around them, people ran, walked, chatted, laughed. Some pushed strollers. Some held hands. Some wore shirts with Bible verses on the back.

Willow Creek didn't require people to have it all together to belong.

That was the beauty.

Grace walked a little ahead, waving at strangers like she was running for mayor. "You've got this!" she called to a woman jogging slowly. "Yes! Look at you!"

Mara laughed. "She's going to encourage the entire town one person at a time."

Paisley nodded. "Honestly? That's on-brand."

Elle smiled, letting the joy of it wash through her.

As they approached the first mile marker, she noticed an older man sitting on a bench near the path, slightly hunched. He wasn't cheering. He wasn't watching anyone in particular. He just sat there, hands clasped, staring down at the ground like his thoughts were heavy.

Something in Elle's spirit tugged.

She slowed without thinking.

"Hey," Mara said softly beside her. "You okay?"

Elle nodded. "Yeah. I just..." She glanced back toward the bench.

Mara followed her gaze and nodded slowly. "Go."

Elle stepped off the path and approached the man gently.

"Hi," she said softly. "Good morning."

He looked up, startled, then guarded. "Morning."

"I'm Elle. I just noticed you sitting here. Are you okay?"

The man blinked, like he hadn't expected anyone to ask.

He opened his mouth, closed it, then let out a breath. "My wife," he said quietly. "She's in the hospital. I came out here because I couldn't sit in that waiting room anymore."

Elle's heart clenched. "I'm so sorry. That's really heavy."

He nodded, eyes shining. "I don't know what to do with myself."

Elle hesitated only a moment. "Would it be all right if I prayed for you? Just right here?"

His eyes widened slightly. He looked like he might say no out of habit.

Then his shoulders sagged.

"Yeah," he whispered. "I'd like that."

Elle bowed her head, standing on the damp edge of the path in the spring sunlight.

"Jesus," she prayed softly, "thank You for seeing him right now. Thank You that You are near to the brokenhearted. I pray for his wife, for healing, for peace, for strength. I pray for him, Lord, that You would hold him up when he feels like he can't stand. Let him feel Your presence today. Let him know he isn't alone."

She paused, then added quietly, "Be his Shepherd. Lead him."

When she lifted her head, the man wiped his cheek quickly.

"Thank you," he said, voice rough. "I needed that."

Elle smiled gently. "I'll keep praying."

She stepped back toward the path.

Mara waited there, eyes soft. "You're you," she said quietly.

Elle blinked, emotion rising unexpectedly. "I just felt like I was supposed to."

Mara didn't say anything. She just fell back into step beside her.

Grace leaned back toward them from a few steps ahead. "Okay, are we stopping to start a revival or can we keep walking?"

Paisley laughed. "Let the girl pray, Grace."

Grace grinned. "Fine. But if we miss the post-walk snacks, I'll pray too."

Elle laughed, wiping at her eyes quickly.

Joy and tenderness, all mixed together.

That was Willow Creek.

* * *

Near the two-mile marker, the path opened into a wide stretch with a view of the mountain in the distance. People slowed to take photos. A few kids cheered loudly.

Elle was laughing at something Paisley said when Mara's eyes lifted past them.

"Oh," Mara said, nodding toward the trailhead entrance. "Look who Luke brought."

Elle turned.

Eli walked into the park beside Luke, both of them moving with easy confidence. Luke wore his usual calm expression, already scanning the group. Beside him, Eli carried himself the same way he always did. Grounded, unhurried, like he didn't need to prove he belonged somewhere to belong there.

He wasn't wearing work clothes today. Just a simple jacket, athletic shoes, hands in his pockets.

Something about seeing him outside the cafe caught Elle slightly off guard.

She had filed him neatly into the category of contractor. Professional. Practical. A person who existed in a specific context with a specific purpose.

He looked different here.

More present somehow.

She looked away before he could catch her looking.

Grace's eyes widened. "Oh! Luke brought Eli. This is becoming a whole thing."

Mara gave Grace a look. "Don't start."

Grace leaned in anyway. "I'm just saying. I sense a theme."

Paisley's grin grew. "I'm listening."

Janelle smiled softly, like she was already praying about it.

Luke reached them first, offering Elle a friendly nod. "Hey. How's the walking ministry going?"

Elle laughed. "Apparently it's active today."

Luke's mouth tilted. "Good."

He glanced toward Grace with that carefully neutral expression, and Grace returned it with equally careful brightness, and Elle watched the two of them not quite look at each other and filed that away for later.

Eli's gaze met hers.

"I was starting to think you only existed on trails and construction sites," he said lightly.

Elle smiled. "I was starting to think the same about you."

They fell into step together as the group widened naturally. Conversation flowed easily. Grace teasing Luke, Paisley asking Eli about the cafe renovation, Mara sharing how she almost didn't come.

Elle listened, smiling, at ease.

Until Paisley asked the question.

* * *

"So Eli," Paisley said, with the particular brightness of someone who didn't realize they were walking into something. "What brought you to Willow Creek originally? Elle said you're not from here."

Eli was quiet for a half step.

"Work, mostly," he said. "I moved around a fair bit after I finished my apprenticeship. Followed the jobs. Eastern Washington, then a few towns over toward the coast." He paused. "I came through Willow Creek on a small job about four years ago and just...stayed."

"What made you stay?" Grace asked.

"The Gathering Place," he said simply. "And the people in it."

There was nothing complicated about the way he said it. Just a man who had been looking for something without knowing exactly what, and had recognized it when he found it.

Elle understood that completely.

"That's beautiful," Paisley said warmly. "Did you leave much behind? Back east?"

Another half-beat pause.

"Not much," Eli said.

His tone was easy. Unbothered. But there was a quality to the simplicity of it that Elle recognized the way you recognize a locked door. Not because anything dramatic had happened. Just because someone had chosen not to open it.

She knew that choice intimately.

What she didn't expect was what came next.

Eli glanced at her briefly, something like curiosity in his expression. "What about you?" he said. "What did you leave behind in the city?"

The question was easy and natural. The kind you asked someone you were getting to know.

Elle felt it land somewhere it wasn't supposed to.

"Oh, you know," she said, keeping her voice light. "The usual. Long hours. Meeting after meeting. Traffic."

She smiled as she said it.

Eli nodded, accepting the answer.

She kept walking, face forward, smile still in place. The smile wasn't dishonest, exactly. Those things were true. She had left them behind.

She just hadn't mentioned what she'd left behind that still followed her. The version of herself who had gone quiet to keep a peace that was never real. The relationship she'd shaped herself around until she couldn't find the edges of herself anymore.

She hadn't lied.

She just hadn't said the thing beneath the thing.

She never did. Not yet. Not with someone whose opinion was still being formed.

That thought stopped her in a way the first thought hadn't.

Since when did his opinion matter?

The question landed somewhere unexpected. She walked another ten steps before she trusted herself to notice it without flinching. Then she named it, the way she was learning to name things now. Set it down. Kept walking.

Professional, she reminded herself.

The word sat differently than it had a week ago. Less like a guideline. More like something she was gripping too hard.

* * *

As they neared the finish line, cheers rose again. People clapped. Kids ran alongside runners. Volunteers handed out water and oranges.

Elle stepped across the line with her friends, breath warm in her chest, sunlight on her face.

She glanced sideways.

Eli was beside her.

Not close enough to touch.

Just there.

Grace leaned toward Paisley and whispered loudly, "This is adorable."

Paisley whispered back, "I know."

Mara sighed. "You two are going to get yourselves in trouble."

Elle heard none of it clearly.

She was thinking about a door she'd closed too fast.

And wondering, for the first time, whether she would ever be willing to open it.

*　*　*

She didn't go straight home.

She told Grace she needed air and peeled away from the group near the park entrance, walking an extra lap alone on the quieter side of the trail where the trees were close and the noise of the finish line faded behind her.

She needed to think.

Or not think.

She wasn't sure which.

The thing she was feeling didn't have a name yet, and that was the problem. Elle Whitaker was good with names. She had spent years in boardrooms translating emotion into language, taking the complicated and making it manageable. She named things. That was how she handled them.

But this.

She stopped on the path and looked up at the mountain, still snow-capped even in spring, completely unhurried by everything happening at its feet.

Since when did his opinion matter?

She had asked herself that question at mile two and then set it down and kept walking. But it had come back. It kept coming back. The way it had felt to give him the partial answer, traffic and long hours and meetings, and know, while she was saying it, that the real answer was right underneath. Close enough to touch. Close enough that she had felt it pressing upward the whole rest of the walk.

She hadn't said it.

She never did. Not yet. Not with someone whose opinion was...

There it was again.

His opinion.

She exhaled slowly.

It wasn't fear, exactly. It was more specific than that. It was the carefulness of a woman who had learned the hard way, in small increments, over one quiet dinner at a time, that showing someone the full version of yourself was a choice, and that once you made it, you couldn't take it back.

She had made it with Daniel.

Or the opposite of it. She had hidden the full version from Daniel, and that had cost her something she was still recovering.

She wasn't sure which was more frightening.

Eli hadn't asked for the full version. He'd just asked a natural question. What did you leave behind in the city?

And something in her had wanted to answer it.

That was the part she was still standing with, hands open, trying to understand.

Something in her had wanted to answer.

She said it to God, quietly, the way she said most honest things these days, not as a request, just as a fact she was handing over.

"I think I like him."

A pause.

The mountain didn't respond. The trail stayed quiet.

But somewhere underneath the carefulness and the history and the part of her that still knew all the reasons to wait, something small and warm and certain said:

I know. I've been here the whole time.

She stood there for another moment.

Then she turned and walked back toward the sound of her people.

***

The plans were spread across his kitchen table when he finally sat down.

He'd been carrying them in his truck since Tuesday.

Rolling them out. Rolling them back up.

Taking measurements he didn't technically need yet because it gave him something to do with his hands while he thought.

He pulled the table lamp closer.

The entry dimensions were marked clearly.

The counter placement. The wall where she wanted the prayer boards. The corner by the left window with the morning light.

He'd drawn it the way she'd described it, carefully, honestly, with room left in the margins the way his dad had taught him, because the person you were building for always thought of something they hadn't told you yet.

He stared at the corner by the window for a moment.

He knew what she'd told him about it. The woman with her coat still on. The cup she wasn't drinking. The person who had come in out of more than just the rain.

He had added a few inches of extra depth to that window seat without telling her.

Not because she'd asked.

Because the woman she'd described would need it.

He leaned back in his chair and rubbed a hand over his jaw.

This wasn't a complicated job. Structurally, it was straightforward, cosmetic repairs, updated electrical, the flooring restoration, new millwork for the counter.

He'd done harder work half asleep in worse conditions.

But he'd never felt this particular weight on a job before.

He'd thought about that a lot this week, trying to be honest with himself the way he'd always tried to be honest with himself, because pretending was expensive and he'd learned that the hard way.

He wasn't just thinking about the building.

He reached forward and touched the corner she'd described. The sketched seat. The window. The light.

Sarah had wanted him to be someone with a plan.

A trajectory.

A destination she could point to at dinner parties and feel certain about.

He had loved her and tried, genuinely, to want what she wanted. But he had learned something in those years that he hadn't been able to explain at the time and understood better now:

You couldn't build a life on someone else's blueprint.

You could only honor the one you'd been given.

He had spent four years since then being careful.

Not closed. He wasn't closed. He believed in love the way he believed in good timber, it existed, it held weight, it was worth the work.

He just hadn't found someone who understood the same things he understood.

Until Tuesday.

He exhaled slowly, a little annoyed at himself for thinking it so plainly.

He had watched her stand in the center of that empty room with worship music filling the high ceilings, hands lifted, eyes closed, completely unaware she wasn't alone.

He had watched her kneel on those old floors, not for effect, not to be seen, but because that was simply what she did when something mattered.

He had watched her share the vision for that corner, the woman, the untouched cup, the coat still on, and he had felt something in his chest recognize it the way you recognized a song you hadn't heard since you were a child.

She wasn't building a cafe.

She was building a home for people who didn't know yet that they needed one.

He understood that completely.

He also understood that understanding it was not the same as knowing what to do with it.

He rolled the plans carefully and set them beside his Bible on the counter.

Eli closed his eyes.

"Lord," he said quietly, in the kitchen, alone, to no one but God, "let me build what You want here."

He paused.

"And help me figure out the rest."

He didn't elaborate.

God already knew the rest.

He went to bed without looking at the plans again.

The next morning, he was at the bakery by nine.

CHAPTER TEN

The Foundation

Morning light filled the old bakery like mercy.

It spilled through the tall front windows in long, clean stripes and warmed the worn wooden floors where generations had once stood waiting for fresh loaves. Dust floated lazily in the beams, turning the empty air into something almost sacred, like the building itself was holding its breath.

Elle stood near the old counter with a paper cup of coffee warming her hands. She'd worn a simple sweater and jeans, hair pulled back, sleeves already pushed up. Not because she planned to do heavy work, today was Eli's day, but because she couldn't seem to keep herself from being part of it.

The Overflow Cafe didn't feel like an idea anymore.

It felt like a beginning.

* * *

Eli arrived just after nine with a tool bag slung over one shoulder and a small stack of plans tucked under his arm.

He paused the moment he stepped inside, eyes lifting instinctively the way they had the first time. A slow survey. A quiet respect.

He stood in the doorway. Looked up before he looked around. The ceiling told you more about a building's history than the floor did, because ceilings bore the weight of everything that had happened below them.

"Morning," he said, voice warm.

"Morning." Elle smiled. "I made coffee."

His mouth curved slightly. "That's already a strong start."

She laughed softly and handed him a cup.

He took it, nodding once in approval, then set his tool bag down and moved toward the entrance the way he always moved through a space he was learning. Unhurried. Attentive. He crouched near the doorway, ran his palm lightly over the boards, then tapped one with his knuckle as if listening for a story.

These floors have seen a lot, he thought.

You could feel it.

The way you could feel a table that had held a thousand meals, or a porch step worn smooth by decades of the same boots. Objects absorbed the living that happened around them. His dad believed that. Eli had spent enough years working with his hands to believe it too.

"All right," he said, rolling out his measuring tape with practiced ease. "If we're starting construction phase for real, first thing is the entry. That's where people decide if they feel welcome before they even know why."

Elle watched him work, the ease in his movements grounding her. Not rushed. Not careless.

Intentional.

It made the whole thing feel possible.

They spent a few minutes talking logistics. What needed repair, what could be preserved, what should be updated. It was practical, steady work. The kind that built trust without trying.

* * *

Then Elle felt her heart press forward, gentle but insistent.

This wasn't just about wood and nails.

Not for her.

She had come carrying something that morning, wrapped carefully like a treasure.

Now she reached into her tote bag and pulled it out.

A Bible.

The cover was worn soft at the edges. The pages held history. Pencil marks, underlines, prayers she had whispered in the dark when she couldn't find her way.

Eli glanced up as she stepped closer.

His expression shifted. Not surprise. Not confusion.

Attention.

Reverence.

Elle swallowed, suddenly aware of the weight of what she was about to ask.

"Before we do too much..." She let out a small breath and steadied herself. "Can we do something here?"

Eli straightened slowly, eyes still on the Bible in her hands. "Yeah," he said quietly. "What is it?"

Elle held the Bible against her chest for a moment, feeling her pulse beneath it.

"I want this place grounded in the Word," she said softly. Then she gave a small, almost self-conscious laugh through the emotion rising in her throat. "Not just as a phrase. Not just on a wall. I mean literally."

Silence settled.

Not awkward.

Holy.

Eli didn't rush to fill it.

He just looked at her, steady and present, like he understood she wasn't talking about decor.

Finally, he nodded once.

"Show me where," he said simply.

Something in Elle's chest loosened, as if she'd been bracing for misunderstanding and instead found honor.

She turned toward the doorway. "Right here," she said quietly. "The entrance. The first step in. I want the Word to be under every step we take to build this."

Eli followed her gaze.

Then he set his coffee down carefully on the counter, as if even that needed to be done with respect.

He walked to the doorway, knelt, and looked up at her once more. Silent question.

Elle nodded.

He reached for his pry bar.

* * *

The first board resisted.

Wood creaked as he eased it upward, the sound low and old, like the building exhaling.

A nail squealed softly against grain.

Dust rose in a faint cloud.

Elle's throat tightened.

She hadn't expected the emotional weight of it. Watching him pull up those boards...old, worn, scarred...felt like watching something in her own life being opened. The careful, patient work of someone who understood that you didn't tear into old things. You listened to them first. You honored what they'd been before you changed them.

She could see it in every movement.

The board lifted free.

Eli set it aside gently, not tossing it like scrap, but placing it like something worth respecting.

He moved to the next.

Then the next.

Each one came up slow, stubborn, aged. Each one held years.

Elle crouched beside him, not touching anything yet, just watching.

The entryway opened like a wound becoming visible.

Below the boards, the darker underlayer appeared. Foundation exposed, raw and honest. No polish. No pretending.

Eli paused, resting back on his heels.

Light fell into the open space.

The silence deepened.

He glanced at the exposed foundation and said quietly, almost to himself, "Most people never see what holds everything up."

Elle's eyes filled.

She didn't say anything.

Eli looked at her then. Really looked.

His expression softened, something steady and tender settling behind his eyes.

He didn't say much.

He didn't need to.

His quiet presence felt like permission to be moved without apology.

Elle blinked, a tear slipping free.

She thought, briefly and without meaning to, of every time she had been vulnerable in front of someone and had it used against her somehow. Not violently. Just quietly. The way someone could take what you showed them and hold it over you without ever meaning to be cruel.

Eli wasn't doing that.

He was just watching her with steady eyes and staying exactly where he was.

She didn't know why that felt so unfamiliar.

She didn't examine it long.

"Okay," she whispered, more to herself than to him. "Okay."

* * *

Eli shifted slightly to make space at the edge of the opening.

Elle understood.

This was shared ground.

She knelt beside him.

Her knees pressed into the old wood. Her fingers trembled slightly as she opened the Bible to a page worn soft from use.

Psalm 23.

Not because she wanted to make it dramatic.

Because it was the place God had met her.

Her eyes landed on the line that had changed everything:

My cup overflows.

She swallowed hard.

Overflow.

The name had come from that verse. A promise. A whisper in the middle of burnout. A reminder that God didn't just restore. He filled. Then He overflowed.

She closed the Bible gently.

Then she looked at Eli.

He nodded once, steady consent.

Together, they lowered it into the open space.

Their hands moved carefully, reverently.

Her fingers brushed his for the briefest moment as they guided the Bible into place.

It wasn't romantic.

Not in the usual way.

It was deeper than that.

It was two people placing something holy at the center of what they were about to build.

When the Bible rested flat beneath the threshold, the air felt different.

Still.

Full.

Elle's tears fell quietly now, not from sadness, but from gratitude so deep it felt like it lived in her bones.

She drew a slow breath.

Then she prayed, softly, out loud.

"Jesus," Elle whispered, voice shaking just slightly, "this place belongs to You. Not to me. Not to a dream. To You." She paused, blinking hard. "Let everyone who walks through this door feel loved. Let the weary find rest. Let the lonely find family. Let this be a place where people encounter You, even if they came in for coffee."

Her words weren't perfect.

They were real.

When she finished, she stayed still, palms open on her knees.

Eli's voice followed. Low, steady, unhurried.

"Lord," he said quietly, "build what You want here. Keep us aligned with You. Let us do this work with integrity. Protect it. Provide for it. And if we ever forget why we started, remind us."

His prayer wasn't long.

It was strong.

The kind of prayer a man prayed when he didn't talk much but meant every word.

Elle's chest tightened again.

Not because she was overwhelmed.

Because she felt safe.

She turned the feeling over once, carefully, the way you handle something fragile when you're not sure it belongs to you yet. Then she set it down.

It had been a long time since she'd felt that in the presence of another person.

She wasn't sure what to do with it.

So she let it be.

* * *

When the silence returned, it didn't feel empty.

It felt full.

Eli exhaled slowly, then reached for the boards they'd removed.

Carefully, one by one, he placed them back.

The wood settled into its old grooves like it belonged there.

Old boards.

New foundation beneath them.

He aligned each piece, then reached for his hammer.

The first nail drove in with a firm, clean sound.

Then another.

Then another.

Each strike echoed softly through the space, a steady rhythm like a heartbeat.

Elle watched, tears drying on her cheeks, something in her spirit settling with each nail.

This was construction.

But it felt like worship.

Eli finished, then ran his hand once along the restored threshold, palm flat, slight pressure, listening.

He stood slowly.

Then, almost without thinking, he tapped the floor once with the heel of his boot.

Solid.

He looked at Elle, the faintest smile at the corner of his mouth.

"All right," he said gently, his voice lighter now, like he was bringing them back to the practical world without breaking the sacred one. "Now we can build."

Elle stared at the doorway.

No one would see it.

No one would know.

The Word resting beneath their feet.

Except her.

Except God.

Except, now, Eli.

Her voice came soft, full of quiet awe. "Most people will never know it's there."

Eli nodded once. "But it's there."

The sunlight warmed the floor.

And the old bakery stood quiet around them, holding what had just been placed inside it.

CHAPTER ELEVEN

Written on the Walls

The cafe smelled like fresh possibility and open primer cans.

Morning light streamed boldly through the tall front windows, warming the old brick and catching in the soft dust that still lingered in corners. Drop cloths covered the floors. Ladders leaned against walls. Sample swatches lay scattered across the counter like a patchwork of future decisions waiting to be made.

Natalie Grant played softly from Elle's phone on the old bakery counter.

Your Great Name...

The music wasn't loud.

It didn't need to be.

It simply filled the room like a steady undercurrent of worship, the way a river moves beneath ice in winter. Present and alive even when you couldn't see it.

Elle stood in the center of the space with her hands wrapped around a warm cup and felt her chest tighten.

Not with nerves.

With gratitude.

She had prayed over this morning for a week. Prayed for each woman who would walk through the door today. Prayed for their hands and their hearts and for the kind of holy mess that happened when people who loved God gathered to build something together.

She hadn't expected them to come so readily.

She should have known better.

* * *

Grace burst through the door first, carrying iced coffees and a bag of pastries like she was delivering relief supplies to a disaster zone.

"Okay," she announced, looking around dramatically. "This is happening."

Behind her came Mara with neatly labeled paint brushes tucked under one arm, Paisley with a full armful of rollers, and Janelle with a quiet smile and a folded paper tucked carefully in her hand.

They came.

Without hesitation.

They came ready to build something that wasn't technically theirs.

Elle's throat tightened in a way she didn't try to hide.

"Before we start," Janelle said gently, glancing around at the bare walls, "can we pray?"

The room stilled immediately.

No one made a joke.

No one rushed.

Grace set her coffees down. Paisley lowered the rollers. Mara stood quietly, her hands folding together in a way that looked like habit.

They formed a loose circle near the center of the cafe, hands loosely linked, paint supplies scattered around them like witnesses.

Mara prayed first.

Her voice was soft, careful with each word.

"Lord, thank You for bringing this dream home," she whispered. "Thank You for obedience. Thank You for second beginnings."

She paused on those last two words just a half breath longer than necessary.

Second beginnings.

Elle felt Mara's fingers tighten slightly around hers.

Paisley followed, voice warm and direct the way she was direct with everything.

"Let this be a place of healing," she said. "For tired nurses. For overwhelmed moms. For anyone who just needs to sit somewhere and feel like they can breathe."

Grace squeezed Elle's other hand before speaking, as if she needed the contact to steady herself.

"God, let this place be loud with joy. Let it be full. Let it be safe." Her voice trembled slightly. "Let it be the kind of place where people walk in heavy and leave lighter."

Janelle's voice was the quietest of all, but it landed the deepest.

"Build it on You," she said simply. "Not on us. On You."

When the circle loosened, the silence that followed wasn't empty.

It was full.

The kind of full that didn't need to be explained.

* * *

Elle looked at the blank walls.

Raw.

Uncovered.

Open.

And suddenly, the idea formed the way her best ideas always did. Not from planning or strategy or a list in her notebook. From the Spirit pressing gently at the center of her chest.

"What if..." she began softly.

They turned toward her.

"What if before we prime the walls... we cover the walls in prayer?"

Grace blinked. "Like... actually write on them?"

Elle nodded slowly, emotion rising unexpectedly into her throat. "Prayers. Declarations. Scripture. For the town. For the people who will sit here. For things we don't even understand yet."

Mara's eyes softened, understanding settling into her expression. "So they'll be under the primer."

"Yes," Elle whispered.

A quiet stillness settled over them again.

Deeper this time.

Holier.

Then Paisley grinned, wide and bright. "Okay. That's beautiful."

Grace grabbed a permanent marker from her bag. "Oh, we are absolutely doing this."

* * *

They spread out across the room.

Natalie Grant's voice moved into another song as the first marker touched the wall.

The sound was soft.

Sacred.

Intentional.

Elle moved toward the wall nearest the entrance. She pressed her palm briefly against the wall before writing, a gesture that had become instinctive whenever she touched something in this building. Like she was listening first.

Then slowly, carefully, she began:

The Lord is my Shepherd; I shall not want.

Her hand trembled slightly as she wrote.

He restores my soul.

She paused.

That line had carried her home.

She swallowed hard and added:

My cup overflows.

Then beneath it, smaller, more personal:

Build this place on You. Let it gather the weary. Let it overflow with Your love. Let every table hold hope.

She stepped back.

Her tears came without asking permission.

She didn't stop them.

Grace was already halfway up a ladder, writing boldly across a high stretch of wall in her large, looping handwriting:

Joy lives here.

And beneath it:

For I know the plans I have for you, declares the Lord. Jeremiah 29:11

Mara stood near the windows, her handwriting smaller than the others. More careful. The handwriting of someone who had learned to be precise about what she asked for.

Elle watched without meaning to watch.

Mara wrote:

Restore what was lost.

She paused for a long moment, marker resting against the brick.

Then she wrote beneath it, slower:

Make beauty from ashes.

Elle looked away.

Not because the moment was too small to notice.

Because it was too large to intrude upon.

Mara's prayer wasn't for the cafe.

Elle understood that with a quiet certainty she didn't examine. Some prayers were too personal to ask about. Some wounds showed themselves only in what a person asked God to do.

She filed it away the way she filed away things that mattered. Gently. Carefully. Without forcing them into the light before they were ready.

Paisley knelt near what would become the children's corner, her hospital-trained hands steady and sure.

Let this be safe for families.

Then: *Heal the brokenhearted.*

Janelle wrote near the back wall in a script that was steady and elegant.

Surely goodness and mercy will follow us.

And beneath it:

Let this place be mercy.

* * *

They moved slowly around the room for the better part of an hour.

Sometimes reading each other's words aloud softly.

Sometimes wiping tears.

Sometimes laughing through the emotion of it, because grief and joy had always lived closer together than people liked to admit.

Grace stepped down from her ladder, looked at her work, and said: "Okay, but I'm also writing: 'Strong coffee. Strong faith.'"

Paisley burst out laughing. "That might be the most Grace thing you've ever said."

"It's accurate though," Grace replied, uncapped marker poised.

Elle laughed too, warmth moving through the laughter, gratitude for the way Grace always knew when to break a holy moment open before it became too heavy to hold.

Elle wandered further along the wall, writing words that rose from deep places she hadn't known she'd been carrying:

Belonging.

Restoration.

Overflow.

Return home.

Trust Him.

In one quiet corner, she wrote smaller than everything else:

Even though I walk through the valley... You are with me.

She didn't explain it.

She didn't need to.

Mara paused nearby and read it gently. She didn't say anything, didn't ask. She simply pressed her shoulder lightly against Elle's for one quiet second before walking on.

The gesture said everything.

I see you.

I understand more than you know.

You are not alone in the valleys you don't talk about.

Elle stood still for a moment after Mara moved away.

Something in her chest loosened.

She thought of Daniel.

Not the whole wound. Just the edge of it. The hollow of having gone quiet in herself for too long, of having shrunk away from being fully known because being known felt dangerous.

She had written those words for herself.

Even though I walk through the valley.

She was still walking out of it.

But she was not walking alone.

She pressed her palm flat against the brick one more time.

Then she moved on.

Prayers for the town covered the walls now, sentences layered between Scripture, different hands and different hearts speaking the same hope into brick and primer:

Let prodigals come home.

Let marriages be strengthened.

Let loneliness end here.

Let this be a gathering place.

Let Jesus be known.

The walls began to look wild and beautiful, covered in ink and hope and handwriting that reflected each woman differently. Grace's declarations large and bold. Mara's requests careful and measured. Paisley's petitions direct and specific. Janelle's affirmations steady and sure. Elle's prayers a mixture of all of them.

Time blurred.

Sunlight shifted.

Natalie Grant's voice moved into another song.

And slowly, something deeper than paint was happening.

They weren't just decorating.

They were covering the cafe in faith.

* * *

The door opened quietly near midday.

Elle turned.

Eli stepped inside first, Luke close behind him.

They both stopped.

The room looked nothing like it had that morning.

Every wall was covered in words. Scripture. Prayers. Declarations written in five different hands, layered over each other, prayers stacked on prayers.

Grace stood in the center holding her marker like a trophy. "Welcome to phase two."

Luke's brows lifted slowly as he scanned the walls. "Well," he said calmly, "this is thorough."

Eli didn't speak immediately.

He walked slowly along the nearest wall, reading.

His expression wasn't amused.

It was moved.

His gaze paused on Restore what was lost.

He stayed there longer than the others.

He didn't know who had written it. The handwriting was careful, measured, the kind of precision that came from choosing words deliberately rather than quickly. Someone who had learned to be exact about what they asked for because approximations hadn't been enough.

He understood that.

He had written prayers like that himself, once. Prayers so specific they embarrassed him. Prayers that asked for the same thing in fourteen different wordings because he wasn't sure God had understood him the first time, and the truth was he wasn't sure he understood himself.

He moved on and read.

Let this place gather the weary.

Then on *My cup overflows.*

He looked toward Elle.

Not dramatic.

Not loud.

Just steady recognition, the way he looked at everything that mattered.

"You've been busy," he said quietly.

Elle smiled softly. "We didn't want to miss anything."

Luke gave a small nod. "That's a lot of prayer."

"Exactly," Janelle replied gently.

Grace crossed her arms. "Do you want to add one?"

Luke hesitated for half a second, the way he hesitated before anything that required him to put words to what he felt. Then he shrugged lightly and took the marker Grace held out.

He walked to the wall near the entrance, studied the prayers already there, then wrote simply:

Protect this place.

Simple.

Strong.

Luke Callahan in three words.

Grace read it and something in her expression went soft and quiet in a way she couldn't quite hide before looking away.

Eli stood still for a moment longer.

He looked at the walls. At the prayers of five women who had stood in this unfinished space and believed before there was anything to believe in yet.

Something settled into him.

He walked toward the wall near where the Bible rested beneath the floor, the place he had knelt and prayed with Elle weeks ago. He uncapped a marker.

And wrote:

Let what is built here honor You.

Nothing flashy.

Nothing long.

Just steady.

He stepped back and read it once. Then looked at Elle.

She didn't say anything.

She just nodded slightly.

And something passed between them that wasn't romance, exactly.

Alignment.

The quiet recognition of two people building from the same foundation.

Grace clapped her hands together. "Okay! Before I start crying again, can we please prime the walls?"

They laughed.

Drop cloths shifted.

Rollers dipped into soft, white paint.

* * *

They began to cover the walls.

Not erasing.

Layering.

Each stroke of the roller sealed prayer beneath it. Each pass preserved what had been written, hidden now but present, the same way the Bible lay under the doorway. The same way the strongest foundations were always the ones you couldn't see.

As the primer rolled forward, the words disappeared one by one.

Grace watched her own bold handwriting vanish under white and pressed her lips together hard.

Paisley painted steadily, jaw set with a kind of gentle resolve.

Janelle moved her roller with the unhurried attention she brought to every act of faith.

Mara painted slowly, methodically, covering Restore what was lost with steady, careful strokes.

Elle watched her for a moment.

Mara's face was composed.

But her eyes were far away.

Elle didn't ask.

She simply moved her roller alongside Mara's for a few minutes, working in the same quiet rhythm, saying nothing. Sometimes presence was the most faithful thing you could offer.

When the last visible prayer disappeared under paint, Elle stepped back and pressed her palm gently against the wall.

Still warm.

Still full.

Hidden beneath the surface:

Hope. Scripture. Longings. Unspoken battles. Future testimonies. The prayers of women and men who had stood here and believed.

She closed her eyes briefly.

"Let it overflow," she whispered.

And somewhere under fresh primer and steady hands, the cafe became more than a business.

It became covered ground.

* * *

Late in the afternoon, when the primer had dried and the drop cloths had been folded and the rollers cleaned, they gathered near the old counter.

Grace passed out the last of the pastries.

Janelle poured water into paper cups.

Paisley flopped into a folding chair with the boneless relief of someone who had been on their feet for eight hours straight.

"Okay," Grace announced, looking at the smooth white walls around them, "you cannot tell me this doesn't feel different."

It did.

The room felt lighter than it had before.

Not because of the paint.

Because of what was underneath it.

Mara sat quietly on an overturned bucket, hands around her water cup, looking at the wall nearest the window. The wall where she had written Make beauty from ashes.

Elle sat down beside her.

They didn't speak for a moment.

Then Mara said softly, almost to herself, "I believe He can."

Elle looked at her.

"Make beauty from ashes," Mara clarified, glancing at Elle with a small, careful smile. "I believe He actually can."

She didn't say more.

She didn't need to.

Elle reached over and rested her hand briefly over Mara's.

"I do too," she said.

Mara nodded once, something quiet and resolved settling across her face.

The conversations around them continued. Grace recounting the dramatic moment her ladder wobbled. Paisley insisting her roller technique was superior. Luke asking from the doorway whether there were any pastries left and being answered by Grace throwing a napkin at him.

The laughter was real and warm and holy in its own way.

Because this was what it looked like when God's people gathered.

Not perfectly.

Not without their wounds and questions and careful prayers and things too deep for easy words.

But together.

And together, it turned out, was exactly enough.

The friendships formed in that sacred, ink-stained afternoon would carry secrets, promises, and answered prayers far beyond the walls of The Overflow Cafe.

They just didn't know it yet.

***

He stayed after the others left.

Not long. Just a few minutes. Long enough to walk the room once more after the drop cloths had been folded and the rollers cleaned and the laughter faded down the street.

The walls were white now. Smooth. Unmarked from the outside.

He knew what was underneath.

He had read most of it before the primer went on. Prayers in five different hands, layered over each other, asking God for things that mattered. He had written his own and meant it and that part was simple.

It was the one he kept coming back to that wasn't simple.

Restore what was lost.

He didn't know who had written it. The handwriting was careful, deliberate, the handwriting of someone who measured their words the way he measured boards. Someone who had learned to be precise about what they asked for because they had asked imprecisely before and it had cost them.

He understood that.

He walked to the wall where it had been and pressed his palm flat against the primer, the way Elle had done before she prayed. He didn't know why he did it. It just felt right to acknowledge what was underneath before he left.

Restore what was lost.

He exhaled slowly.

The thing he had never said out loud, not to Luke, not in any of the towns before this one, not even to God in words that felt honest enough to count, was this:

He had not just lost Sarah.

He had lost his own certainty.

Not his faith. He was clear enough to know the difference. He still believed. Still prayed. Still showed up on job sites and in churches and at kitchen tables and meant every word he said to God.

But he had trusted his own judgment about her. Had looked at what they were building together and decided it was sound. Had checked the bones of it the way his father taught him and concluded it would hold.

And it hadn't held.

Not because of a sudden collapse. That would have been easier to understand. It had held and held and held and then one day he looked at it and understood that what he had believed was weight-bearing had never been weight-bearing at all. He had been reading the structure wrong from the beginning.

He pulled his hand back from the wall.

Lord, he said quietly, to the empty room, to the white walls, to the God he had been talking to since he was a boy in his father's truck on early mornings. *I don't know how to trust what I see anymore.*

He let that sit.

It was the first time he had said it that plainly.

I thought I knew what I was looking at. I thought I understood the difference between something that was sound and something that only looked sound. My father spent thirty years teaching me how to read a structure.

He stopped.

He was not talking about a building.

He pressed two fingers against the primer the way he pressed them against old walls to take a pulse.

What if I'm wrong again?

The question landed in the empty cafe and stayed there.

He didn't get an answer.

He had not expected one. He had learned enough about prayer to know that the honest ones didn't always come back with an immediate reply. Sometimes you said the true thing and sat in the quiet of having said it and waited.

He was learning to wait.

He picked up his tool bag.

He looked at the doorway. At the threshold he had lifted and replaced and nailed back down with care. At the floor beneath which something solid and true rested, invisible, load-bearing, present whether anyone thought about it or not.

He thought about what he had said to Elle when they knelt there together.

Most people never see what holds everything up.

He walked to the threshold.

He pressed the heel of his boot against it once.

Solid.

He stood there for a moment. Just standing on it. Letting it hold him.

I don't know if I can trust what I see, he said again, quietly. *But I trust what You build.*

He picked up his bag.

Switched off the work light.

And walked out into the evening, leaving the question behind him in a room full of hidden prayers, trusting, the way he trusted every foundation he had ever stood on, that the thing underneath was doing its work whether he could feel it or not.

Chapter Twelve

Market Days

By the time Saturday arrived, Willow Creek smelled like summer trying its best.

Not the full heat of July. Not yet. But the warm promise of it. Sunlight poured down on Main Street, bright enough to make the painted storefronts glow and the window boxes overflow with color. A breeze moved through town carrying the scent of lilacs and fresh-cut grass and something sweet baking somewhere nearby, close enough to smell but too far to identify.

The farmers market was already buzzing when Elle and her friends arrived.

Tents lined the street in cheerful rows, canvas tops fluttering gently in the breeze. People wandered with tote bags and coffee cups, laughing in small clusters and stopping to examine honey jars and handmade soap and early strawberries so red they looked impossible. Kids darted between booths with sticky fingers and wide grins. A local musician played guitar near the fountain, the melody light and familiar enough that you could hum along without thinking about why you knew it.

Elle stopped at the edge of it all and just breathed it in.

This was Willow Creek in its truest form. Unhurried. Generous. Alive with the warmth of people who had chosen to stay.

* * *

Grace hooked her arm through Elle's like she was afraid she might float away.

"Okay," she announced, scanning the vendors with the focus of a general surveying a battlefield. "This is my favorite day of the week. And I swear if The Overflow Cafe does not have market-day specials eventually, I will file a formal complaint."

Elle laughed. "Duly noted."

Mara walked on Elle's other side, calm and observant, taking in the crowd the way she took in every room she entered. Not just seeing it but reading it. The tired mother with the double stroller. The elderly couple walking slowly with their hands linked. The teenager at the edge of a group who wasn't quite part of it yet.

Mara saw people.

It was one of the things Elle loved most about her.

Paisley was already three steps ahead, waving at someone in line for flowers. "Oh my gosh, look at that booth," she called back, pointing. "Handmade cinnamon rolls. This is the kind of ministry I understand."

Janelle smiled quietly beside her, gaze lingering on a vendor handing small bouquets to a little girl who looked overwhelmed by the options. "It's beautiful," she said softly. "It feels like the whole town is here."

Elle looked around, letting the noise and color fill her.

It was.

And for the first time in a long time, the sound of people didn't feel like chaos.

It felt like community.

It felt like exactly what she was trying to build.

* * *

They stopped at a stall overflowing with tulips and ranunculus, Grace insisting that everyone needed flowers because "it's practically biblical to celebrate joy," and Mara buying a small bundle of daffodils without saying why.

Elle didn't ask.

Some things were sacred and personal and didn't need explaining.

They wandered booth to booth: jars of jam and handmade soap and fresh berries and baskets woven from local reeds. At one table, someone had carved wooden signs with Scripture verses burned into the grain, each one unique, each one clearly made by someone who understood that words needed to be held in something lasting.

Grace picked one up with great drama.

"'As for me and my house,'" she read aloud, then looked up. "Yes. I'll take four."

Mara laughed. "For who?"

Grace shrugged. "My future children."

Paisley choked on laughter. "Grace. You don't even have a boyfriend."

Grace smiled sweetly. "Faith is the substance of things hoped for."

Elle laughed so hard she had to press her hand to her stomach, and in the middle of that laughter, she felt the Saturday open up around her like something she had almost forgotten how to inhabit.

Joy.

Simple, unhurried, unearned joy.

She had missed this. Not the market specifically. But this. The ease of being surrounded by people who knew her name and wanted nothing from her except her company.

* * *

And then she noticed him.

Eli stood a little distance away near the edge of the market, talking with Luke. Both of them held iced coffees from one of the vendor stands, both of them carrying the easy posture of men who weren't in any hurry. Luke said something and Eli tilted his head with a quiet smile.

Luke spotted Grace and lifted a hand in a calm wave.

Eli's gaze followed Luke's and found Elle.

Warm recognition moved across his face. Subtle but clear.

Not dramatic.

Just steady.

Elle's heart gave a small, quiet thump that she filed away without examining.

Grace leaned toward Mara immediately, whispering with absolutely zero subtlety, "Do not say anything. Do not ruin this."

Mara lifted an eyebrow. "I wasn't going to say anything."

Paisley grinned, eyes sparkling. "What exactly is 'this'?"

Janelle's smile was soft, like she was already praying for everyone involved and had been for some time.

Eli reached them, hands in his pockets, shoulders relaxed. "Hey," he said simply.

Elle smiled. "Hey."

Luke joined a moment later, nodding at the group with his usual grounded warmth. "Good turnout."

"It's Willow Creek," Grace said. "We show up for produce and friendship."

Luke's mouth tilted. "Accurate."

Eli glanced toward the pastry bag in Grace's hand. "Cinnamon rolls?"

Paisley clutched hers protectively. "These are sacred."

Eli chuckled softly, then looked at Elle with an ease that had been building between them for weeks now. "You're here for inspiration?"

Elle blinked. "Inspiration?"

"For your menu," he said, tone light but not teasing. Genuine curiosity. "Seems like something you'd do."

She felt the accuracy of that land with a small warmth in her chest. "I... yes. Actually."

Grace raised her chin proudly. "The Overflow Cafe will have the best menu in Washington."

Luke leaned slightly toward Eli. "She's already decided that."

Eli's eyes held quiet amusement. "I can tell."

* * *

They kept walking as a loose, comfortable group, drifting deeper into the market.

Conversations around them rose and fell like waves. Someone greeted Luke by name near the bread booth. Someone called out to Mara from across the way. Paisley stopped twice to talk with people from the hospital, her voice shifting into the particular warmth she saved for people who were still carrying something hard.

Elle watched it all with a soft heart.

This wasn't just her dream anymore.

It was becoming the town's dream too.

She didn't know exactly when that had happened. Somewhere between the prayers on the walls and the permitting paperwork and the slow, steady work of building in public view. People had started watching. Leaning in. Hoping along with her.

The weight of that was beautiful and terrifying in equal measure.

She pressed her fingers briefly against the small key on her lanyard. Old habit. Grounding herself.

Then they stopped.

Because a scent caught the air. Rich and warm and sweet in a way that had nothing to do with pastries.

Coffee.

Elle's head turned instinctively.

* * *

A booth stood near the middle of the market; the table covered in burlap and wooden crates stacked with quiet intention.

Bags of coffee beans were arranged neatly, each labeled with hand-stamped tags that looked like someone had stayed up late getting them exactly right. Small jars of honey glowed amber in the morning sun beside them, lined up like little lanterns.

Behind the table stood a young man with an easy smile and sleeves rolled up to his elbows, pouring small samples into tiny paper cups with the relaxed confidence of someone who loved what he was doing.

The sign above him read:

WILLOW AND WILD COFFEE AND HONEY

Small Batch. Local Harvest.

Grace made a delighted sound. "Oh. Yes."

Paisley's eyes widened. "This is dangerous."

Mara nodded slowly. "We should absolutely stop."

Janelle smiled gently. "It smells amazing."

The vendor looked up as they approached, smile widening as if he'd been hoping for exactly this kind of group. "Morning," he called warmly. "Coffee sample? Honey drizzle? Both? We don't judge here."

Elle laughed softly, something in his energy instantly familiar. Not in a way she could name. Just comfortable. Like someone who fit Willow Creek the way a good piece of furniture fit an old room.

Grace stepped up first, because Grace never hesitated. "Hi," she said, leaning in to read the labels. "Are you new here?"

The man grinned. "I'm Caleb. And newish. Been doing markets for a while, but I'm expanding this season. Bringing in a few specialty roasts. I also harvest honey on my family's property."

Paisley gasped. "You are a walking Pinterest board."

Caleb laughed easily. "I've genuinely never been called that before."

Elle accepted a sample cup and took a sip.

Her eyes widened.

It was good. Really good. Rich and smooth, with something bright underneath that she couldn't identify but immediately wanted more of.

"Wow," she breathed. "That is really good."

Caleb's smile warmed. "Thank you. That roast is called Rainier Sunrise."

Grace practically squealed. "Of course it is."

Eli stood slightly behind Elle, watching the exchange with calm interest, arms loosely crossed. Luke had moved toward the table and was reading labels with the careful attention of a man deciding which one could survive a firehouse.

Caleb's gaze returned to Elle, friendly and curious. "You look like someone who appreciates coffee."

The statement landed more personally than he probably meant it. "I do," she said.

Grace beamed proudly. "She's opening a cafe."

Caleb's eyes widened. "Seriously?"

Elle blinked at Grace. "Grace."

Grace held up her hands innocently. "What? It's exciting!"

Elle laughed softly, then nodded. "Yes. The Overflow Cafe. In the old Daily Bread building on Main."

Caleb's expression shifted into genuine interest. "That's a great space. People have been talking about it."

Mara nodded. "They definitely have."

Caleb leaned forward slightly, lowering his voice like he was offering something real. "If you want coffee beans with a story, I'm your guy. Small batch, locally roasted, honest sourcing."

Elle smiled. "I might take you up on that."

"And local honey in the lattes?" he added. "Game changer. I'm just saying."

Paisley leaned toward Elle and stage-whispered, "Honey latte ministry."

Janelle covered her smile with her hand.

Luke nodded toward the jars. "You sell to local businesses?"

"Some," Caleb said. "Hoping to expand. I want to partner with places that care about people, not just profit."

Elle felt something tighten gently in her chest at that.

Care about people.

She understood that language.

* * *

She glanced toward Eli, but he had already moved slightly to the side of the booth.

He stood near a small display she hadn't noticed until now, handcrafted ceramic mugs arranged carefully on a wooden shelf. Each one was unique, glazed in soft earth tones, shapes slightly different from the others, imperfect in the particular way that made handmade things more beautiful than factory-perfect ones.

One mug near the center had a simple cross etched into the clay.

Clean. Unhurried. Grounded.

Elle stepped closer, drawn to it without quite deciding to move.

Eli stepped at the same moment.

Their hands reached for the same mug.

And touched.

Not a brush. Not a casual accidental bump in a crowded market.

A clean contact. Fingers against fingers. And something moved through Elle's hand and up her arm that she could not have explained to anyone who asked.

She went still.

Completely still.

The world didn't stop around them. The market noise continued. Grace was saying something three feet away. Caleb was explaining honey varietals. A child nearby dropped a strawberry and burst into tears.

But inside the small radius of her and Eli and the mug with the cross, everything paused.

She lifted her eyes slowly.

He was already looking at her.

No teasing in his expression.

No flirtation.

Just the quiet, steady recognition that he had felt it too. Whatever it was. This thing they had not named and were not rushing and were not entirely pretending wasn't there.

Elle pulled her hand back slowly, her heart beating just a little faster than it had been ten seconds ago.

"I'm sorry," she said softly, though she wasn't entirely sure what she was apologizing for.

Eli's mouth curved faintly. "No need."

His voice was calm. But the slight warmth underneath it settled into her like something that would take a while to cool.

He picked up the mug carefully this time, holding it out toward her. "You were reaching for it."

Elle hesitated. "Are you sure?"

He nodded once. "Yeah."

She took it gently, her fingertips brushing the cool ceramic. The cross etched into the clay felt rough beneath her thumb.

Grounded.

Simple.

She looked down at it, focusing on the mug because focusing on his eyes felt like too much right now. Her heart needed a moment to settle back into its usual rhythm.

"It's beautiful," she said quietly.

Caleb's voice came in from behind the booth. "That one's handmade by a local artist, Hannah. People are drawn to it. I think because it's honest. Nothing decorative about it. Just the cross and the clay."

Elle nodded slowly.

She turned it over in her hands, feeling the weight of it.

Something in her wanted to examine what had just happened between her and Eli. To take it out and look at it in the light the way she took out difficult things and tried to understand them.

But she recognized the old instinct underneath that impulse.

The one that had ruined things before.

The one that picked things apart before they had a chance to become anything.

She filed the moment away instead. Set it gently to the side. Let it exist without forcing it into a shape.

That was new for her.

She wasn't sure when she had learned to do that.

She glanced up and met Eli's gaze briefly.

He was watching her, not intensely, just with that steady attentiveness that had become as familiar as the sound of his drill in the mornings.

As if he saw her.

Not the cafe. Not the project. Not the calling.

Her.

Elle's cheeks warmed.

She looked back at the mug and laughed softly. "I think this might be a future Overflow mug."

Grace appeared at her elbow like she'd been summoned. "OH," she said, staring at the mug with absolute conviction. "YES. That is absolutely an Overflow mug."

Mara stepped closer and looked at the cross, eyes soft. "It fits."

Paisley leaned in and stage-whispered, "It's giving 'signature drink.'"

Janelle smiled gently. "It's giving 'purpose.'"

Elle laughed, grateful for the way her friends could hold a moment without making it heavier than it needed to be.

Caleb nodded with an approving grin. "If you ever want a set for the cafe, I can connect you with the artist directly. She'd love knowing where they ended up."

Elle nodded. "When we're closer to opening, I'll reach out."

Eli's gaze flicked toward her at that, something knowing in it.

Building.

Yes.

In more ways than one.

* * *

Luke cleared his throat lightly, scanning the market. "We should keep moving before Grace buys the entire street."

Grace pointed at him. "Do not underestimate me."

They laughed and began walking again, the sun warm on their shoulders, the market alive around them.

Elle held the mug carefully as they walked, fingers curled around the cross etched into the clay.

It wasn't just ceramic.

She knew that.

It was the moment that had happened beside it. The jolt she wasn't ready to name. The feeling of being seen in a way that didn't ask her to perform or achieve or explain herself.

She had felt it before.

Not like this.

With Daniel, being seen had eventually felt like being watched. Like she was always slightly on trial for whether she was enough. And she had gone quieter and quieter trying to pass a test that kept changing its criteria.

This didn't feel like that.

This felt like standing in good light.

She almost let herself stay with the thought.

Then she tucked it away again, gently, and looked ahead at her friends laughing in the morning sun.

Not yet.

Not because she was afraid, exactly.

Because some things deserved to grow slowly in the right soil before you put them in the window.

As they drifted away from the booth, Elle glanced back once and saw Caleb chatting with a new customer, smiling like a man who loved what his hands produced.

She thought about what he had said.

Partner with places that care about people, not just profit.

She would be calling him soon.

She could already feel it.

* * *

Near the far end of the market, Grace stopped at a booth run by a quiet man with weathered hands and a hand-lettered sign:

MILLER FAMILY DAIRY

Fresh Cream. Local Delivery. Willow Creek and Surrounding Areas.

Small glass bottles lined the table, cream rising visibly to the tops of several of them.

"Okay," Paisley said. "This is what lattes are supposed to be made with."

Grace picked up a bottle and turned it over. "Can you do deliveries to a cafe?"

The man behind the table nodded. "That's most of our business. We supply four places in town already."

Elle made a mental note.

Miller Family Dairy.

She wrote it in her phone under cafe suppliers before she could forget it.

Eli had already picked up a bottle and was reading the label with the same quiet attention he brought to everything. He set it down and looked at Elle. "You should talk to them before you finalize your order list."

"I will," she said.

He nodded once.

Simple as that.

He didn't need to say more and neither did she. They had fallen into a rhythm over these past weeks that still surprised her sometimes. Not finishing each other's sentences. Just understanding each other's direction.

She wasn't sure when that had started.

She wasn't sure she wanted to examine it too closely yet.

The sun climbed higher over Willow Creek as the morning deepened into midday. They bought jam and flowers and wooden signs and cinnamon rolls that Grace declared were transformative. They laughed and wandered and let the market hold them for a few hours.

And Elle walked through all of it carrying a ceramic mug with a cross etched into the clay, and a moment she was not yet ready to name, and the quiet gathering sense that God was connecting things around her with the same patient care He had always used.

Not rushing.

Not forcing.

Just building.

Under the bright Willow Creek sun, Elle walked on, quietly holding both a mug and a morning she knew she would not forget.

CHAPTER THIRTEEN

The Art of the Blend

Morning light poured into The Overflow Cafe like it had been invited.

The walls had dried, leaving the space soft and bright and holding its breath in that particular way unfinished rooms did, full of potential and the faint smell of possibility. The scent of fresh primer still lingered faintly, but beneath it, something far more important had already begun to take over.

Coffee.

Real coffee. The kind that reached you before you saw the source.

Elle stood behind a temporary folding table she had transformed into a makeshift tasting bar with the focused pleasure of someone returning to a language they thought they had forgotten. Four small glass carafes sat in a row, steam rising gently from each one. Beside them, small white tasting cups lined up like an audience. Spoons. A notebook already filled with scribbles in her handwriting, margins crowded with arrows and stars and circled words.

She had tied her hair back with a loose clip. Sleeves pushed up. Eyes bright with a kind of electricity that hummed through her entire posture.

For ten years she had led coffee tastings in sleek corporate conference rooms, for executives who checked their phones and buyers who needed to be impressed before noon.

Today she was leading one in her own cafe.

For Jesus.

For community.

For something that mattered more than any quarterly report had ever mattered.

It felt entirely different.

It felt like coming home to a skill she had always carried but never been allowed to fully inhabit.

* * *

Eli stepped through the front door carrying his tool bag and paused the moment the smell hit him.

He stood just inside the threshold the way he always stood when he first entered the cafe, taking the room in before moving into it. His gaze landed on the table. On the carafes. On Elle behind them looking like she had been waiting for this exact morning for years.

He set his bag down slowly. "Well," he said, a small smile forming, "this looks official."

Elle beamed. "Good. You're right on time."

He walked closer, studying the setup with the same quiet attention he gave to blueprints and building materials. "Should I be nervous?"

"Only if you refuse to participate fully."

He folded his arms loosely. "Define fully."

She slid a small tasting cup toward him across the table. "You're about to experience coffee the way it was meant to be experienced."

He picked it up carefully. "I already drink coffee."

Elle shook her head with playful seriousness. "No. You consume coffee. Today you will taste it."

His mouth twitched. "All right. I'm teachable."

She clapped once, genuinely delighted. "Perfect."

She moved into position behind the table like a seasoned instructor stepping back into a classroom she loved. But this time there were no executives checking watches. No sales targets hovering in the background like uninvited guests. No pressure to perform or impress or justify the time.

Just sunlight through old windows.

An unfinished cafe.

And a man willing to learn.

* * *

"For ten years," she began, eyes alive with it, "I led coffee tastings before every major meeting. Buyers, leadership teams, new colleagues. It was how we started every conversation. Build common ground over something sensory before you get to the numbers."

Eli leaned against the counter frame, listening the way he listened to everything. Completely.

"But this," she said softly, gesturing around the unfinished space, "is the first time it has ever felt like mine."

He nodded once, quietly. The way he received things that mattered.

She lifted the first carafe and poured a small amount into his cup.

"Step one," she said, slipping into expert mode as naturally as breathing. "Aroma. Don't sip yet. Just smell."

He brought the cup toward his nose and inhaled.

"Okay," he said after a moment. "Coffee."

Elle burst out laughing, the sound filling the high ceilings. "We are going deeper than that."

He smiled. "All right, coach."

She leaned in slightly beside him. "Close your eyes. Smell again. What does it remind you of? Not the word coffee. Something else. A place. A feeling. A memory."

He did.

This time he paused longer.

She watched his face, the small furrow of concentration between his brows, the slight tilt of his head.

"Warm," he said slowly. "Like something toasted. Like a morning that doesn't have anywhere to be."

Her smile softened instantly.

"Yes," she said. "That is exactly right. That is a medium roast. Balanced. It doesn't shout. It welcomes."

He opened his eyes. "That feels accurate."

"It does," she agreed. "And it's important. The first sip someone takes in The Overflow Cafe needs to feel like that. Like a morning that doesn't have anywhere to be."

Something shifted in his expression, quiet and pleased.

She poured from the second carafe. "Now this one."

He inhaled again.

His brows drew together. "Brighter. Almost citrus."

Her eyes lit. "You're good at this."

He shrugged lightly. "I pay attention."

The words landed simply, without performance. Just true.

She moved to the third carafe, voice dropping slightly with excitement. "Now we taste."

He lifted the cup.

She held up one finger. "Wait. There is a method."

He looked at her.

"Take a sip," she instructed, "but don't swallow immediately. Let it sit on your tongue. Feel where it lands. Then."

She demonstrated.

A full, unapologetic, thoroughly audible slurp.

The sound echoed in the nearly empty cafe.

Eli blinked.

She grinned. "Yes. Like that."

He stared at her for a beat. "You're serious."

"Completely."

He looked around the empty room as if checking whether anyone was watching, then lifted his cup and made a small, polite, barely-qualifying sound.

Elle gasped. "No. Bigger."

"Bigger?"

"Bigger," she said, laughing now. "Slurp like you mean it. The sound is what aerates it. It changes the flavor profile."

He shook his head once, but there was a smile pulling at the corner of his mouth that he was very clearly not trying hard enough to suppress. Then he tried again.

This time the slurp echoed properly off brick.

She clapped, delighted. "Yes! That's it!"

He swallowed and blinked. "That actually does change it."

"I know," she said triumphantly.

"The aeration thing is real."

"The aeration thing is absolutely real."

He looked at her with the expression of a man who had just been proven wrong about something and found it more enjoyable than expected. "Now where do I taste it? Is that what you're about to ask?"

"Front of your tongue? Back? Sides?"

He considered. "Middle. Smooth. Bold but not bitter."

She nodded, deeply pleased. "Dark roast. Steady. Like it knows what it is and doesn't need to prove it."

He glanced at her. "You love this."

The observation landed with a gentleness that made her look up from her notebook.

She did.

She really, genuinely did.

"For years," she said quietly, "this was my job. But it always felt like it was pointing somewhere else. Somewhere slower. Somewhere I hadn't arrived yet."

She looked around the unfinished space.

"Here," she said. "It was always pointing here."

He looked around the cafe too. At the walls. The drop cloths. The old bread board leaning against the counter.

Then back at her.

"Worth the wait," he said simply.

She wasn't sure if he was talking about the cafe.

She didn't examine it.

* * *

"And now," she said, energy building again, "we get to create something no one else has. A signature blend. Something people can only get here."

He leaned back against the counter, attentive. "What would make it special?"

She lit up the way she always lit up when this topic surfaced.

"Balance," she said immediately. "Warmth. A little brightness underneath so it doesn't feel heavy. Comfort but not boring. Something that feels like home on the first sip and like belonging on the second."

She had been thinking about this for years. She had notes in seven different notebooks about it. She had dreamed about it twice that she could remember.

"We could blend a medium roast for the warmth, a lighter roast for brightness, maybe a hint of something darker for depth. A blend that feels like community. Different notes coming together into something better than any of them alone."

He watched her pace lightly, hands moving as she talked, and his expression held something she had learned to recognize over the past weeks.

Quiet admiration.

Not flattery. Not performance.

Just a man paying attention to a woman doing what she was made to do.

"You've thought about this for a long time," he said.

"For years," she admitted.

She paused suddenly.

Caleb.

The market booth. The Rainier Sunrise. The small-batch roasting. The offer.

Her eyes widened slightly.

"Oh."

She typed quickly, thumbs moving fast.

Reminder: Text Caleb re Overflow blend samples

She looked up. "He roasts small batch locally. He understands flavor and story both. He could help craft something completely unique. Not corporate. Not mass-produced."

"Ours," Eli said.

She smiled at the word.

Ours.

She let it sit there a moment before moving on.

"The drinks," she continued, excitement building through her. "Lattes, breves, cortados, honey drinks. Seasonal specials. Comfort drinks for hard days. Celebration drinks for good ones. Coffee flights in summer. An Overflow Blend featured every single morning."

He watched her with that familiar quiet attention, and she was so deep in the vision that she almost missed the warmth in it.

Almost.

"You've dreamed this," he said.

"I just never had a place to put the ideas," she said softly.

He nodded slowly. Understanding more than she said aloud. The way he often did.

A brief, companionable silence settled.

Then Eli pushed off the counter and glanced toward the primed walls. "So if this place is going to feel like home, we need the colors right."

She blinked. "Paint."

"Warm. Welcoming. Nothing sterile."

Her smile came back slowly. "You care about that."

"I care about how people feel when they walk into a space," he said. "Before they order anything. Before they sit down. The room has already told them whether they belong."

Her chest warmed.

"Okay," she said. "Hardware store."

* * *

The bell over the door at Willow Creek Hardware chimed as they stepped inside.

Wood floors creaked under their feet. The scent of lumber and varnish hung comfortably in the air, familiar and grounding. Paint samples lined an entire wall in soft, endless gradients, creams and sage greens and warm whites that all looked subtly different and somehow the same.

An older man behind the counter looked up immediately, his expression shifting from idle to genuinely pleased.

"Well now," he said warmly. "You must be the ones bringing life back to Daily Bread."

Elle laughed. "We're trying."

"Best kind of work there is," he replied, with the certainty of someone who had watched a lot of things come and go in this town. "People have been talking. Good things."

Elle felt the warmth of that settle into her. "Thank you."

They moved toward the paint section together.

Elle's fingers moved over swatches slowly, reading them the way she read menus. Creamy whites that leaned warm. Soft taupe's with honey undertones. A sage green that whispered rather than announced itself.

"Nothing cold," she murmured. "Nothing that makes people feel assessed when they walk in."

Eli studied the samples beside her, close enough that she was aware of his presence without it crowding her. "What do you want people to feel in the first three seconds?"

She didn't hesitate.

"Safe."

The word came out simple and unguarded.

The way honest answers did when you stopped managing them.

He nodded once. "Then warm tones. Soft edges. Nothing that shouts. Places people want to stay in instead of move through."

She looked at him then.

Really looked.

At the way he stood beside her at a paint rack in a hardware store in a small Washington town, talking about how rooms made people feel safe, with the same steady seriousness he brought to load-bearing walls and building codes.

He wasn't performing sensitivity.

He just had it.

Built in, the same way the carpenter instincts were built in.

"You're good at this," she said.

He considered for a moment, then gave a quiet half-smile. "Years of listening to what a space needs before I touch it."

Elle pulled two swatches from the rack and held them side by side. A warm cream with the faintest honey undertone. A soft taupe that felt like a late afternoon in October.

"These two," she said.

He looked at them. Considered. Then pointed to the cream. "That one for the main walls. It will hold the light differently through the day. Warmer in the morning, softer by evening."

She stared at him.

"How do you know that?"

He looked slightly amused. "I've painted a lot of rooms."

She laughed, shaking her head. "Of course you have."

They stood there a moment longer beneath fluorescent lights and rows of color cards, holding the future between them in two small squares of painted paper.

It wasn't dramatic.

It was better than dramatic.

It was two people who understood what they were building and trusted each other enough to build it well.

Outside, Willow Creek moved through its ordinary Saturday afternoon.

Inside the hardware store, Elle held her paint swatches and thought about mornings that didn't have anywhere to be, and rooms that made people feel safe before they understood why, and a man who paid attention.

She thought about the signature blend she would create with Caleb.

About the mugs with crosses etched into the clay.

About the prayers written beneath the primer on every wall.

About what it meant to build something on the right foundation.

She didn't think about Daniel.

And the fact that she didn't, for the first time in longer than she could remember, felt like the first dry ground after a very long flood.

CHAPTER FOURTEEN

Framing the Future

The scent of fresh-cut wood greeted Elle before she even stepped fully inside.

Morning light poured through the tall front windows of The Overflow Cafe, catching in the fine sawdust that floated through the air like golden breath. It settled across the primed walls and along the old brick near the entrance and glimmered in the sunbeams the way dust did in spaces that were being remade. The building smelled like effort. Like intention.

Like something real being built inside something old.

Elle paused just inside the doorway, coffee in one hand, keys still looped around her finger. She took the room in the way Eli had taught her to take rooms in, not rushing past the first impression to get to the work, but letting the space tell her something before she changed it.

What it told her this morning was this: it was becoming.

No longer just an old bakery. Not yet a cafe. But in the particular in-between space where things that were being built with care and patience lived. Alive with the sound of a saw humming somewhere deeper in the room.

Eli was already there.

Of course he was.

* * *

She followed the sound toward the front counter area and found him kneeling beside a long stretch of newly cut lumber, pencil tucked behind his ear, tape measure extended across the floor with the ease of a man who had done this ten thousand times.

The skeletal frame of what would become the main service counter had begun to take shape. Clean lines marked in wood. Corners squared. Joints fitted with the kind of precision that came from caring about what happened inside the wall as much as what people would see from the outside.

His father had built that into him.

She could see it in every choice he made.

He glanced up when he heard her footsteps.

"Morning," he said, pushing to his feet with the unhurried ease of someone who had been on his knees working since before she arrived and didn't need her to notice.

There was a faint smear of sawdust along one sleeve and the soft crease of focus between his brows.

Elle smiled. "You've been busy."

He looked at the framework behind him and nodded once. "Getting the counter footprint mapped out. Wanted to see how it felt in the space before locking anything in. Paper plans are one thing. Standing inside it is another."

That was Eli in a sentence. He needed to stand inside something before he committed to it. Needed to feel the weight of it, the actual dimensions, not just the measurements on a page.

She stepped closer, moving slowly around the outline of the counter.

Even unfinished, raw wood and pencil marks and sawdust on the floor, it changed the room. Gave it direction. You could feel where the energy of the space was being gathered and intentionally shaped.

"This is where people will order," she murmured softly. "Where they'll stand and decide what kind of morning they're about to have."

He glanced at her. "That's a lot of pressure for a counter."

She laughed. "Coffee is serious."

He smiled faintly. "So I'm learning."

He handed her the tape measure. "Stand there a second?"

She moved where he gestured, just behind where the register would eventually live.

He stepped back and studied the proportions. Not the measurements. The feel.

"Line space here for customers," he said, pointing toward the door. "Pickup there. Espresso machine along this section, which keeps the workflow moving left to right and gives you visibility to the whole room while you're working."

Her eyes lit. "You thought through the flow."

He shrugged lightly. "People like knowing where to go when they walk into somewhere new. Makes them feel comfortable before they've even decided whether they like the place."

She watched him for a moment, this man who thought about how people felt when they walked into rooms and designed spaces accordingly, and said quietly, "You're really good at this."

He met her gaze briefly. "I care about doing things right."

She nodded.

That mattered to her more than she could have explained to anyone who asked.

* * *

The hum of a drill filled the space for the next hour as Eli secured the first sections of the counter frame into place.

Elle moved around the room with her notepad and pencil, jotting down ideas as they came. Where the pastry case might sit. Where a small shelf for prayer journals could go near the door. How the afternoon light fell across the corner that might hold the cozy reading chair she had been imagining since April.

Charity Gayle played softly from her phone on the windowsill.

Every so often Eli asked for her input on spacing or height, and she found herself stepping into the role easily, naturally, as if she had always been meant to work beside someone rather than alone.

Partner in something tangible.

Not just dreaming anymore.

Building.

When the main counter base was secured, Eli wiped his hands on a cloth and glanced toward the back of the cafe.

"Want to take a look at the coffee bar area? I want to check electrical and plumbing before we get much further. Better to know now."

Elle followed him through the seating area toward the back, where the original bakery kitchen had once operated. The space still held old tile flooring and exposed sections of wall where earlier work had begun and paused.

The history of the building was visible back here in ways the front room had been painted over.

She liked it.

She liked that the bones were honest.

Eli crouched near the future espresso station and pulled aside a loose panel. A cluster of older wiring appeared behind it, dark with age, running in patterns that made sense for a bakery in 1952 and considerably less sense for a cafe in the present.

He studied it quietly.

The quality of his silence when he was thinking was something Elle had come to recognize. It wasn't the silence of someone who didn't know what to say. It was the silence of someone assembling information before they spoke, because they intended to be accurate.

Finally he exhaled.

"Okay," he said.

That one word.

"Okay good, or okay not great?" she asked.

He gave her a small, wry smile. "Somewhere in the middle."

She folded her arms and waited.

"This building is just older," he said calmly. "Nothing unusual for the age. But we'll need to bring some of this up to current code before we install anything that draws real power." He tapped a section gently. "Especially an espresso machine running all day. Commercial equipment pulls a different load than a residential kitchen."

Elle nodded slowly. "Which means permits."

"Most likely. Electrical updates usually do. And we'll want to walk it with an inspector before we go too far." He glanced up at her, reading her expression. "Nothing we can't handle. Just steps."

His tone was level. Grounded.

No false reassurance. No alarm. Just truth delivered by someone who had encountered versions of this problem before and come out the other side of all of them.

She appreciated that more than she could say.

He moved toward the small hallway leading to the bathroom and crouched again, checking a pipe beneath the old sink with practiced hands.

"Same idea here," he said. "Some updates. Adds cost and a little time, but nothing that changes the vision. We build it right."

We.

She noticed that word every time he used it.

"Okay," she said softly.

He glanced up at her.

"We'll handle it," he added, quieter.

Not as a promise to fix everything. Not as a guarantee against difficulty.

As a steady presence beside her in whatever came next.

She nodded. "I trust that."

He gave a small nod in return, then rose and dusted off his hands.

She thought about the old wiring in the walls. About how the building had been carrying this limitation for decades, not broken exactly, just not designed for what it was about to hold.

She thought about herself.

She had been carrying some outdated wiring of her own.

Some circuits designed for a life she was no longer living.

Maybe that needed updating too.

* * *

A knock at the open door drew their attention.

Grace burst in like a weather system, ponytail swinging, tote bag slung over one shoulder.

"Quick visit!" she announced. "I have exactly nine minutes before I need to be somewhere responsible."

Elle laughed. "Come see what's happening."

Grace stepped toward the counter frame and made a sound that was half gasp, half something spiritual. "Oh my gosh. It's actually happening."

She walked around the outline with her hands clasped. "People will stand here. Order here. Spill life stories here."

"Preferably not spill," Eli said mildly.

Grace grinned at him. "Metaphorically spill."

She turned back to Elle. "This is going to be the coziest place in the entire Pacific Northwest."

"We're working on it," Elle said.

Grace nodded with great seriousness, then leaned closer, lowering her voice the way she did when she had useful information she had been waiting for the right moment to deliver.

"Have you confirmed your milk supplier?" she asked.

Elle blinked. "I have the name, Miller Family Dairy, the one we met at the market."

Grace's eyes widened. "Yes. That's exactly who you want. Everyone in town swears by them. Owen Miller runs it now, took it over from his parents a few years ago. Fresh cream, local delivery, and he actually cares where his milk ends up."

Eli made a quiet note on his clipboard.

Elle added it to her phone under suppliers, right above Caleb's name.

Miller Family Dairy. Owen Miller.

She had already written it once after the market. Writing it again felt like confirmation.

Grace checked her watch and sighed with the grief of someone being pulled away from something important. "Okay. I must go be productive." She hugged Elle quickly, waved at Eli with genuine warmth, and disappeared as suddenly as she had arrived, the door swinging softly behind her.

Eli watched the door settle. "High energy."

Elle smiled. "Always."

A beat.

"She's good for you," he said.

Elle looked at him.

He was back to examining the counter frame, not making a moment of it.

Just true.

"She is," Elle said quietly.

* * *

Mara stopped by mid-afternoon with a folder tucked under one arm and the kind of unhurried attentiveness she brought everywhere.

She walked through the space slowly, taking it in with thoughtful eyes. Not evaluating it. Receiving it.

"This feels good," she said finally, voice quiet. "It already feels like somewhere people will want to stay."

She offered a few gentle observations about furniture placement and traffic flow, practical things that came from understanding how people moved through rooms and what made them linger or leave.

Then, before she left, she paused near the doorway and looked back at Elle with something careful in her expression.

"Hey," she said softly. "You seem different lately."

Elle blinked. "Different how?"

Mara considered. "Lighter. Like something you were carrying is starting to set down."

Elle held her gaze for a moment.

"Yeah," she said quietly. "I think it is."

Mara nodded once, something knowing and glad in her eyes. She squeezed Elle's hand before heading back to work.

Neither Grace nor Mara had stayed long.

But each visit had left something behind.

Encouragement.

Belief.

The gift of people who showed up for the in-between stages when there was nothing impressive to see yet.

* * *

By late afternoon the counter frame stood fully outlined and secured, the back wiring exposed but understood, and a clear list of next steps organized on a page in Elle's notebook.

She stood near the entrance as Eli packed up his tools for the day, moving through the familiar closing ritual with the quiet efficiency of someone who treated the end of the workday with the same care as the beginning.

He switched off the work light.

She locked the back door.

They stepped outside together into the evening.

The sun hung low over Willow Creek, painting the storefront windows in warm gold that made the old brick look like something in a photograph. The street had quieted into that particular stillness of early evening, the day's business done and the night's quiet not quite arrived.

They stood side by side on the sidewalk without needing to decide to.

Both looking through the glass at the space inside.

Wood framing standing clean against primed walls.

Wires waiting to be brought forward.

A dream assembled piece by piece in the bones of something old.

"Lot left to do," Eli said.

"Yeah," Elle agreed softly.

But her chest felt full in a way that had nothing to do with completion.

It felt like hope made tangible. Like faith with a tape measure.

"We'll get there," he said.

She glanced at him, then back at the cafe.

"We are," she said.

Not we will.

We are.

Present tense.

Already happening.

Eli's gaze stayed on the window a moment longer. Something in his posture shifted, barely perceptibly, the particular quality of stillness that meant he was sitting with something rather than moving past it.

"My dad used to say that the most important work on any building happened before anyone could see it," he said. "Foundation. Framing. The bones."

Elle looked at him.

"He said if you got those right, everything else was just finishing."

She was quiet for a moment.

"I think that's true about more than buildings," she said.

He glanced at her.

She held his gaze.

The evening light settled warm around them, and neither of them looked away.

Then Eli slipped his keys into his pocket, the small sound of it returning them gently to the practical.

"Same time tomorrow?" he asked.

"Same time," she said.

The sun dipped lower, light spilling across the front windows of The Overflow Cafe like a benediction.

And as they stood there in the quiet warmth of early evening, watching the outline of something new taking shape inside old walls, it felt clear to both of them in the way that true things sometimes felt before you had the words for them:

They weren't just renovating a building.

They were building something meant to last.

Chapter Fifteen

The Bridge

Early summer had settled gently over Willow Creek.

Hydrangeas bowed heavy with blooms along white picket fences, their blues and violets softened by morning light. Lavender lined the edges of gardens and walkways, releasing its calm fragrance into the air with the unhurried generosity of something that had been waiting all year for exactly this moment.

Elle stepped onto the winding river path just outside town and pressed play.

Elevation Worship filled her ears, layered harmonies rising steady and sure. She exhaled slowly and began walking.

Upstream.

The river moved beside her, strong and clear, its current pressing forward with quiet determination. The path rose gradually, not steep but firm enough that she felt it in her calves after the first ten minutes. Gravel shifted beneath her shoes. The air smelled of water and wildflowers and early summer warmth, the kind of morning that felt like a gift before you had done anything to deserve it.

Upstream always required effort.

She had been walking this way for years without fully understanding that.

* * *

"Thank You," she whispered first.

Gratitude came easily now. That was one of the things coming home had done for her. Restored her access to it.

Thank You for bringing me home.

Thank You for peace returning.

Thank You for the cafe and Grace and laughter and second chances.

She breathed the words more than spoke them, the rhythm of her feet carrying the rhythm of her prayer.

Then the worship shifted.

A different song. Slower. More intimate.

And something in her chest shifted with it.

"God," she breathed, quieter now. "I tried to build something without You."

The path curved ahead, narrowing slightly as it approached the small wooden bridge that crossed over a narrower section of the river. The current was pressed tighter here, moving faster between the stones, louder.

She felt the incline deepen beneath her feet.

And something inside her mirrored it exactly.

* * *

For years she had walked like this.

Pushing forward. Striving upward. Building and achieving and advancing. Calling it ambition. Calling it impact. Calling it success because the people around her called it success and she had learned to borrow their certainty when her own ran out.

But never asking whether she was moving with God.

Or against Him.

Or simply beside herself, too exhausted to feel the difference.

Her chest constricted.

She stepped onto the bridge.

The wood creaked softly beneath her weight, the familiar sound of old things still holding. Water rushed below, louder here than anywhere on the path. She could feel it in her feet through the boards.

She stopped in the center.

The worship built around her, drums rising slowly under the melody.

And the tears came.

Not quiet this time. Not the gentle, manageable kind she sometimes allowed herself on these walks, the kind she could blink back and keep moving through.

A deep, aching release. The kind that had been waiting for a bridge.

She gripped the railing and bowed her head.

"I was so tired," she said aloud, her voice swallowed immediately by the sound of the river and the trees and the wide morning air. "I built everything I thought I was supposed to build. I did everything right. I hit every number. I impressed every person I was supposed to impress."

Her shoulders shook.

"And I felt nothing."

The river rushed harder below her feet, indifferent and constant.

"I was successful and I was empty and I did not understand why, and I was too proud to admit that to anyone, including You."

Her voice cracked on the last words.

She pressed her forehead to her hands on the railing.

And then the other thing surfaced.

The thing underneath the burnout.

The thing she had been circling for months without landing on directly.

* * *

Daniel.

Not his face. Not the specific details she still sometimes replayed at two in the morning. Just the feeling of it. The particular shape of what that season had cost her.

She had gone quieter and quieter in that relationship, and she had called it compromise. She had made herself smaller and called it maturity. She had stopped talking about the things that mattered most to her because his discomfort with them mattered more to her than her own voice, and she had told herself that was love.

It wasn't love.

It was fear wearing love's clothing.

She had been so afraid of losing him that she had already lost herself long before he left.

And after he was gone, she had strived harder. Worked longer. Built more. As if achievement could fill the particular hollow that came from having been known and found wanting. As if a sales number could answer the question his leaving had planted in her:

What if being fully known always ends the same way?

What if the real version of you is always too much, or not enough, or simply wrong for the life you most want?

She hadn't let herself examine that question directly.

She had outrun it instead.

For years.

Until her legs gave out on an apartment floor in Seattle with her Bible in her lap and Psalm 23 blurring through tears.

She gripped the railing harder now.

"I don't just want to stop striving," she cried, the words tearing out of her with a rawness she hadn't planned. "I want to stop being afraid of being known."

The river thundered beneath her.

"I want to stop making myself smaller so I'm easier to keep. I want to stop going quiet when I should speak. I want to stop choosing smallness and calling it love."

Her voice broke completely.

"I want to be known, and I am terrified of what that costs."

She wept on the bridge in the morning air, the hydrangeas nodding somewhere behind her, the lavender doing nothing to help, the river entirely unmoved by any of it.

Which was, in its way, exactly what she needed.

Something that kept moving regardless.

Something that did not require her to be okay.

* * *

And in that noise, in the rush of water and the ache of finally saying true things out loud, something holy broke open.

Not shame.

Not condemnation.

Not the voice she had half-expected that would agree with all her worst assessments of herself.

Release.

The particular release that came from being seen completely and not destroyed by it.

She inhaled sharply.

The truth rose steady and unmistakable, the way truth did when you stopped drowning it out:

You are not too much.

You were never too much.

You were just in the wrong places, building the wrong things, trying to earn what was already freely given.

She pressed her forehead to her hands again.

"I surrender," she whispered.

The words weren't dramatic.

They were exhausted.

The surrender of someone who had finally run out of alternatives.

"I don't want to be in control anymore. I don't want to chase what looks impressive if You're not in it. I don't want to keep making myself small to feel safe. I want You to build what You want to build in me, and I want to stop trying to be the architect of my own worth."

A breath.

Shaky.

Then steadier.

"Heal what Daniel broke," she said softly. "Not just the loneliness. The part of me that decided being known wasn't safe anymore. The part that went quiet and called it wisdom."

She exhaled slowly.

"I want to be known. I want to be actually known. And I am asking You to make that feel possible again."

Her grip on the railing loosened.

The river kept moving.

Unbothered by her breakdown.

Unimpressed by her credentials.

Unmoved by her striving.

Just flowing.

Forward.

Constant.

She closed her eyes and let the silence after the tears settle into her like something that had been waiting a long time for this exact moment of entry.

Not instant euphoria.

Not lightning.

Just calm.

Deep.

Steady.

Unmistakable.

The weight in her chest began to lift.

Not all of it.

Healing didn't work like that. She understood that now.

But enough.

Enough to breathe.

Enough to believe.

Enough to turn around.

* * *

She straightened.

Wiped her cheeks with the back of her hand.

Looked downstream.

And turned.

The difference was immediate.

Her steps felt lighter. Not because the path was different. The path was identical. The same gravel, the same morning air, the same distance back to town.

But she was moving with the river now instead of against it.

The incline that had pressed against her on the way up was barely perceptible going down. The current moved in the same direction as her stride. The lavender came toward her instead of passing behind.

Worship rose in her ears, lyrics about surrender and trust and the freedom of letting go of what you were never meant to carry.

She prayed as she walked, easy and unhurried.

For the cafe. For it to be His, fully, every cup and conversation and crumb on the floor.

For Willow Creek. For the tired hearts she hadn't met yet who would one day sit in the corner with a latte and cry and feel less alone.

For Grace, who loved so loudly and so well.

For Mara, who carried something she hadn't named yet, but that Elle could feel like weather.

For the man she hadn't let herself think about directly.

She paused on that one.

Then let it be a prayer without words.

Sometimes that was the most honest kind.

* * *

Eli had left early that morning for a supply run, an errand that took him past the edge of town and back before most people had finished their first coffee. He knew this path. He had driven alongside it a dozen times since coming to Willow Creek, had watched the river from the road and understood why people walked here.

He noticed her immediately.

She was on the bridge.

He slowed, not enough to stop, not enough to intrude. Just enough to see.

Her hands gripped the railing. Her head was bowed. Her shoulders held the shape of someone in the middle of something important, something that required every part of them.

He watched her stand still.

He watched something shift in her posture.

He watched her straighten.

Wipe her face.

And then turn.

And begin walking downstream with a quality of movement that was new. Not faster. Not triumphant.

Just free.

He didn't understand the full story.

He didn't need to.

He understood this:

Her faith was real.

Not decorative. Not the Sunday morning kind that came out for company and went back in a drawer the rest of the week.

Foundational.

The kind that held weight.

The kind that showed up on a bridge alone in the morning and wrestled with God and came away walking differently.

He had prayed for a woman like this.

He had almost stopped believing she existed.

He drove on quietly, one hand on the wheel, the road ahead of him, the river beside him, something settled and certain moving through his chest that he did not yet have the words for but recognized the way you recognized your own name being called across a distance.

* * *

Elle reached the end of the path as sunlight warmed fully over the trees.

The river beside her moved steady and strong.

She slipped one earbud out and listened to it for a moment without music. Without words. Without asking anything of the silence or filling it with the next thought.

Just the river.

Forward.

Constant.

Unforced.

She smiled.

Softly. Slowly. The kind of smile that came from somewhere deeper than happiness.

"Downstream," she whispered.

The word felt like a name for something she had been trying to find for years.

Not downstream as in giving up. Not downstream as in taking the easy path or choosing comfort over calling.

Downstream as in moving with the Shepherd instead of ahead of Him.

Downstream as in letting the current carry what she was not strong enough to carry alone.

Downstream as in trusting that the river knew where it was going even when she couldn't see around the bend.

She stood there a moment longer, the morning full around her, Willow Creek waking up somewhere behind her, the cafe waiting with its primed walls and its prayers written unseen, and its Bible under the floor. You never thought about foundations. You only knew them by what they held.

And for the first time in years, she wasn't striving toward something she hoped would finally satisfy her.

She wasn't building to prove she was worth knowing.

She wasn't going quiet to make herself easier to keep.

She was walking with the Shepherd.

And He already knew her name.

And that was enough.

That was more than enough.

That was everything.

CHAPTER SIXTEEN

The Space Between the Lines

The next morning felt different.

Not louder. Not brighter. Nothing you could point to on the surface and name.

Just settled.

Elle had slept deeply for the first time in longer than she could easily calculate. Not the shallow, restless sleep of a woman with too many open tabs in her mind, but the real kind. The kind that left you feeling returned to yourself when you woke.

She walked to the cafe in the early morning quiet, coffee in hand, and noticed things she had been moving past too quickly to see. The dahlias outside the storefront were fully open now, their blooms heavy and unhurried in the early sun. Daisies along the neighboring sidewalk brushed the air with calm.

Summer had stopped approaching. It had simply arrived, the way things did when you stopped watching for them and just let them come.

She slipped her key into the lock and stepped inside.

The scent of sawdust met her first. Then the steady rhythm of a drill.

Eli was already there.

Of course he was.

* * *

He stood behind the partially framed counter, securing a support beam into place with the focused quiet of someone who was somewhere between prayer and craft. The wood structure now reached mid-torso height, clearly becoming something real. Not just lines on a blueprint. A thing with weight and dimension and a smell of fresh-cut lumber that Elle had started to associate with progress in a way that had nothing to do with any job she had ever held before this one.

Blueprint pages lay open on a nearby crate, pencil markings deepened where adjustments had already been made.

He glanced up when he heard the door close.

"Morning."

"Morning," she replied softly.

He studied her for half a second longer than the greeting required.

"Good walk yesterday?" he asked.

She paused.

She hadn't told him she was going walking. She hadn't mentioned the bridge or the river path or any of it. He had simply driven past and seen what he had seen, and now he was asking about it the way he asked about everything. Quietly. Without pressure. Leaving her complete freedom to answer as much or as little as she chose.

"Yeah," she said, a small smile forming. "It was."

He nodded once, like that was exactly the right amount of information. "Good."

He turned back to his drill.

But there was something in his posture that felt subtly different from his usual focused efficiency. A quality of awareness that told her he had not entirely moved on from the question.

He had seen something on that bridge.

He wasn't going to make her explain it.

She was more grateful for that than she knew how to say.

* * *

She moved behind the counter frame, setting her coffee on a temporary shelf and stepping into the space she had been imagining for months.

She closed her eyes briefly. Let the room tell her what it needed.

Espresso machine here. Milk fridge below. Syrup pump rack here. Pickup window there.

She reached toward the imaginary espresso handle and shifted her weight the way she would shift it during a morning rush, when eight drinks were queued and someone was asking about the gluten-free options and the milk steamer was singing.

Her brow furrowed.

She stepped to the right. Then left. Her hand hovered where the milk pitcher would sit. She pivoted. Reached. Pivoted again.

Her stomach tightened just a little.

The spacing wasn't wrong exactly. But it wasn't right.

She opened her eyes.

Eli was tightening a bolt along the base frame, focused, unhurried.

She stood with the realization for a moment, feeling the old pull of two competing instincts. The first was the one she had always trusted before: fix it immediately, loudly, with total confidence in her own assessment. The second was newer and harder: choose respect. Ask rather than correct. Trust that the person across from her could receive honest feedback without it being a confrontation.

She had not always known how to do that.

She was learning.

"Can I ask you something?" she said gently.

He looked up immediately. "Of course."

She stepped fully into the counter space and motioned him closer. "Can you stand here for a second?"

He wiped his hands on a cloth and walked over without question, without the slight defensive tightening she had seen in other people when their work was being examined.

"All right," he said lightly. "Am I in trouble?"

She laughed softly. "No."

"Then I'm comfortable."

She positioned him where she indicated. "Okay," she said. "I need you to imagine you're making a latte."

He blinked once. "We're role-playing barista now?"

"Very serious role-playing," she said.

He raised an eyebrow but complied without further negotiation, placing his hand where the espresso machine would be with the good-natured willingness of a man who had decided somewhere along the way that this woman's requests were worth honoring even when they were unexpected.

"Now," she continued, stepping into the workflow beside him, "you pull a shot here. Then you turn for the milk."

She pivoted slightly, demonstrating. He followed her movement, his shoulder briefly near hers.

"Then you step to set it down for pickup."

She demonstrated again.

He paused. Then looked at the counter frame. Then at her.

"You don't like the spacing," he said. Not a question. Not an accusation. An observation from someone paying attention.

She shook her head slightly. "I don't dislike it. I just..." She exhaled carefully. "I think it will slow the flow during a rush. I need the milk fridge a little closer to the machine. And the pickup area slightly farther forward."

She braced internally. Not because she thought he would be unkind. But because she had learned in a different season to brace for the particular coldness of a person whose ego was housed inside their work.

It didn't come.

He looked at the layout again. Walked the steps himself. Pull the shot. Turn. Pour. Step. Set.

He paused at the end. "Yeah," he said simply. "You'd be reaching more than you should. Especially on a long shift."

Relief moved through her like warm water.

"I didn't want to say something after you'd already built part of it," she admitted.

He gave her a small, amused look. Not patronizing. Fond.

"Elle."

She blinked.

"I'd rather get it right than get it done fast."

The words landed steady and complete.

Her shoulders dropped a full inch. "Okay," she breathed.

* * *

He grabbed the tape measure and crouched, rechecking dimensions with the same unhurried precision he brought to everything. "Shift it six inches forward," he murmured, more to himself than to her. "Fridge tuck here instead. Widen this section."

She knelt beside him without thinking about it, holding the tape end steady as he marked new lines on the floor in pencil. Their shoulders brushed lightly. Natural. Unforced. The kind of proximity that had been building gradually over weeks of shared work until it no longer registered as significant and simply registered as right.

He glanced at her sideways. "You know, most people don't analyze counter placement like this."

"Most people haven't spent years reviewing coffee bar designs and workflow efficiency reports," she said.

He chuckled, a quiet sound that she had started to collect without meaning to. "Fair."

They worked in rhythm then. Unscrewing. Repositioning. Re-measuring. He didn't rush. Didn't sigh. Didn't make a single moment of the adjustment feel like an inconvenience. He approached the correction with the same care he had brought to the original build, which told her something important about the kind of man he was.

At one point he leaned back on his heels and said lightly, "Next time, maybe we do the barista role-play before I install anything."

She laughed, warmth rising in her chest. "Deal."

When the new layout was taped out on the floor, she stepped back into position behind the revised frame.

Pull the shot. Turn. Pour. Step. Set.

It felt right. Not just functional. Right. The way a sentence felt when every word was exactly where it needed to be.

She looked up at him, eyes bright. "This works."

He nodded once. "Good."

She studied him for a moment. "You're not frustrated?" she asked.

He tilted his head slightly. "Why would I be?"

"Because I changed the plan."

He shrugged lightly. "Plans change. Vision gets clearer. That's part of building." A pause. Then, with the faintest hint of humor underneath the calm: "I'm just glad you told me before we installed marble countertops."

She laughed, the sound filling the high ceilings.

He rose to his feet and picked up his drill again. "I've built cafes in a few different towns," he said. "They all look good on paper. But the ones that last, the ones people actually love being in, those are always the ones where the person running them speaks up. Even when it's uncomfortable. Even after the work has started."

She looked at him.

A few different towns.

She let that sit for a moment, hearing the shape of something larger inside it.

"Are you glad you're here?" she asked quietly. "In Willow Creek."

He met her eyes. The question had come out more personally than she had planned, and she almost softened it, almost added in Willow Creek specifically or working on this project to give them both a smaller version of it to answer.

She didn't. She let it stand.

He held her gaze for a moment, something moving behind his expression that wasn't quite readable but wasn't closed.

"Yeah," he said. "I am."

The answer felt layered.

She didn't press for the layers. But she didn't pretend she hadn't felt them either.

*　*　*

He returned to securing the revised frame, and she filled two cups from the thermos she had brought. She held one out to him.

"Coffee break?"

He accepted it. "I won't slurp."

She grinned. "Coward."

He laughed under his breath, the sound low and warm, and they settled onto overturned buckets in the middle of the half-built cafe the way people settled into things that had become familiar. Without ceremony. Without needing to make a moment of it.

Sunlight streamed across primed walls. Fresh pencil markings lined the floor. The counter stood stronger than it had an hour ago, not because it hadn't needed adjusting, but because they had adjusted it together and the adjustment had made it truer.

Elle sipped her coffee and looked at the revised layout markings on the floor.

"Can I ask you something?" she said.

"You can always ask," he said. She appreciated that he said always and not sure.

"The other towns," she said. "How many?"

He considered the question with his cup in both hands, looking at the floor. "Four, maybe five where I stayed long enough to actually finish something," he said. "A few others where the work was short."

"What made you move?"

He exhaled slowly. "Work, mostly. At first."

At first.

"And then?" she asked gently.

He was quiet for a moment. Not the closed quiet of someone shutting a door. The open quiet of someone choosing their words because the words mattered.

"I think I was looking for something," he said finally. "And I kept thinking it might be in the next town. The next project." A pause. "Turns out that's not how finding works."

Elle looked at him.

He glanced at her sideways, a faint, self-deprecating smile at the corner of his mouth. "Took me longer than it should have to figure that out."

She thought about her own version of that story. The promotions and the titles and the sales numbers that kept promising to be the thing that finally made her feel like enough.

"I understand that," she said quietly.

He looked at her then. Really looked. "Yeah," he said. "I think you do."

They sat in the quiet of that shared understanding for a moment, two people who had both spent years looking in the wrong directions and had both, somehow, ended up in the same small town at the same time building the same thing.

Elle looked down at the fresh pencil lines on the floor. The revised layout. Truer than the first version. Better for having been corrected.

Partnership wasn't about getting it right the first time.

It was about being willing to re-measure together.

And sitting here on overturned buckets in the middle of an unfinished cafe, she thought that might be the truest thing she had learned since coming home.

***

She couldn't sleep.

It was late enough that the house had gone completely quiet and early enough that even the street outside was still. She had been in bed for an hour. She had not been close to sleeping for any of it.

She got up.

She pulled on the cardigan from the hook by her door and slipped her feet into her shoes without tying them and went out to the back porch.

The summer night was warm and close. No breeze. The stars were out but hazy, filtered through the heat that had settled over Willow Creek and decided to stay.

She sat down.

She did not open her Bible.

She did not put in her earbuds.

She just sat with her hands in her lap and let the thing she had been outrunning all day catch up with her.

It was the way he had looked at her when she asked if he was glad he was here.

Yeah. I am.

The layering of it. The way she had felt it and not pretended she hadn't.

And the question that followed, the one she had gotten good at not asking directly:

What happens when someone sees who you actually are and then decides to leave anyway?

She pressed her fingers against her eyes.

Daniel had not left because she was too much. She knew that now. She had done enough work with God on that bridge to understand it. He had left because they had wanted different things and neither of them had been honest enough to say so until it was too late.

But knowing the truth of something and being unafraid of it were different things.

She exhaled slowly.

Lord, she said. Not out loud. Just inward. The way she prayed when she was too tired for full sentences. *I don't understand what You're doing.*

She sat with that.

The porch lights were off. She hadn't turned them on. The dark felt appropriate for what she was doing.

I came home. I said yes. I signed the lease and I knelt on those floors, and I surrendered the striving and I am trying to build something real.

A pause.

And now there is this person. And I don't know if he is part of what You're building or if I am just hoping he is because I am lonely and he is good and I am tired of being afraid.

The hazy stars did not rearrange themselves into an answer.

The warm night did not shift.

She had been here before. She knew God was present even when He was quiet. She believed that with the part of her that had been formed on this very porch over years of exactly this.

But believing it and feeling it were also different things.

What if I let myself be known, she said, *and it costs me again?*

The question sat there.

Small and true and unanswered.

She did not try to answer it herself. She had learned the hard way that the answers she manufactured at midnight were not to be trusted.

She just left it.

For Him.

After a while she went back inside. She did not feel peace. She did not feel certainty. She felt the specific tiredness of someone who had said a true thing and received no immediate reply and was learning, slowly and against her nature, that sometimes that was exactly what trust looked like.

She got into bed.

She lay in the dark.

Still Yours, she whispered. The same words she pressed against the cafe window the first night she stood outside it.

She meant it.

But tonight it cost her something to mean it.

She was asleep before she decided to be.

CHAPTER SEVENTEEN

When Summer Settled In

The heat arrived without warning.

One week Willow Creek had still carried the gentle cool of early summer mornings, the kind that made you grateful for a light sweater on the walk to wherever you were going. The next, summer pressed in fully and without apology, warm air settling over the town like a heavy quilt that no one had asked for, and no one knew quite how to remove.

By mid-morning, Main Street shimmered.

By noon, the sidewalks felt warm through the soles of shoes.

And by early afternoon inside The Overflow Cafe, every window was propped open and two box fans hummed in opposite corners, doing their earnest, limited best to move the air from one part of the room to another without meaningfully cooling any of it.

They were not succeeding.

Elle stood behind the newly framed counter area with her hair pulled into a loose knot and a chilled glass jar pressed briefly against the side of her neck, eyes closed, letting the cold seep in.

"Okay," she declared to the room. "This officially qualifies as hot."

From across the counter framing, Eli didn't look up from the cabinet hinges he was aligning with careful precision. "You've said that every fifteen minutes."

"Because it keeps being true," she replied.

He gave a quiet chuckle and tightened one last screw before straightening. A faint sheen of effort touched his forehead, but he didn't seem particularly bothered by it. He had the constitution of a man who had worked in all kinds of conditions and had made a practical peace with the ones he couldn't change.

Elle, who had spent a decade in climate-controlled offices, had not yet achieved that peace.

She set the jar down and moved toward the folding table that had become her semi-permanent coffee lab.

"If we're going to survive this," she said, sliding her notebook open, "we need a summer menu strategy."

He leaned against the counter frame, folding his arms loosely. "Strategy."

"Yes," she said, with the seriousness of someone who had given this real thought. "No one wants hot coffee when it feels like this. We need cold brew. Iced options. Things that make people feel human again."

He nodded slowly. "That tracks."

She poured chilled coffee from a mason jar into two glasses filled with ice, the sound of it cool and immediate and exactly right for the day.

"Cold brew test number one," she announced, sliding one across to him.

He accepted it. "I'm honored."

"You're essential," she corrected.

He took a sip and his eyebrows lifted slightly. Just slightly. But she had learned to read the register of his expressions, and slightly was significant.

"That's good," he said.

"Too bold?"

He shook his head. "Smooth. Not bitter. Finishes clean."

She brightened immediately, reaching for her pen. "Okay. Good. Because I want to pair this base with Caleb's honey once the blend samples are ready. Something that works both hot and iced."

She made a note. Then another.

"Imagine this," she continued, energy lifting despite the heat. "Honey iced latte with local milk from Miller Family Dairy. Light cold foam on top. A summer sampler flight. Cold brew with a hint of vanilla. Something citrus for people who don't drink coffee."

He watched her move through the vision with the attentiveness she had come to trust completely.

"You've been thinking about this for a while," he said.

She smiled. "Years. I just never had a place to put the ideas."

He nodded. The same nod he gave when she said things that landed differently than their surface. Understanding more than the words.

* * *

The bell above the open door gave a soft jingle as the breeze shifted.

Paisley stepped in first, cheeks flushed from the heat outside, hospital badge still clipped to her scrubs from a shift that had apparently ended recently. She stopped just inside the door and looked at them both with the direct expression of a woman who had urgent needs.

"Tell me you have something cold."

Elle immediately slid her a glass. "Taste test."

Paisley took one long sip, closed her eyes, and exhaled with the relief of someone who had been waiting for exactly that sensation for several hours.

"Bless you," she said.

Eli returned quietly to adjusting cabinet alignment near the back wall, giving the women space while remaining present in the comfortable way he had of doing both at once.

Grace arrived ten minutes later, dramatically fanning herself with a notebook she had apparently grabbed from her bag for exactly this purpose.

"It is approximately one thousand degrees outside."

"It's ninety-two," Eli said calmly from across the room, not looking up.

"Exactly," Grace replied, as if this confirmed her point entirely.

She grabbed the remaining cold brew glass and took a long, grateful sip. "Okay. I have an important announcement."

Elle looked at her.

"If this heat continues into tomorrow," Grace said, with the authority of someone who had made a decision and was simply informing the relevant parties, "we are all going to the lake."

Elle blinked. "The lake."

"Yes. Everyone. No work. No measuring tape. No permits. Just water and shade and not dissolving into puddles."

Paisley nodded immediately. "I support this completely."

Elle laughed. "We have a cafe to build."

Grace waved a hand with the particular dismissiveness of someone who had already accounted for this objection and found it insufficient. "It will still be here in one day. We however will not survive if we turn into overheated raisins first."

Eli glanced over from across the room, mouth tilting. "Strong argument."

Grace pointed at him. "You're coming too."

He lifted one shoulder in a small, easy shrug. "I go where I'm sent."

Elle smiled despite herself, her mind already moving toward the image of it. A full day away from measurements and decision-making and the steady accumulation of responsibility. Just water and sun and the people she had come to love in this town.

She had not let herself rest like that in a long time.

"Okay," she said finally. "If it's still this hot tomorrow, lake day."

Grace clapped once, sharp and triumphant.

Paisley raised her cold brew glass.

Eli returned to his cabinet hinges.

* * *

By late afternoon the heat had pressed itself even more firmly into the building, the afternoon sun finding angles through the open windows that the fans couldn't answer.

Work slowed naturally. Tools were set aside more often. Water breaks stretched a little longer. Elle found herself standing in the open doorway more than once, just letting the faint breeze move across her face and remembering what slightly cooler air felt like.

The flowers in the planter near the storefront drooped slightly under the weight of the afternoon, their petals heavy but still holding their color. Still blooming in spite of the conditions.

She thought about that.

Still blooming in spite of.

She had been doing that for a while now too.

Behind her, she heard Eli set down a tool and step outside. He moved to stand beside her on the sidewalk, leaning lightly against the brick exterior, both of them facing the quiet street.

He pulled a water bottle from his pocket and handed it to her without comment.

She took it.

They stood in comfortable silence, the town slow and warm around them, the kind of afternoon that didn't ask anything of anyone.

"Long day," he said after a while.

"Hot day," she corrected.

The corner of his mouth lifted. "Both."

She looked out at Main Street. A couple walked past holding iced drinks. A dog stretched out flat on a shaded porch. Somewhere down the block a sprinkler ran in someone's yard and the sound of it was the most refreshing thing she had heard all afternoon.

"Can I ask you something?" she said.

"Go ahead," he said. The same easy openness he always offered.

"Do you ever get tired of it?" she asked. "The building. The moving. Setting something up and then not always being there to see it finished."

He was quiet for a moment. She had learned to trust his quiet the way she trusted the river. It was going somewhere even when it was still.

"Sometimes," he said honestly. "There's a job site in eastern Oregon I still think about. School gymnasium. We framed it and got the roof on and then the contract shifted to another crew." A pause. "I drove past it two years later. It was full of kids."

Elle looked at him.

"That was enough," he said simply. "Didn't matter that I wasn't the one who finished it. It got finished. Kids were in it."

She thought about that.

"That's a generous way to see it."

He shrugged. "My dad used to say that every craftsman builds more than he sees completed. Most of what we make gets lived in by people who never know our name." A faint smile. "He thought that was the point."

"This one will be different though," she said softly, looking back at the cafe window. "You'll see this one finished."

He looked at the window too.

At the counter framing visible through the glass. The primed walls. The outline of something becoming.

"Yeah," he said. And there was something in the single word that told her he understood she wasn't only talking about the building.

She didn't examine that too closely.

She just let it be true.

* * *

The sun moved lower, the heat finally beginning to concede just slightly to the late afternoon.

Inside, tools were packed away. Drop cloths folded. The folding table cleared and the coffee supplies covered for the night.

Tomorrow there would be lake water and shade and a full day of nothing that needed to be decided.

And the day after that there would be more framing and more planning and more steps toward October.

But tonight there was just this.

Two people on a sidewalk in the fading heat of a summer day, looking at a building that was becoming something neither of them could have fully built alone.

"Tomorrow," Elle said, pushing lightly off the wall.

"Tomorrow," he agreed.

She started toward her car.

Then stopped and turned back.

"Eli."

He looked at her.

"Thank you," she said. "For today. For all of them, actually."

He held her gaze for a moment, something steady and unhurried in his expression.

"That's what building together looks like," he said.

She nodded.

Turned toward her car.

And smiled the whole drive home in a way she did not try to explain to herself.

Tomorrow would hold water and laughter and a different kind of rest.

And as Elle glanced in her rearview mirror at the road leading back toward Main Street, she felt something light and easy settle into her chest.

Summer, it seemed, had fully arrived.

And for the first time in a long time, she was fully present enough to feel it.

CHAPTER EIGHTEEN

Lake Day

By ten in the morning the heat had already settled in.

Sunlight stretched wide across Willow Creek in that bright, unwavering way that only happened a few weeks each summer, when Washington decided, briefly and intensely, to feel like somewhere much warmer than it had any business feeling. The sky was the shade of blue that made everything beneath it look more saturated. More real. Like the world had turned up its own contrast.

Elle pulled her car into the gravel lot beside the lake and laughed softly when she saw everyone already there.

Grace had claimed a shady stretch of grass with the focused authority of someone who had done reconnaissance. Towels spread. A cooler positioned just so. A striped umbrella tilted at an optimistic angle that suggested it was doing its best.

Paisley waved from a folding chair, sunglasses pushed up on her head. Mara stood near the water's edge rolling up the legs of her jeans with the careful deliberateness of someone who had not fully committed to getting wet but was leaving the door open. Janelle sat beneath a tree with a book in her lap and looked up with a soft, unhurried smile as Elle approached, the kind of smile that said she had been praying for everyone present and intended to keep doing so quietly for the rest of the afternoon.

It felt like stepping into a memory she hadn't known she had been missing.

"Finally," Grace called, standing. "We were about to send someone."

Elle laughed and lifted the tote she was carrying. "I stopped for extra ice and watermelon."

Grace made a sound of pure approval. "You are the favorite today."

"Today specifically," Paisley said.

"The watermelon secured it," Mara agreed.

Elle set the tote down and glanced toward the lake, letting her eyes adjust from the brightness of the parking lot to the wide shimmer of the water.

Luke stood knee-deep at the edge, testing the temperature with the careful seriousness of a man who approached all assessments methodically. A few feet away, Caleb crouched near a second cooler, organizing drinks with the same attention he gave to his coffee booth at the market. Several bottles of honey lemonade stood in a neat row, their labels hand-stamped in the same style as his market signs.

And at the end of the dock, hands resting loosely at his sides, stood Eli.

He was looking out across the water. Not at anything specific. Just at the expanse of it. The way he looked at rooms before he worked in them. Taking it in before he changed it.

Something shifted gently in Elle's chest at the sight of him there, at ease, unhurried, holding no tool and measuring nothing.

Just present.

Just himself.

Grace appeared at her elbow without warning. "You're looking."

"I am not," Elle said.

Grace said nothing.

Just smiled to herself in a way that suggested she had all the time in the world and intended to be right.

* * *

Within minutes shoes were kicked off, towels spread, bags dropped.

The lake shimmered under the climbing sun, water lapping softly against the dock in a rhythm that felt immediately calming, the way certain sounds did when the body recognized them as permission to stop.

Paisley waded forward with a small gasp at the temperature, then laughed. "Oh, this is exactly right."

Luke assessed the water, nodded once as though he had received the data he needed, and then dove cleanly off the end of the dock. He surfaced with a grin that was considerably less restrained than his usual expression. "Come on in."

Grace followed with a shriek that was equal parts cold water and delight, dissolving almost immediately into laughter.

Caleb handed out bottles of honey lemonade from the cooler, easy and generous, and Elle accepted hers with genuine gratitude, the cold of it moving through her hands and up her arms.

"This is incredible," she told him.

He grinned. "Summer recipe, honey Lemonade. I figured it would pair well with something eventually."

She smiled. "I'm thinking that something might be The Overflow Cafe."

His expression warmed. "I was hoping you'd say that. And those blend samples should be ready by next week."

"I'll clear my schedule," she said, which made him laugh because they both understood her schedule was the cafe. The cafe was everything.

Elle stepped slowly into the water, letting the coolness rise around her ankles, then calves, then knees. Relief moved through her almost instantly. Not just from the heat.

From the weight of the past several weeks.

Decisions and permits and wiring codes and paint swatches and the fatigue of caring so much about something that every small setback felt enormous.

The lake received all of it without comment.

"This was a good idea," she admitted.

Eli had waded in from the dock and was nearby in the shallows, water at his knees, the ease of him in this setting striking her the same way it had struck her when she first saw him on the dock. No tool belt. No blueprint. Just a man in a lake on a hot day.

"Grace rarely has a bad idea," he said.

Elle laughed.

* * *

The afternoon moved in the unhurried way that afternoons at lakes in summer were designed to move.

Swimming. Floating. A beach ball that kept drifting toward Luke no matter how carefully it was aimed elsewhere. Paisley insisting at regular intervals that everyone try the honey lemonade as though some of them had not already had two.

Luke attempted a flip off the end of the dock that was more ambitious than technically successful and was received with exactly the response it deserved.

Mara floated on her back near the shallows with her eyes closed and her face turned toward the sun, still and quiet in the way she was always still and quiet, as though peace was her natural resting state even when Elle suspected it cost her something to maintain it.

At one point Elle found herself standing with Caleb near the cooler while the others swam.

"How long have you been in Willow Creek?" she asked.

"Three years," he said. "Moved back after my grandfather passed and left me the property. The bees were already there. The roasting came later." He smiled. "Turns out honey and coffee have a lot in common."

"Both take patience," Elle said.

"Both reward it," he agreed.

She liked Caleb. She had liked him from the first sample cup at the market. There was a quality of contentment in him that felt hard-earned and genuine, the kind that came from a person who had found the shape of their own life and settled into it without apology.

She hoped she was becoming that.

She thought maybe she was starting to.

* * *

By late afternoon the sun had softened, turning the light golden as it began its slow descent toward the tree line.

The energy of the group shifted naturally from swimming to settling. Towels draped over the dock. Shoes retrieved. Someone had produced a bag of chips from somewhere and it was being passed around without anyone asking where it had come from.

Grace eventually gathered Mara and Paisley for a walk toward a snack stand she had spotted near the parking lot, pulling Luke along with an insistence that left no room for negotiation. Janelle followed at a gentler pace with her book tucked under her arm.

Caleb carried the cooler back toward the cars.

And without anyone announcing it or planning it, the dock grew quiet.

Elle sat at the very end, feet dangling in the water, watching the colors move across the lake. Gold and pale pink and the soft orange that only appeared in the last hour of a summer day, reflected back by the water in gentle ripples that made the whole surface look like it was breathing.

She heard the dock shift behind her.

Eli.

He sat down beside her without speaking first, lowering his feet into the water the same way she had, the same unhurried ease. The dock held them both steadily.

For a long moment they just watched the light.

Crickets had begun their soft evening chorus somewhere in the grass behind them. A faint breeze moved across the lake, finally carrying the promise of cooler air.

"Good call coming here," he said quietly.

Elle nodded. "I didn't realize how much I needed a day that didn't ask anything of me."

He rested his forearms loosely on his knees, gaze still on the horizon. "You've been carrying a lot."

"We both have," she said.

He gave a small nod.

The silence that followed was the kind that didn't need to be managed. The kind that two people only found together after enough shared hours that the quiet between them had become its own language.

Elle watched a ripple move outward from where her foot had broken the surface and thought about what she wanted to say next.

She had been thinking about it since the bridge.

About how much of her story she was still carrying alone. About the wound she had named out loud to God on that bridge and had not yet named to anyone else. About whether she was ready to let someone else hold a piece of it.

She looked at the water.

"When I first moved back," she said softly, "I kept wondering if I'd made the right decision. Left everything. All of it. The title and the apartment and the life that looked right from the outside."

He listened.

Just listened.

"Part of why I left," she said, and then she paused.

Something tightened in her chest.

Not panic. Not the old instinct to shut the door and change the subject.

Something more like standing at the edge of something real and feeling the height of it.

She almost said his name.

Almost said: part of why I left was a man named Daniel and what happened with him changed the way I understood myself for a long time.

She held the words for a moment.

Beside her, something in Eli's stillness shifted almost imperceptibly. Not pushing. Not pulling back. Just present in the particular way of a man who had noticed the door she had opened and was choosing to wait quietly beside it.

She filed that away.

Then let them settle back down.

Not yet.

Not because she was afraid of Eli exactly. But because the story deserved more than the end of a long afternoon on a dock. It deserved a moment she chose deliberately rather than stumbled into.

She would tell him.

She knew that now with a quiet certainty she hadn't felt before the bridge.

She would tell him and it would be okay.

But not today.

"Part of why I left," she said again, redirecting gently, "was that I had stopped knowing who I was outside of what I produced. And I needed to come home to remember."

He looked at her.

"And?" he asked quietly.

"And I'm remembering," she said.

Something in his expression settled.

"Good," he said.

One word.

Warm and complete.

* * *

The sky deepened toward evening, the colors softening into dusk.

Lights flickered on in distant houses along the far shoreline. Somewhere across the water someone laughed, the sound carrying cleanly over the surface in the way sounds did over water in the evening.

Elle shifted slightly on the dock, adjusting her position, and her shoulder came to rest against his.

Gently.

Naturally.

The way things happened between two people when the space between them had finally become small enough that contact was simply the next honest thing.

Neither of them moved away.

Neither of them commented.

The moment simply existed, her shoulder against his, warm and unhurried, the lake in front of them and the evening coming in around them.

She thought about the bridge. About turning downstream. About asking God to make being known feel possible again.

She thought about the way he had driven past without stopping. The way he had simply asked if it was a good walk and accepted her answer without pressing.

She thought about the mug with the cross etched into the clay, still sitting on her kitchen counter at home, the cross rough under her thumb every morning when she picked it up to look at it.

She thought about his father teaching him to look past what a space was to what it could become.

She stayed where she was.

Shoulder against his.

Not moving away.

Choosing it.

Grace's voice echoed from the shoreline, calling them back with dramatic urgency about mosquitoes and packing up before dark.

Elle laughed softly and the movement of it shifted her shoulder against his just slightly.

She pushed herself to stand, brushing water from her legs. Eli rose beside her, steady as always, and for a moment they stood at the end of the dock together before turning back toward shore.

The lake behind them.

The evening ahead.

Their friends waiting in the warm last light.

Elle walked back along the dock beside him, close enough that their arms nearly touched with each step, and felt something she had not felt in a very long time.

Not the nervous awareness of someone hoping she was enough.

Not the careful management of someone trying not to want too much.

Just warmth.

Simple.

Real.

The kind that didn't ask permission and didn't need to be examined.

The kind that simply was.

And as the last of the sunset stretched golden across the lake behind them, Elle walked toward shore and understood quietly, without forcing it into words, that something was beginning.

Not rushing.

Not forcing.

Just beginning.

The way all the best things did.

CHAPTER NINETEEN

The Clock Starts

The heat wave broke the way it had arrived.

Quietly.

One morning Elle stepped outside and the air was simply different. Not cold. Not even close to cold. But the pressing weight of the past week had lifted, replaced by something breathable and clean that carried the faint green scent of the hills beyond town.

Willow Creek exhaled.

The flowers in the planters along Main Street perked back up as if they had merely been waiting for permission. The lavender swayed in the morning breeze with a kind of forgiveness for the week it had just endured. Even the old brick of The Overflow Cafe seemed to have released something in the cooler air, its color warmer and more welcoming than it had appeared under the flat white weight of the heat.

Elle unlocked the front door and stepped inside with a grateful exhale of her own.

The space looked different every single day now.

That was the thing about building. You could not always see the progress while you were inside it. But every morning when she stepped through the door, the accumulation of all the days before was visible in a new way. The counter framing standing sturdier. The back area taking shape. The bones of the place becoming less like bones and more like a body.

From the coffee bar area came the steady sound of Eli's level being checked against trim.

Real progress.

Not measuring. Not planning.

Building.

* * *

An older man had stopped by earlier that morning, before Eli arrived.

He had knocked on the open door frame with a gnarled knuckle and held up a folded piece of paper when Elle turned around. A photocopy of an old photograph, she realized. The Daily Bread Bakery, in what looked like the 1960s. The storefront bright and busy, women in aprons visible through the window, a handwritten chalkboard sign out front.

"Thought you might want this," he said simply. His voice had the unhurried quality of a man who had lived long enough to know which things were worth saying and which weren't.

"I'm Elle," she said, stepping forward. "I'm the one opening the cafe."

He nodded as though he had already known that. "Frank Alderman. My mother used to bring me here every Saturday when I was small. Best cinnamon rolls in the county." He looked around the unfinished space without rushing, taking it in the way people did when they were comparing what they saw to something held carefully in memory. "Good bones," he said finally.

"That's what we keep finding," Elle said softly.

Frank gave a slow, satisfied nod, the kind that meant more than agreement. "She'd be glad," he said simply, and Elle understood he wasn't talking about anyone she had ever met.

He hadn't stayed long. Just handed over the photograph with both hands, the way you handed someone something that belonged to them, and walked back out into the morning.

Elle had set the photograph carefully on the folding table beside her notebook. She kept looking at it without meaning to.

The same door. The same brick. Different hands, different season, same purpose.

Feed people.

Gather them.

Make somewhere worth coming back to.

* * *

She found Eli kneeling near the espresso station, securing the final bracket on a trim piece with the focused patience she had come to understand was simply how he moved through his work.

Unhurried. Precise. Treating every small piece as though it mattered, because to him it did.

He glanced up when she appeared in his peripheral vision.

"Morning."

"Morning." She set her bag down and slid a cold bottle of water along the counter frame toward him without breaking stride.

He caught it easily. "You're learning."

"I'm adapting," she corrected. "Summer is humbling."

He gave a quiet chuckle and returned to his work.

Elle moved through the space slowly, notebook open, letting the morning tell her what it had to say before she started asking things of it. She ran her hand along the new shelving near the back wall. Smooth boards, mounted level and secure, waiting patiently for the mugs and glasses that would one day line them.

She thought about the mug with the cross etched into the clay, sitting on her kitchen counter at home.

Soon.

She had just opened her notebook on the folding table, beside Frank's photograph, when the bell over the front door chimed.

She looked up, expecting Grace.

A woman in her late fifties stepped inside instead, wearing a light linen blouse and carrying a folder with the organized confidence of someone who had spent decades making orderly things out of complicated ones. Her hair was swept up neatly. A name badge was clipped to her pocket with the understated professionalism of a person who took her role seriously without taking herself too seriously.

She stepped just inside the threshold and took the space in with warm, experienced eyes. Not evaluating it the way an inspector might. Receiving it the way someone did when they wanted to understand what a place was becoming.

"Good morning," she said. "Is this The Overflow Cafe?"

Elle stood. "Yes. Hi. I'm Elle. I'm the owner."

The woman's face opened into a genuine smile. "Wonderful to finally meet you. I'm Linda Hart. I work with the town on permitting and business openings." She paused, then added with the ease of someone who had said this line before but still meant it: "In Willow Creek we like to think of it as helping dreams come to life."

Elle let out a small, surprised laugh. "That's actually beautiful."

"I try," Linda said warmly.

Eli appeared from the coffee bar area, wiping his hands on a cloth. He didn't step in front of the conversation. Just positioned himself nearby with the quiet readiness of someone who understood that his role in this particular moment was to support rather than lead.

Linda's gaze moved to him briefly. "Contractor?"

"Eli," he said simply, offering a nod. "Renovations."

Linda looked back at Elle. "Do you have a few minutes to walk through some things?"

Elle's heart gave a small, involuntary thump.

She recognized the feeling. It was not fear exactly. It was the awareness that came when something she had been building in faith was about to encounter the reality of systems and requirements and the practical machinery of the world. The moment where vision met process.

She had learned to stop interpreting that feeling as a sign she had made the wrong choice.

It was just the feeling of things becoming real.

"Yes," she said. "Absolutely."

* * *

Linda stepped further into the space, taking it in with the appreciative eye of someone who had seen a lot of storefronts in various states of becoming and could recognize the difference between a project and a place.

"First of all," she said, "this is going to be darling. The town is already talking."

Elle's cheeks warmed. "They are?"

"Oh, enthusiastically," Linda confirmed. "People remember The Daily Bread Bakery. They miss having somewhere to gather that feels like it belongs to them. And the name, The Overflow Cafe, everyone loves it. The church community especially."

Elle's throat tightened with quiet gratitude. "That's the hope."

Linda nodded, then opened her folder with the gentle efficiency of someone who respected other people's time. "Now. Before you get too far into the build, I want to make sure you're aware of a few requirements. Since you'll be serving food and beverages, there are specific codes that apply."

Elle's stomach tightened slightly.

Not panic. Just the quiet bracing of someone who had learned that good things usually came with paperwork.

Linda moved toward the coffee bar area, pointing as she spoke with the clarity of someone who had explained these things many times and understood that clarity was itself a form of kindness.

"Handwashing sink placement needs to be within a specific distance of the service area. The bathroom will need to meet current accessibility standards. Older buildings often need some updating there." She turned a page. "And you'll want to plan for an inspection schedule once your build is closer to complete. Final approvals usually require a couple of visits."

Eli listened without interrupting, his expression steady and attentive. Elle could feel him beside her absorbing the information the same way she was, organizing it into steps rather than letting it accumulate into weight.

Linda paused and her voice softened slightly, the way a person's voice did when they had enough experience to recognize the invisible load someone was carrying.

"I know this can feel like a lot," she said gently. "It's not meant to be. It's just the process. And we want you to succeed here."

Elle's throat tightened unexpectedly.

We want you to succeed.

Not the metrics-driven, conditional version of success she had chased for a decade. Just the simple human declaration of a woman who worked with small business owners and genuinely meant what she said.

Eli shifted slightly closer to Elle's side. Not dramatically. Just near.

Linda continued. "One more thing worth knowing. The Fall Harvest Festival brings the whole region into Willow Creek. It's one of our biggest weekends. Families, visitors, vendors, music. The town comes fully alive."

Elle's attention sharpened.

"It's a wonderful opportunity for a new business," Linda said. "Visibility, foot traffic, community goodwill. If you're hoping to open around that time, we'd want to map your inspection dates carefully to make sure everything lines up."

Elle felt it immediately. The weight and the possibility of it arriving in the same breath.

The cafe open. Doors welcoming people in on the busiest weekend of the year. Warm drinks and cozy chairs and the community she had been praying for already gathered and waiting.

A dream.

And then Linda added, gently: "Timing matters if the festival is your target."

Timing matters.

Something tightened in Elle's chest.

The old whisper tried to rise. *What if it doesn't happen in time. What if the costs exceed the budget. What if she had told people and built hope and it wasn't ready and she let the whole town down.*

She pressed her hand lightly against the edge of the counter frame.

The wood was solid beneath her palm.

Real.

She closed her eyes for just a second.

Jesus. You led me here. You will lead me through. Give me wisdom and peace and help me not rush ahead in fear. Help me not let the weight of what people are hoping for become the thing that drives me instead of You.

She opened her eyes.

"Thank you," she said, her voice steadier than she felt. "I'm genuinely glad you came now rather than later."

Linda smiled warmly. "That's exactly why I do it this way."

* * *

Eli spoke for the first time since Linda had arrived, his voice calm and direct.

"Do you have a checklist? Something we can follow step by step?"

Linda's expression brightened with the particular pleasure of someone who had been asked the right question. "I do."

She pulled a printed packet from her folder and handed it to him.

"You're my favorite kind of contractor," she said approvingly. "The kind who isn't threatened by government paperwork."

Eli's mouth tilted slightly. "I save my frustration for more important things."

Elle laughed, the tension in her shoulders loosening for the first time since Linda had walked in.

Linda flipped to a final page. "There may be some additional costs depending on what your inspector identifies. But nothing that should derail you, just things to plan for. And Willow Creek tends to be cooperative with local businesses that are doing things right."

She said it like a promise built on experience.

Then she looked at Elle one more time with the directness of someone who meant to be remembered.

"You're doing something good here," she said. "The town can feel it. That matters more than you might think when it comes to how things go."

Elle swallowed. "I hope so," she said quietly.

Linda closed her folder with the satisfying efficiency of a completed task. "Call me anytime. I would far rather answer ten questions early than watch someone stress about something preventable later."

She started toward the door, then paused with her hand on the frame, turning back with a warm afterthought.

"Oh. And when you're closer to opening, let me know. I'd like to be among the first customers." A beat. "What's the signature drink going to be?"

Elle smiled, the question landing like a small gift. "A honey blend. Local roast, local milk, local honey. Something that tastes like coming home."

Linda's expression settled into something deeply satisfied.

"Perfect," she said simply.

And she stepped out into the morning, the bell chiming softly behind her.

* * *

The cafe fell quiet.

Not empty. Just returned to itself after the visit.

Elle stood with her hand still resting on the counter frame and looked at the checklist packet Eli had set beside Frank's photograph on the folding table. Several pages. Neat columns. The practical architecture of a dream meeting the world.

Her pulse was still slightly elevated.

Not panic.

But pressure. Real pressure. The kind that came from caring and from having told people and from the particular vulnerability of a dream that had moved from private to public and was now being held by more hands than just her own.

Eli picked up the packet and turned to look at her.

He read her expression the way he read rooms. Quickly. Accurately. Without making a performance of it.

"You okay?" he asked.

Elle nodded once. Then exhaled. "I think I just... it suddenly feels very real."

"It was already real," he said. "But I know what you mean."

She looked at the checklist. "The festival..."

"Is a good goal."

"And a real deadline."

He didn't argue with that. He didn't rush to reassure her with something easy and hollow. He simply looked at the packet in his hands, turned it to the first page, and set it down flat on the table between them.

"Okay," he said. "Then we make a plan."

She looked at him.

He met her gaze with that steadiness that had become, over these past weeks, one of the things she trusted most in the world.

"We do it right," he continued. "Step by step. We get the inspections scheduled in the right order. We adjust where we need to. We don't do it alone and we don't do it afraid."

Something in her chest eased.

Not because the checklist disappeared.

Not because the deadline moved.

But because she was not facing either of them by herself.

Elle nodded slowly, feeling the steadiness of his words move through the pressure like light through water.

"Okay," she said. And meant it this time with her whole chest.

Eli's expression shifted just slightly, the faintest hint of warmth beneath the calm. "And maybe we order a third box fan while we're at it."

She laughed, a real laugh, and wiped quickly at the corner of one eye before anything could fall.

"Deal," she said.

* * *

They spent the next hour working through the checklist together.

He asked questions she wouldn't have known to ask. She flagged sections with a highlighter and built a running list in her phone titled Harvest Festival Opening Plan that made her stomach flutter every time she looked at it.

Not fear.

Awe and responsibility in equal measure.

A goal worth working toward.

At one point Elle looked up from the pages and found herself watching Eli work through the inspection timeline with the same methodical patience he brought to every task, pencil moving in quiet, sure lines across the margins.

She thought about what he had said on the dock.

He had been looking for something. And he had kept thinking it was in the next town.

Turns out that's not how finding works.

She understood that completely.

She had spent years looking for herself in the next promotion, the next achievement, the next person who might finally confirm she was worth staying for.

And then she had come home.

And the thing she had been looking for had been here all along, waiting under the old brick and the papered windows and the Bible beneath the floor.

Not a thing.

A belonging.

She looked back at her notebook.

Frank's photograph sat at the edge of the table, quiet and certain.

The same door. The same brick. The same purpose moving through time like a river that had always known where it was going.

In the quiet of the half-built cafe, with sunlight warming primed walls and the checklist organized into clear and manageable steps, Elle felt the shift settle into her fully.

A clock had started.

Not to frighten her.

Not to rush her.

To focus her.

To remind her that calling was worth working for.

And with Jesus leading, and steady hands beside her, she believed with her whole heart that they would build The Overflow Cafe in time.

Step by step.

Together.

CHAPTER TWENTY

Under the Same Light

Linda had barely cleared the doorway before Eli rolled the permitting packet and tucked it under his arm.

"We need that bracket hardware anyway," he said. "Bring your notebook."

Elle looked at him. Then at the packet. Then at the door Linda had just walked through.

"You want to do this at the hardware store."

"I want to do this somewhere that doesn't feel like we're under a deadline," he said simply. "Different walls help."

She picked up her notebook.

* * *

The bell above the door at Willow Creek Hardware chimed as they stepped inside.

The scent of lumber and varnish settled over them immediately, familiar and grounding. The older man behind the counter looked up from whatever he was reading, recognized Elle, and gave a slow nod of approval.

"Back again."

"Back again," she confirmed. "Can we use a corner of your counter for a few minutes? We have some paperwork."

He gestured broadly. "Counter's yours. Water's on the left if you need it."

They spread the permitting packet on the wide wooden counter near the window, the afternoon light falling across the pages in the same clean way it fell across the paint samples the last time they'd stood here. The same fluorescent hum overhead. The same smell of possibility.

Different from the café.

Quieter in a way that had nothing to do with sound.

* * *

"Handwashing sink placement. Bathroom accessibility. Inspection timeline." Eli ran his finger down the first column without urgency. "None of this is unusual for a building this age."

Elle frowned at the page. "It's still more."

"More steps," he said. "Not more chaos. Steps have a beginning and an end."

She sat with that for a moment. She had spent years in a professional culture that treated urgency like a virtue. Everything had been a crisis or a victory. Nothing had simply been a step.

"Steps," she said. "Okay."

They worked through the list methodically. Sink placement. Electrical capacity. Bathroom plumbing. She marked sections, built the running list in her phone under the name that still made her stomach lift every time she opened it:

Harvest Festival Opening Plan.

"What's the festival date?" Eli asked.

"Second weekend of October."

He nodded. "Real timeline."

"A deadline," she murmured.

He looked up. "A goal."

The difference settled into her chest.

Goal. Not doom.

"A goal," she agreed.

The silence between the work was the kind that didn't need filling. She had spent years in rooms where silence was uncomfortable, where empty air had to be occupied before anyone could relax. This was different. This was the quiet of two people who had run out of the need to perform for each other.

The older man moved around his store at the other end of the counter, unhurried, occasionally glancing over with the comfortable indifference of a man who had seen plenty of conversations happen over his counter and knew which ones to leave alone.

* * *

"Third: budget review," Eli said, moving down the list.

Elle's smile faded slightly.

He didn't pretend not to notice. "We estimate. We plan. If something changes, we adjust." A pause. "That's not failure. That's building."

She looked at him. "You really don't panic."

He shrugged lightly. "Panic never built anything worth keeping."

The sentence landed with the weight of something learned rather than inherited.

Elle studied him a moment longer than she intended to. "Where did you learn to be like this?"

His expression shifted. A door that didn't open all the way but didn't close either.

"Hard way," he said.

She didn't push. But she didn't pretend she hadn't seen it.

He tapped his pencil against the paper and continued, more measured now. "I've worked in a lot of places. You learn what holds up under pressure and what doesn't. In the work and in yourself."

"A lot of towns," she said.

"Eastern Washington originally. Left early and moved around." A pause. "For a long time I told myself it was the work. Better contracts. Better opportunities."

He was looking at the checklist now, not at her. Not avoiding. Just choosing.

"But eventually I had to be honest that I was also running from something that had nothing to do with job sites." He exhaled slowly. "I trusted someone I shouldn't have. Put a lot of weight on a situation that wasn't built to hold it. And when it gave way, I figured the best thing I could do was keep moving."

Elle's chest tightened.

She understood that logic from the inside.

"That sounds lonely," she said softly.

He glanced at her. "It was."

Simply. Without drama.

A silence settled between them that was full rather than empty.

"What changed?" she asked.

He looked at the pages in front of him for a moment.

"I started realizing I could build a lot of things," he said. "But I wasn't building a life."

Elle didn't say anything.

He glanced at her with the faintest self-deprecating warmth, keeping it from becoming too heavy. "Turns out lumber is simpler than people."

She laughed softly. "Sometimes." A pause. "But people are what make the building worth it."

He held her gaze for a moment. Then nodded once, slowly. Like he was storing it somewhere careful.

* * *

They finished the list as the afternoon light shifted toward evening through the hardware store window. Eli capped his pen and stacked the pages into a neat square.

"That's a plan," he said.

Elle looked at the pages and let out a slow breath. "It is."

She reached for her notebook. Her eyes stung unexpectedly.

He noticed. He always noticed.

"Hey." Not alarmed. Just present.

She blinked quickly. "I'm just grateful."

"For what?"

She smiled at the same time as the sting, which probably looked contradictory and felt entirely true. "For not being alone in this."

Something in his expression shifted. Not dramatically. Just a softening.

"You're not," he said.

Two words.

Elle felt something loosen in her chest that she hadn't fully realized was still tied.

* * *

Main Street had settled into early evening by the time they walked back. The streetlights were just beginning to matter. The storefronts glowed in that particular summer-dusk way, warm and unhurried, the town easing toward the end of its day.

Elle paused outside The Overflow Cafe.

She pressed her hand briefly against the glass. The counter framing visible inside. The primed walls. The tape lines on the floor marking where everything would live.

Still Yours, she thought. Still becoming.

"Can we go in for a minute?" she asked.

He held the door.

Inside, the cafe was dim and quiet, the overhead light off, the last of the evening coming through the front windows and lying across the floor in long soft bars. Elle didn't turn on the light. The room felt right this way.

She stood near the center.

The same place she had stood alone the very first time. On her knees on these floors asking God to let it feed people again.

A lot had happened since then.

"Can we pray?" she asked.

He didn't hesitate. "Yeah."

He stood close enough that she could feel the steadiness of him. Not performing it. Just there.

She bowed her head.

"Jesus," she began softly, "thank You for leading me here. Thank You for bringing me home when I had run out of reasons to stay anywhere. Thank You for providing what I need, step by step, even when I can only see one step at a time."

Her voice steadied as she went.

"Help me not rush ahead of You. Help me trust that Your timing is better than my urgency. And thank You," she added, quieter, "for sending help."

A breath.

Then Eli's voice. Low. Unhurried. The voice of a man who had been talking to God long enough that prayer sounded like conversation.

"Lord, keep us honest and steady. Help us build this right, not just fast. Provide what's needed and guard her heart from fear."

A pause.

"Let this place be Yours from the ground up. And help me show up the way I'm supposed to show up."

"Amen," Elle whispered.

"Amen," he echoed.

She opened her eyes slowly.

The room was the same. The checklist was in her bag where she'd put it. The unfinished counter waited in the dark.

But something in the space had settled. The way rooms settled after prayer. As if the air had been reminded of what it was for.

She looked at him.

He looked at her.

Soft light. Quiet room. Two people standing in the middle of something unfinished with no urgency to force it to completion.

Outside, Willow Creek moved through its ordinary summer evening.

Inside, the prayers under the primer held steady.

The Bible under the floor held steady.

And Elle stood in the space she had been building toward for months and let herself, finally, feel the full weight of how far she had come.

It was a good weight.
The kind worth carrying.

CHAPTER TWENTY-ONE

Notes of Honey and Hope

The morning felt like a gift.

Not the dramatic kind. Not the kind that announced itself with golden light and swelling music. Just the quiet, reliable kind that arrived in Willow Creek on the heels of a good night's sleep and a cooler morning than the week before. The kind that reminded you why you had chosen to build your life in a small town where summer still knew how to be gentle.

Elle unlocked The Overflow Cafe with a bright, particular anticipation pulsing in her chest.

Today wasn't just renovation.

Today was identity.

Inside, light spilled across the walls in long, warm streaks. The sawdust scent had faded to something faint and pleasant. Elle had set her coffee lab back up with the focused pleasure of a woman returning to her element, everything arranged with a care that was equal parts professional habit and personal reverence.

A row of clean tasting cups.

Spoons lined up precisely.

Carafes ready.

Her notebook open to a page with a single line at the top written in her clearest handwriting:

Signature Blend: The Overflow Cafe

She stood back and looked at those words for a moment.

She had written versions of that phrase in notebooks for years. In margins of meeting agendas. In the notes app on her phone at eleven at night when the dream pressed in too close to sleep. In the back of journals she kept under her bed.

She had never written it on a table that belonged to her. In a building that was hers. For a purpose that was His.

She exhaled slowly, gratitude moving through her like warm coffee.

* * *

From the back of the cafe came the sound of Eli's steady footsteps approaching. He emerged carrying a small bundle of trim boards, sleeves rolled, a small dusting of sawdust along one forearm that he hadn't bothered to brush away yet. His gaze landed on the tasting setup and registered it the way he registered everything she built.

With quiet attention.

"Big day," he said.

Elle nodded, eyes bright. "Caleb's bringing the blend samples."

Eli set the trim boards down and glanced at the table again. "I gathered that from the level of organization happening over there."

"This is professional organization," she said.

He gave a quiet chuckle. "Of course it is."

She moved toward him with playful seriousness. "And I want to prepare you now. You will be asked to slurp."

He looked at her. "I thought we had an understanding about that."

"We do not have an understanding about that."

He shook his head once, but the smile pulling at the corner of his mouth was entirely unguarded. "All right."

The bell above the front door chimed before he could say more.

Elle turned.

Caleb stepped inside carrying a cardboard tray in both hands and a small cooler looped over one arm, his expression warm and easy and carrying the energy of someone who had been up early doing work he loved.

"Morning," he said. "I come with samples."

Elle laughed. "You really do."

He set the tray on the table with careful hands, then reached into the cooler and produced four labeled bags and two small jars of honey, each one the same deep amber she had admired at his market booth.

"Four blend samples," he said, touching each bag in turn. "I tried to hold onto everything you described. Warm. Welcoming. A little brightness underneath. Comfort that doesn't feel heavy."

Elle's expression softened. "That is exactly the language I used."

Caleb smiled. "I wrote it down."

Eli offered him a nod. "Appreciate you coming out."

"Of course," Caleb said. "I'm invested now. The whole town is talking about this place like it's already open."

Elle's stomach lifted.

Not with fear this time.

With expectation.

Caleb glanced around the space. "It's coming together."

"One step at a time," Elle said.

He nodded. "Best way to build anything."

* * *

Elle stepped into her element.

The part of herself that had led tastings in conference rooms and training sessions and onboarding days for a decade, the part that knew coffee the way musicians knew their instrument, stepped forward with quiet confidence and took charge of the morning.

"Okay," she announced, clapping once. "We are doing this properly."

Caleb's brows lifted. "You're in tasting mode."

"I'm always in tasting mode," she said. "Eli."

He straightened slightly from where he had leaned against the counter framing. "I know," he said. "Slurp."

She pointed at him. "Good man."

The bell chimed again and Grace appeared in the doorway as if she had been called by the scent alone, which was not entirely impossible.

"Did someone say coffee tasting?" she announced, already stepping inside. "Because I heard that with my whole spirit."

Paisley followed two minutes behind, still in scrubs, cheeks flushed from the walk over between shifts. "I have fifteen minutes," she said, holding up one finger. "But I smelled something and my body moved on its own."

Elle grinned. "Perfect timing. Both of you."

Caleb laughed. "This is the best audience I've ever had."

Eli moved closer and leaned against the counter, arms loosely crossed, watching the whole scene settle into motion with the quiet amusement of a man who had learned to love the particular warmth of this group of people.

Elle handed cups around and positioned herself behind the table.

"Step one," she said, her voice slipping into the authority she wore like a second skin in this context. "Smell. No sipping yet. Eyes closed if you're serious about it."

Grace inhaled with exaggerated concentration. "Notes of..." She paused dramatically. "Holiness."

Paisley snorted.

Eli's mouth twitched.

Elle laughed. "Okay. But actually. What does it remind you of?"

Paisley sniffed again, more thoughtfully. "This one smells warm. Like toasted sugar and something just slightly sweet underneath."

Caleb nodded. "That's the medium base in Sample Two. Good."

Elle looked at Eli. "And you?"

He lifted his cup and inhaled with the careful attention she had come to recognize as his version of taking something seriously. "Brighter," he said after a moment. "Almost like citrus but softer than that."

Elle's eyebrows rose. "Yes. Keep going."

He considered. "Like early morning before it gets warm. That kind of bright."

She stared at him. "That is exactly right. That is a lighter roast woven into the base. It lifts the whole thing."

Grace raised her cup again. "Mine smells like I need it in my life daily."

Elle smiled warmly. "Also accurate."

"Okay," Elle said, producing a spoon. "Step two."

Eli's shoulders shifted almost imperceptibly.

"Slurp," she confirmed.

She demonstrated first, full and unapologetic, the sound filling the unfinished room.

Grace stared at her. "Like that?"

"Like that," Elle confirmed.

Grace tried a polite, careful version that barely registered.

"Grace," Elle said.

"I am a woman of dignity," Grace said.

"You are not," Paisley said immediately.

"Bigger," Elle said. "You need to aerate it."

Grace sighed with the weight of someone being asked to compromise their values, then produced a proper slurp that bounced off the walls.

Everyone burst out laughing.

"There it is," Elle said, delighted.

Eli took his turn without further prompting. A full, audible, genuine slurp. He swallowed and blinked. "Smooth. Finishes clean."

"Front of the tongue? Back?"

"Middle," he said. "Like it knows where it's going."

Elle wrote that down immediately.

* * *

They tasted all four samples.

Sample One was good. Balanced. A little predictable.

Sample Two was warm. Comfortable. Paisley closed her eyes and said softly, "This feels like comfort."

Elle's pen moved.

Sample Three was brighter, more complex. Grace tilted her head. "This one feels hopeful."

Elle wrote that down too.

Then Sample Four.

Elle lifted the cup to her nose and inhaled slowly.

And went still.

It was warm the way the best things were warm. Not hot. Not aggressive. Just the kind of warmth that met you where you were and didn't ask you to go anywhere else. But underneath it, like light behind a curtain, was something alive and bright and quietly present.

She took a sip.

Slurped gently.

Let it sit.

Swallowed.

Her eyes stung.

She didn't try to stop them.

Caleb watched her carefully, a man who had learned to read the room at market booths and understood that Elle Whitaker's silence was not disengagement. "That one felt right when I was blending it," he said quietly. "Something about it wanted to be what it is."

Elle nodded slowly, fingertips pressed lightly to the edge of the table.

"It tastes like..." She searched for the right word. Not caramel. Not nut. Not citrus. Something deeper than notes. Something that landed in a different register entirely.

"It tastes like returning," she whispered.

The room went still.

Even Grace didn't fill the silence.

Elle looked up at Caleb. Then at Eli. Then at her friends.

"This is it," she said. "This is the one, The Returning Blend!"

Paisley's voice was gentle. "It feels like a hug."

Grace nodded, eyes shining. "It feels like the kind of thing people cry into and then feel better."

Elle laughed through the sting in her own eyes. "Yes."

Caleb smiled slowly. "That's what I was trying to build into it."

Eli cleared his throat lightly, keeping the moment from tipping into sentiment they couldn't carry back to the day. "If the goal is 'people cry into it and feel better,' I'd say that's a yes."

Grace laughed, the tension releasing beautifully.

Elle exhaled, grateful.

* * *

Caleb reached into his bag and set a small jar of honey on the table beside the Sample Four bag. "The honey works in this one specifically," he said. "It rounds the brightness without killing it. Warm finish."

Elle picked up the jar. Turned it in the light. The amber of it glowed.

"Local?" she asked, though she already knew.

"From my property," he confirmed. "Same bees, same flowers, same hills. Every jar is a little different because the seasons are a little different. But the character stays the same."

Elle set the jar down carefully.

She thought about that for a moment.

Every cup a little different. But the character stays the same.

That was what she wanted for this place. Not a formula. A character. Something that was recognizably itself in every season.

"I want to use it," she said. "In the signature latte. The Overflow Honey Latte."

Caleb grinned. "I was hoping you'd say that."

"And," Elle said, the idea arriving fully formed the way the best ideas did, "I want ceramic mugs with a cross etched into the clay. I saw them at your booth the morning of the market."

Caleb's expression shifted to surprised pleasure. "You remember those."

"I bought one," she said. "It's been sitting on my kitchen counter since that Saturday. I pick it up every morning."

She did not say what had happened the moment her hand had reached for it. Some memories were personal enough to be kept. But she felt Eli's stillness beside her and understood he remembered too.

"The artist who made them," Elle continued, "I want to order a full set for the cafe. Enough for every table. I want the Overflow Honey Latte served in a mug with a cross etched into the clay."

Caleb looked genuinely moved. "Her name is Hannah. She lives about twenty minutes outside town. She makes everything by hand. She's going to love that."

"Can you connect us?" Elle asked.

"Today if you want," he said.

Grace pressed both hands to her chest. "A handmade mug with a cross. A honey latte made with local bees. A signature blend that tastes like returning." She looked at Elle. "You are going to ruin people in the best possible way."

Janelle, who had slipped in quietly sometime during the tasting and settled near the back without anyone quite noticing, covered her smile and said softly, "That is what it looks like when a dream is built on the right foundation."

Elle looked at her.

Grateful. Full. A little overwhelmed by the goodness of it all.

* * *

Caleb paused before packing up and glanced toward Elle casually. "When you're closer to menus and signage and all of that," he said, "my friend Micah does graphic design. He's the kind of designer who actually listens to what something is trying to say before he decides how it should look. I think he'd get this place."

"Micah," Elle said.

"Micah Reyes," Caleb confirmed. "He's been in Willow Creek about a year. Quiet guy. Thoughtful. His work is the kind that feels personal even when it's professional."

Elle nodded, filing the name carefully. "When we're ready, I'll reach out."

"Just tell me," Caleb said. "I'll make the introduction."

Grace leaned toward Paisley and stage-whispered, "Micah. Is he single?"

Caleb laughed. "Grace."

"What," she said with complete innocence. "I'm just thinking about the narrative arc of this town."

Everyone laughed, including Eli, a quiet sound that Elle had started to catalog without meaning to.

Paisley checked her watch and made the face of a woman being returned to reality against her will. "I have to go save lives," she announced. "I'm offended by that."

Elle hugged her quickly. "Thank you for coming."

Paisley held on an extra second. "This place is going to change people, Elle. I can feel it in my bones and I have very reliable bones."

Elle laughed and let her go.

Grace lingered just long enough to suggest the blend be named Holy Grounds, be firmly outvoted, argue her case one more time, and then accept defeat with considerable grace for someone named Grace.

Caleb packed his cooler, exchanged a warm handshake with Eli, and headed for the door. "I'll text you Hannah's information today," he told Elle. "And I'll start on a refined version of Sample Four. Get it consistent before you commit."

"Thank you," she said. "For all of this."

He paused in the doorway. "I meant it when I said I'm invested. This place is going to matter." A beat. "Let me know what you need."

"I will," she promised.

He stepped out into the morning and the bell chimed gently behind him.

* * *

The cafe settled into quiet.

Elle and Eli stood near the tasting table, the four sample bags arranged in a row, the honey jar glowing amber in the morning light. The cups still held faint traces of the blend that had undone her.

She looked at Sample Four, "The Returning Blend" for a long moment.
Then at Eli.

"Can we pray over it?" she asked. "Before we move on."

He didn't hesitate. "Yeah."

They stood beside the table. Not formal. Not performative. Two people who had built a practice of bringing things to God before carrying them forward.

Elle bowed her head. "Jesus, thank You for providing. For creativity. For Caleb and the work of his hands and the bees on his family's land and the way You connect things that seem unrelated until suddenly they're exactly right."

She paused.

"We dedicate this blend to You. Every cup that comes from it. Every conversation that happens over it. Every person who wraps their hands around a mug with a cross in the clay and feels something they can't quite name."

Her voice softened. "Let that thing they feel be You."

A breath.

"Let it taste like returning. Because You are always the One we're returning to."

Eli's voice followed, unhurried and sincere. "Lord, thank You for her. For the way she sees what things can become and then actually builds them. Bless the work of these hands. Let this cafe be a place where people feel safe and seen and fed in ways they didn't know they needed."

A pause.

"Use it for Your glory. Provide what we need for the festival. And keep our hearts right while we build."

"Amen," Elle whispered.

"Amen," Eli echoed.

Her phone buzzed on the counter.

A text from Caleb.

I'll text you Hannah's information today.

Elle looked at it for a moment. Then at the mug on her kitchen counter at home that she could see in her mind as clearly as if it were in front of her. The cross in the clay. The weight of it exactly right in both hands.

She typed before she could talk herself out of it.

Hi Hannah, my name is Elle Whitaker. I'm opening a cafe in Willow Creek and Caleb thought we should meet. I have one of your mugs and I'd love to talk about ordering a full set for the café.

Three dots appeared almost immediately.

I know who you are. Everyone in town is talking about The Overflow Cafe. When can you come?

Elle smiled.

* * *

Hannah Stroud lived twenty minutes outside Willow Creek on a gravel road that climbed gently into the foothills before leveling out into a property that looked like it had grown up rather than been built. Raised beds along the south fence. A small orchard just past the barn. And at the back of the property, separate from the house, a low-roofed studio with a kiln exhaust pipe visible through the trees and a hand-painted sign above the door that read simply:

MADE BY HAND

Elle parked and sat for a moment in her car, looking at it.

The morning air came in through her cracked window carrying the scent of pine and damp earth and something underneath it, clay, she realized. Warm. Mineral. Ancient.

She stepped out.

The studio door was propped open with a river stone.

* * *

Hannah was already at her wheel when Elle stepped inside.

She was older than Elle had imagined, somewhere in her late fifties, hands moving through wet clay with the unhurried authority of someone who had been doing this long enough that the work no longer required her full concentration, only her full presence. Her hair was pulled back loosely, silver threaded through brown. A smear of clay along one forearm. Reading glasses pushed up on her forehead that she clearly had no intention of using.

She looked up when Elle's shadow crossed the threshold.

"Elle." Not a question. A recognition. Her eyes moved quickly over Elle's face the way craftspeople looked at things, not evaluating, reading. "Come in. Don't worry about your shoes."

Elle stepped inside.

The studio was warm and organized in the way of a place that had been worked in for decades. Shelves lined every wall, rows of pieces in various stages of completion, bisque-fired bowls, glazed mugs, small vessels Elle did not have names for. The light came through two east-facing windows and fell across the worktable in long, clean strips.

And there, on a shelf near the window, a row of finished mugs.

Elle recognized them instantly.

The same quiet shape. The same earth-toned glaze. The same cross etched into the clay on each one, clean, unhurried, grounded.

She crossed to them slowly.

"May I?" she asked.

"Please," Hannah said.

Elle lifted one from the shelf.

The weight of it settled into both palms exactly the way she remembered. The cross rough under her right thumb. She pressed it the way she pressed it every morning at home, instinctively, the way you pressed something that had become a habit of comfort.

She stood with it for a long moment without speaking.

"You have one already," Hannah said. Not a question either.

"From the market," Elle said. "Several months ago." She paused. "I've picked it up every morning since."

Hannah's expression shifted into something that was not quite a smile and not quite something else. Something in between. The look of a craftsperson hearing that something they made had been used the way it was meant to be used.

"Then you understand them," she said simply.

* * *

They sat with tea at Hannah's worktable while the kiln hummed at the back of the studio. Hannah asked about the cafe, with genuine, focused attention that made Elle feel like the vision she had been carrying for months had finally found someone who could hold it without reducing it.

She told Hannah about the old Daily Bread Bakery. About coming home. About the Bible under the threshold and the prayers written on the walls. She shared about Caleb's blend and the feeling she kept trying to name, that she wanted the cafe to be a place where people who were hurting could walk in and set something down.

Hannah listened.

She did not offer quick affirmations.

She did not fill pauses.

She just listened the way Elle had come to recognize as its own spiritual gift. The full, undivided kind that made the speaker feel like what they were saying mattered enough to be heard completely.

When Elle finished, Hannah looked at the mug between Elle's hands.

"Can I tell you why I make those?" she asked.

"Please," Elle said.

Hannah set her own mug down. "My husband was sick for three years before he passed. Lung cancer." She said it plainly, without the careful management that came from fresh grief. This was older pain, worn smooth. "The last year was very hard. There were a lot of days when I couldn't pray. Couldn't speak. Couldn't do anything except sit with him."

Elle went still.

"I started making these during that time," Hannah continued, gesturing toward the mugs. "Not for anyone. Just to have something to do with my hands while I was sitting in rooms that were too quiet. I'd sketch the cross into the clay before it dried."

She paused. "It wasn't art. It was just, I needed something to hold onto. And I kept thinking about other people. People sitting in hospital waiting rooms or quiet houses or difficult mornings, wrapping their hands around a cup of something warm."

Her voice was steady. Not performing the grief. Just telling the truth of it.

"I figure," she said, "if someone is going to hold something while they're hurting, they might as well hold something that reminds them who holds them."

Elle's breath caught.

She looked down at the mug in her hands.

The cross rough under her thumb.

The weight of it exactly right.

She had been picking this up every morning for months without knowing the story behind it, and somehow it had always done exactly what Hannah described. On the mornings when the permit checklist felt impossible. On the mornings when she held it and thought about Eli and did not yet have words for what she was feeling.

She had been holding something that was made to hold her.

She blinked hard. "Hannah."

"I know," Hannah said gently.

Elle exhaled. "I want these mugs in every hand that comes through the door."

Hannah smiled, a full smile this time. "How many do you need?"

* * *

They spent another hour at the worktable together.

Hannah showed Elle the different glaze options, the earth tones she returned to most, the way the color shifted depending on the firing temperature, why each mug came out slightly different from the last. The imperfection was part of it. You could not make them identical by hand, and you would not want to. Every mug was its own.

"Like people," Elle said, without quite meaning to say it aloud.

Hannah looked at her. "Exactly like people."

Elle ordered sixty mugs to start. Enough for every table with extras behind the counter. She asked whether the cross could stay exactly as it was, no refinement, no stylizing. Just the etched cross in the clay the way Hannah had always made it.

As Elle stood to leave, Hannah pressed a second mug into her hands. "For someone else who needs to hold something."

Elle looked at it. Then up at her.

"I'll know who," Elle said.

Hannah nodded. "You will."

* * *

Elle drove back toward Willow Creek, the morning opening around her into the kind of late summer day that felt like a gift with no occasion.

She thought about Hannah at her wheel during the three hard years. About the way grief had shaped something in her hands that she passed forward into the hands of strangers. About the way God had taken a woman's need to hold something and turned it into a way of holding other people.

She pressed her thumb against the cross etched into the clay on the seat beside her.

Rough.

Grounded.

True.

Let that thing they feel be You.

She had just prayed those words over the blend an hour ago.

She understood now that the answer had already been in progress. Long before she arrived. Long before she had the idea. Long before she knew Caleb or Hannah or any of them.

God had already been placing the right hands in the right places, working with unhurried patience toward a morning when a woman would drive down a gravel road into the foothills and hold something that had been made with prayer during someone else's sorrow.

She understood that the whole story, the blend and the mug and the café and the calling, was not hers.

It was His.

It had always been His.

Thank You, she whispered.

The hills opened up ahead of her into the valley. Willow Creek waited below, small and steady in the late morning light.

She drove down toward it, carrying one story home and carrying another one forward.

* * *

She lifted her head.

The afternoon light had shifted slightly, the way it did as summer moved toward midday, warmer and fuller and settling into the room like something that intended to stay.

She looked at the tasting cups. At the honey jar. At the bag labeled Sample Four. At Eli, who was looking at her in that way he had.

Not intensely. Not demandingly.

Just steadily.

As if she was worth paying attention to.

As if he had all the time in the world to do it.

The Overflow Cafe was becoming real.

One blend. One mug. One honest cup at a time.

And in the scent of warm coffee and something that tasted like returning, it felt like something had just been named in the right language for the very first time.

CHAPTER TWENTY-TWO

The Right Kind of Quiet

They didn't plan it as anything.

It started the way most of their best moments did.

Naturally.

One more thing to finish. One more measurement to confirm. One more item checked off the list that had been growing and shrinking and growing again since Linda Hart had walked through the door with her folder and her kindness.

By the time they finally stepped back from the counter framing, the light inside The Overflow Cafe had turned warm and honeyed, spilling long shadows across the primed walls. The scent of coffee still lingered from the morning's tasting, soft and comforting, like it had settled into the bones of the place and decided to stay.

Elle set the last tasting cup in a box and closed the lid.

Eli clicked his pen and laid the permit checklist neatly on top of her notebook.

"That's enough for one day," he said.

Elle smiled, tired in the good way. "Agreed."

They locked up together, the small ritual of it familiar now. Lights off, tools tucked, the front door secured with the turn of her key.

Outside, Willow Creek had softened into evening.

The air carried a faint thread of lavender from somewhere down the block, and the warmth of the day had finally eased into something that felt like a reward for surviving it. A few porch lights glowed. The street was quiet in the particular way of small towns at the end of a summer day, not empty but resting, still full of people just settled into their own evenings.

Elle paused on the sidewalk and looked back through the front window at the cafe.

The counter stood. The shelves were up. The tape lines on the floor marked where everything would live. The primed walls waited.

She pressed her hand briefly against the glass.

Still Yours, she thought. Still becoming.

Eli stood beside her, looking at the same window.

"Good day," he said quietly.

"Really good," she agreed.

A beat of comfortable silence.

Then, as naturally as everything else that happened between them, he nodded toward the street that led down to the river path.

"Want to walk a minute?"

Elle's heart lifted in a way that felt simple and right.

"Yeah," she said. "I would."

* * *

They started down the sidewalk side by side.

Not rushed. Not filling the air with words. Just walking.

Elle had come to love this about him. The way he didn't treat silence as something to be managed or filled. The way he moved through the world without needing it to be louder than it was.

She had spent years in environments where silence was uncomfortable, where the space between words had to be occupied before anyone could relax. She had learned to perform in those spaces. To be the person who kept things moving.

Walking beside Eli, she had unlearned that.

The path curved along the river as the sun continued its long, unhurried descent. The water moved beside them, steady and clear, catching the last of the light in small bright fragments. Trees overhung the path on one side, their summer fullness filtering the evening into something soft and dappled.

Elle breathed in.

"Thank You," she whispered without thinking.

Eli glanced at her, warm. "You pray like it's breathing."

She smiled faintly. "It kind of is for me."

He nodded once, accepting that with the ease of someone who understood it completely.

They walked for a few minutes before Elle spoke again.

"I keep thinking about timing," she admitted.

"Because of the festival?"

"Yes," she said. "And because of everything."

He waited.

"In the city," she continued, watching the river, "timing was always urgent. Everything was a deadline. Everything was pressure. Everything was pushing."

She paused. "And I didn't realize how much that trained my heart to believe God was only in the outcomes."

He was quiet. Just present.

"In the results," she said. "In the big moments. In what I could accomplish and show for it."

She exhaled slowly, watching the current. "But I'm learning He's in the process. In the steps. In the waiting. In the small obedience that nobody applauds because nobody sees it but Him."

Eli's eyes stayed on the path ahead, but his attention was entirely on her.

"Your walk the other morning," he said after a moment. "On the bridge."

Elle's breath caught softly.

"I drove past," he said. "I didn't want to intrude."

"You looked real," he said.

The word landed like something she hadn't known she needed. Not impressive. Not together. Not successful.

Real.

"Thank you," she whispered.

He nodded.

They kept walking.

* * *

"What about you?" she asked, after the comfortable quiet had stretched and held.

He glanced at her. "Timing," she said. "Your version of it."

He was quiet long enough that she wondered if she had asked too far.

Then he spoke.

"My dad was a carpenter."

The words were simple. The weight behind them was not.

Elle turned her face toward him slightly, giving him the full attention the statement deserved.

"He started taking me to job sites when I was still small," Eli said. "Not to work. Just to watch. To be in the space. He'd hand me a piece of scrap wood and a pencil and tell me to measure it like it mattered."

Elle's chest softened. "Did it matter?" she asked gently.

Eli's mouth curved faintly. "He said everything you measured carefully mattered. Because the habit of caring was the same whether you were cutting a doorframe for a cathedral or a shelf for someone's garage."

Elle walked slowly, not wanting to rush a single word of this.

"He used to say, 'If you build with care when nobody's watching, you'll build with integrity when everyone is.'"

She absorbed that.

"He sounds like a man who knew Jesus," she said softly.

Eli nodded. "He wasn't the loud faith kind. Didn't preach on the job site or put verses on his truck. But he prayed every morning before work. In his truck. Quiet. Simple. He didn't make a performance of it."

The path curved gently around a bend, the river widening slightly beside them.

"And he talked about Jesus like He was part of the crew," Eli said. "Not a concept. Not a Sunday thing. A person. Like He was actually there in the work with him."

Elle's throat tightened.

"He'd say Jesus was a carpenter too," Eli added, a faint, fond warmth in his voice. "Like that was the most natural thing in the world. Like of course He understood what it meant to be on your knees on a job site trying to figure out if the floor was truly level."

Elle let out a soft laugh, her chest full. "That's such a dad thing to say."

Eli's eyes crinkled slightly. "It really is."

They walked a stretch in quiet, the evening settling deeper around them, the birdsong thinning as the light thinned.

"When I was old enough," Eli continued, his voice more thoughtful now, "he taught me the tools. Not just how to use them. How to see what a space needed. How to look past what something was, all the damage and the age and the surface problems, and find what it could become."

Elle's steps slowed slightly. Something in her chest pulled.

"That is exactly what you've been doing with the cafe," she said.

He looked at her. A small, quiet smile. The kind that didn't need to fill a room.

"Yeah," he said. "It feels familiar."

She swallowed, blinking quickly.

"He taught you to build with Jesus," she said.

"He did."

A pause.

"Where is he now?" she asked gently.

Eli's expression shifted by a degree. The same small door she had seen before.

"He passed when I was twenty-six," he said. "Heart attack. On a job site." A beat. "At least he was somewhere he loved."

The way he said it told her he had made peace with it. Not that it didn't hurt. But that he had found the frame that held the grief without being destroyed by it.

"I'm sorry," she said.

"Thank you."

They walked in the quiet of that for a moment, the river accompanying them, unhurried.

"He's in your hands," Elle said softly. "The way you work. I see him in it."

Eli looked at her.

Something moved in his expression that she had not seen there before. Something open and unguarded and briefly exposed, the way honest things were when they were received by the right person.

"Yeah," he said.

One word. But the way he said it told her it was the truest thing he had said all evening.

* * *

"What made you start moving after he passed?" she asked quietly, when the moment had settled.

His shoulders shifted slightly. "Work at first," he said. "Then..." He exhaled. "I think I told you. I trusted someone I shouldn't have. Put weight on something that wasn't built for it."

"And when it gave way you kept moving," she said.

"Yeah."

She nodded slowly. She understood that logic from the inside.

"Do you still believe that was the right call?" she asked. "The moving?"

He considered the question with the seriousness it deserved. "I think it got me here," he said finally. "So I can't entirely regret it."

The path bent around a small stand of trees, opening onto a wider stretch of river where the water moved more slowly. The sky above the tree line had deepened to the particular blue that came just before the first stars.

"I've been asking God," Eli said, his voice quieter now, "to let me build something that lasts."

Elle kept her pace steady.

"Not just buildings," he continued. "A life. Community. Something rooted. Something that doesn't require me to keep moving to feel like it has value."

Elle's eyes stung.

Because she recognized those words. She had prayed them herself in different language. On a bridge. Over a river. Downstream.

"I want that too," she said.

It came out simply. Without performance. Without the careful management she had once applied to everything she wanted.

Eli looked at her. The path was quiet around them. The river moved. The evening held them in its soft remaining light.

"I know," he said.

And the way he said it told her he had been paying attention. All along. Every walk. Every morning. Every prayer over coffee grounds and building materials and unfinished walls.

He had been paying attention.

* * *

They kept walking.

The path narrowed slightly around a bend where tree roots had pushed up through the gravel, and Elle shifted to navigate around them.

Her hand swung at her side. His hand swung at his. Close.

She was aware of it the way you became aware of something when your body understood before your mind did.

She thought about the bridge. About asking God to make being known feel possible again. About deciding on the dock that she would tell him. That she would choose it deliberately rather than stumble into it.

About the mug with the cross that she still picked up every morning, the rough clay under her thumb, the weight of it exactly right.

About his hands on the counter framing. On the tape measure. On the level he pressed against every wall to make sure what was being built was true.

Hands that built with care when nobody was watching.

She looked at the path ahead of her.

Then she made a choice.

Not an impulsive one. Not a frightened one. Not the desperate reaching of someone who was afraid of losing something before she had properly held it.

A deliberate one.

The kind that came from standing on a bridge and turning downstream and deciding that being known was worth the risk of what it cost.

Her fingers brushed his.

He went still for half a step.

Not pulling away. Just noticing.

She let her hand settle alongside his.

And then, without either of them fully deciding the moment, without announcement or ceremony or anything louder than the river beside them and the last birds of the evening, their fingers laced together.

Warm.

Steady.

Right.

The way things felt when they had been coming for a long time and finally arrived.

Elle looked ahead at the path.

She didn't look at him yet. She wanted to hold the moment for exactly one breath before it became something they would have to talk about or navigate or be careful around.

One breath of just this.

His hand in hers. The river beside them. The evening coming in. The town somewhere behind them full of people who were rooting for them without knowing it.

Then she turned her head and looked at him.

He was already looking at her.

His expression was open in a way she had not seen it be open before. Not the door half-cracked. Not the careful steadiness. Just him. Unguarded. Certain.

They shared a small smile, soft and unhurried, the kind that said we both felt it and we are both still here and that is enough.

No words. No declarations.

Just the quiet, tender understanding of two people who had both been afraid for a long time and had both, separately and together, decided to stop.

They kept walking.

Hands linked.

As if it had always been this way.

As if their hands had simply remembered where they belonged.

Elle's heart beat steady in her chest. Not racing. Not panicked.

Peaceful.

She thought of the bridge. The river. The turn downstream.

She thought of his thumb moving lightly against her knuckles, absent and gentle and present all at once.

* * *

They reached a small clearing where the river widened, catching the last color of the sky across its surface.

Elle slowed naturally. Eli slowed with her.

They stood at the edge of the path, looking out at the water, hands still joined.

Elle breathed in the evening air and let peace fill her the way she had learned to let things fill her.

Fully. Without managing it.

Then she looked at him.

"Can we pray?" she asked.

His grip didn't tighten. Didn't loosen.

"Yeah," he said simply.

They bowed their heads there on the path, beside the widening river, hands linked, the first evening stars beginning to appear above the tree line.

Elle's voice was soft. "Jesus, thank You. Thank You for Your timing. For the way You do not rush and do not force and do not demand. For the way You simply lead and ask us to follow."

She paused.

"Help us keep You first. Above the cafe, above everything we want and everything we hope for. Guard our hearts. Keep us humble. Make this whatever You want it to be."

A breath.

Eli's voice followed, low and steady, the voice she had come to know as well as the sound of the river. "Lord, thank You for her. For the way she follows You with her whole life. Thank You for bringing me here."

A pause.

"Help me honor You in the way I build. In the way I work. In the way I show up."

His voice quieted further. "And help me deserve the trust she's offering."

Elle's breath caught softly. Quietly. Just enough for the river to hear.

"Amen," she whispered.

"Amen," he echoed.

They lifted their heads slowly.

The last light of the sun had filtered through the trees, turning the river gold.

Eli looked at her with the steady calm that had always carried warmth underneath it, only now the warmth was not underneath.

It was right there. Visible. Present. Unmanaged.

Elle looked back at him, her heart full of a particular kind of gratitude she was still learning the language for.

Their hands stayed linked as they turned back toward town.

And as they walked, Elle understood something quietly holy:

God's timing didn't rush.

It didn't force.

It didn't demand or manipulate or take shortcuts through the hard and necessary work of becoming.

It simply unfolded.

Steady and sure and unhurried.

Until you looked down and realized you had been held up the whole time.

And the thing you had been afraid to want had been walking beside you all along, waiting for you to reach for it.

CHAPTER TWENTY-THREE

Where Two or Three Gather

The air had changed.

Not enough for sweaters. Not yet.

Late summer in Washington had softened. The heat wave was a memory now, replaced by a gentle current that carried the faint scent of river water and distant evergreens instead of heavy warmth.

She had walked to the cafe slowly. Not because she was tired, she had slept better than she had in months, but because the morning felt like something worth moving through carefully. The lavender along the path that ran parallel to Main Street was still blooming, later than it had any right to be in September, and she had stopped once to breathe it in.

She was aware that her hands felt different this morning. Nothing dramatic. Just a quiet, steady awareness of where they had been the night before. Of the decision she had made with them.

She had prayed before she slept. Not a long prayer. Just: Thank You. Keep us. Lead us.

That was enough.

Elle unlocked the front door of The Overflow Cafe; a cool breeze followed her inside like a quiet promise.

Elle propped the door open.

"Let it breathe," she murmured to herself.

The cafe exhaled.

Light streamed through the front windows and moved across the primed walls in slow, golden streaks. The space felt different with the door open, less like a construction site and more like something waking up.

From the back corner came the steady sound of a drill.

Real progress.

Not measuring. Not planning.

Building.

Elle walked toward the coffee bar area where Eli was crouched beneath the counter frame, tightening the final bracket on the new handwashing sink. Copper piping curved cleanly against the wall, and the basin caught the light like something purposeful.

He glanced up when she approached, a faint smudge of dust on his cheek.

"Morning," he said.

She smiled. "Morning."

He nodded toward the open door. "Feels good."

"It does."

She leaned against the unfinished counter and watched him work, steady hands, careful movements, attention to detail. There was something deeply grounding about seeing him physically shaping the place now.

It wasn't a dream sketched on paper anymore.

It was plumbing, brackets, shelves.

He stood and tested the faucet, running water briefly to check the seal.

No leaks.

He shut it off and nodded once in quiet satisfaction.

"One step closer," he said.

Elle let out a breath she hadn't realized she was holding. "Thank you," she said softly.

He wiped his hands on a cloth. "It's coming together."

She turned slightly and took in the rest of the space. On the opposite wall, he had begun installing simple wooden shelves, smooth boards mounted securely, waiting for mugs and glasses that would one day line them.

She walked over and ran her hand lightly across the wood. "Those are beautiful," she said.

"Your idea," he replied.

"Your execution," she countered.

His mouth curved faintly.

The breeze shifted again, stirring the papers on the folding table and carrying the sound of Main Street, car doors, distant laughter, the faint flap of fabric.

Elle stepped closer to the doorway and noticed new banners strung between the lampposts across the street.

WILLOW CREEK FALL HARVEST FESTIVAL

October felt closer than it had yesterday.

Her chest tightened just slightly.

Not panic.

Awareness.

She pressed her fingers briefly against the doorframe.

"Jesus," she whispered under her breath, "keep me steady."

Behind her, Eli moved a ladder into place and climbed up to secure the last bracket for the upper shelf.

The scrape of metal against wood sounded solid. Real.

The bell above the door gave a soft jingle as the breeze shifted again.

Then a shadow crossed the threshold.

"Sorry," a voice said gently from outside. "Didn't mean to intrude. Saw the door open."

Elle turned.

Frank stood just beyond the doorway, cap in hand. His eyes carried both the warmth of recognition and genuine delight as he peered into the space. He had been by before, enough times now that his visits had become their own quiet rhythm. Each time he came, he brought something, a memory, a verse, a piece of the building's history. Each time he left, the cafe felt a little more like itself.

"Frank," Eli said from the ladder, offering a nod of easy recognition.

Frank returned the nod. "Eli. Looking good up there."

He stepped one foot inside, careful not to track dirt. His gaze moved slowly around the room, lingering on the shelves, the sink, the open floor.

"I used to bring my wife here," he said quietly. "Back when it was Daily Bread."

Elle smiled softly. "I've heard it was special."

He nodded. "It was." Then he glanced at her. "But looks like you're building something new."

"That's the hope," she said.

He looked toward the shelves Eli had just mounted.

"Places matter," he said thoughtfully. "You know that, right?"

Elle nodded.

He reached into his pocket and unfolded a small, worn piece of paper. It had clearly been folded and unfolded many times.

"I've been thinking about you since I heard about this place," he said. "About what it could be."

He handed the paper to her.

Elle took it gently and read:

Matthew 18:20

"For where two or three gather in my name, there am I with them."

Her breath caught.

The cafe suddenly felt fuller than it had seconds before.

The man smiled softly. "You're not just opening a business," he said. "You're opening a place for people to gather. And when they gather for Him..." He tapped the verse lightly. "He shows up."

Elle's eyes stung, not with overwhelm, but with confirmation.

"Yes," she whispered. "That's exactly what I'm praying for."

The man nodded, satisfied. "Then you're on the right track."

Eli climbed down from the ladder and stepped forward. "You holding up all right, Frank?" he asked. The ease of the question told its own story, the kind of check-in that came from a man who paid attention to people.

Frank considered this with the unhurried honesty of someone who didn't bother with false answers anymore. "Some days better than others," he said simply. "But today's a good one."

Eli nodded once. That was enough.

Frank glanced once more around the space, then back to Elle.

"You planning to be open by the Harvest Festival?" he asked, nodding toward the banner outside.

There it was again. The question.

This time it didn't feel like pressure.

It felt like anticipation.

"That's the goal," Elle said steadily.

Frank grinned. "Good. Town could use this."

He tipped his cap and stepped back out into the breeze, leaving the door open behind him.

For a moment, the only sound inside the cafe was the soft movement of air and the distant hum of town life.

Elle looked down at the verse in her hand again.

Where two or three gather in my name...

She lifted her gaze slowly.

Eli was watching her, not intrusively, just present.

"It fits," he said quietly.

"It does," she replied.

He leaned lightly against the counter frame. "He's already gathering people."

She nodded.

"He is."

* * *

A young couple paused briefly at the doorway next, peeking in with polite curiosity.

"Is this the new cafe?" the woman asked.

"It is," Elle said.

"When do you open?"

"Fall," she answered. "We're aiming for the Harvest Festival."

The couple smiled. "We'll be here."

Then they were gone, no lingering, no speeches. Just interest.

Natural.

Organic.

The breeze continued moving through the space, lifting the edge of the blueprint on the table.

Elle folded the verse carefully and tucked it into her notebook beside the permit checklist.

It felt like it belonged there.

Beside the plans. Beside the steps.

* * *

Eli's phone buzzed quietly in his pocket.

He glanced at it and hesitated just slightly before silencing the notification.

Elle noticed.

"Everything okay?" she asked gently.

He nodded. "Yeah. Just family."

She didn't press. Instead, she said softly, "Whenever you want to talk about it, I'm here."

He met her eyes and gave a small nod. "I know."

The simplicity of that exchange felt deeper than anything dramatic could have been.

Eli returned to tightening the final shelf bracket.

Elle stood in the middle of the cafe, feeling the movement of air around her, the sound of construction, the echo of scripture.

The place no longer felt empty.

It felt expectant.

She closed her eyes briefly.

"Lord," she prayed quietly, "let this be a place where You meet people. Let it be warm. Let it be honest. Let it be safe. And help me lead it with peace."

When she opened her eyes again, Eli was testing the sturdiness of the shelves with both hands.

Solid. Strong. Ready.

Outside, the festival banner shifted in the breeze.

October was coming.

And The Overflow Cafe was no longer just an idea.

It was becoming a gathering place.

One shelf.

One sink.

One step closer.

CHAPTER TWENTY-FOUR

Measured in Inches

September mornings in Willow Creek carried a quiet kind of clarity.

The air was crisp enough that Elle could see the faintest hint of her breath when she unlocked The Overflow Cafe just after seven. A light sweater felt necessary at dawn now, even though she knew by mid-afternoon the sun would warm the sidewalks and coax everyone back into short sleeves.

The door swung open, and cool air slipped inside ahead of her.

She propped it open with a small wooden wedge.

Let it breathe.

Inside, the space felt less like a project and more like a promise.

The new handwashing sink gleamed under the window light. The shelves along the back wall waited patiently for rows of mugs. But what caught her attention this morning wasn't what was finished.

It was what was coming.

Along the far wall near the front windows, an unpainted stretch of drywall stood marked lightly in pencil.

PRAYER WALL

She could already imagine it.

Handwritten prayers tucked into small wooden slots. Names. Praises. Tears folded into paper and slipped into a place where no one else had to see them, but God would.

Across from it, she'd mapped out the cozy corner. Two deep chairs angled toward one another. A small table between them. A lamp casting soft light. A place where someone could sit with a book and a latte and breathe.

The cafe wasn't just being built in wood and plumbing.

It was being imagined into existence.

From the back, the steady hum of a drill echoed briefly, then stopped.

Eli stepped out from the restroom area, wiping his hands with a cloth. He had already removed part of the interior framing in preparation for today's inspection.

"Morning," he said.

Elle smiled. "Morning."

"You sleep?" he asked lightly.

"A little," she admitted.

He nodded once. "It'll be fine."

The words weren't dramatic. They weren't overconfident.

Just steady.

* * *

At exactly nine, a white city vehicle pulled into the gravel lot behind the building.

Linda Hart stepped out first, her expression friendly as always. Behind her came a tall man with a clipboard tucked under one arm and a tape measure clipped to his belt.

"Morning," Linda called as they stepped inside. "This is Eric Henderson," she said. "He's handling compliance and code."

Paul gave a brief nod. "Morning."

His tone wasn't unfriendly. It just wasn't warm. Professional. Direct.

He scanned the space quickly with experienced eyes before saying, "Let's begin."

No small talk. No commentary about how lovely it would be. Just the job.

Elle appreciated that, in a way. It kept things clear.

Eric tested the sink first, checking water flow and clearance beneath. He measured distances between the counter and the wall. He examined electrical placements without commentary.

When he reached the restroom, he stepped inside, closed the door, and measured carefully.

He measured again.

Then he stepped out.

"There was a code update in January," he said evenly, referencing his clipboard. "ADA turning radius requirements expanded. Your interior wall is short by approximately three inches."

Three inches.

He tapped his pen against the paper.

"You'll need to shift the framing here to meet updated clearance. Additionally, grab bar placement needs to move slightly higher to meet the current standard."

He walked toward the main sink again.

"This front sink clearance is close. But it requires modification to meet updated ADA guidelines."

He wasn't critical. He wasn't encouraging. He was precise.

Elle nodded slowly, absorbing the words without letting them multiply into panic.

"Understood," Eli said calmly.

Eric looked at him. "You'll need adjustments completed before final approval. Once corrected, schedule re-inspection."

He checked one final measurement, scribbled something on his clipboard, and stepped back.

"You're close," he said simply. "Just not compliant yet."

Eric handed a copy of the notes to Eli.

Linda offered Elle a small, sympathetic smile. "Call me when you're ready for the follow-up," she said.

And then they were gone.

The door swung slightly in the morning breeze before settling.

Silence filled the cafe.

Elle stood in the middle of the room, eyes drifting from the restroom doorway to the prayer wall space to the cozy corner outline.

Three inches.

She let the number sit there without letting it grow.

Eli didn't speak immediately. He stepped back into the restroom and began measuring again, this time not to evaluate, but to plan.

Elle joined him at the doorway.

"Talk to me," she said quietly.

He kept his voice even. "We'll shift the wall. It's framing and drywall. It's work, but it's doable."

"How long?" she asked.

"About two weeks with scheduling."

"And the festival?"

He looked at her directly.

"It tightens things," he said honestly. "But it doesn't end them."

She nodded slowly. "And cost?" she asked.

He didn't hesitate. "Some increase. But manageable."

No panic in his voice. No over-promising. Just grounded leadership.

She breathed out. "Okay."

He rested his hand lightly against the unfinished doorway. "If we build it, we build it right."

She nodded.

"If we're going to welcome everyone," he added quietly, "we make sure everyone has access."

That shifted something inside her.

This wasn't an obstacle.

It was alignment.

The breeze moved through the cafe again, stirring the papers on the table.

Three inches.

A small adjustment that made space for more people.

* * *

Around noon, Grace slipped inside carrying two iced coffees and wearing concern on her face.

"So?" she asked gently.

"Updated code," Elle said.

Grace made a face. "That sounds expensive."

"It's precise," Eli corrected mildly.

Grace blinked. "That's worse."

They laughed softly, tension easing.

Grace perched on the edge of the future gathering table area and looked around.

"It already feels different," she said quietly.

Elle followed her gaze.

Sunlight now filled the front of the cafe, illuminating the prayer wall section and casting long light toward the imagined reading corner.

"It feels closer," Elle said.

Grace hesitated, then shifted slightly.

"I need to tell you something," she said.

Elle turned fully toward her.

"I really feel called to teach at a Christian school," Grace said quietly. "Not just anywhere. Somewhere where I can pray with my students. Talk about Jesus openly. Build something lasting."

Elle's heart softened.

"But there aren't any openings here right now," Grace continued. "And I don't want to leave Willow Creek. I don't want to leave our church. Or..." She hesitated, cheeks faintly pink. "...everything."

Everything included Luke. That didn't need to be spoken.

Eli leaned casually against the counter, listening.

"Doors don't always open when we expect," he said evenly.

Grace looked at him.

"But when they do," he added, "they usually open wide."

Grace exhaled slowly. "I just don't want to build roots somewhere else if this is where I'm meant to be."

Elle reached for her hand.

"Maybe it's just a matter of inches," Elle said quietly.

Grace frowned. "What?"

Elle glanced toward the restroom wall. "Sometimes the adjustment is small," she said. "It just makes room for something better."

Grace studied her sister thoughtfully.

"Okay," she said finally. "Then I'll keep praying."

* * *

Later that afternoon, when the crisp morning had fully given way to warm sunlight and the open door carried the gentle sounds of Main Street, Eli's phone buzzed again.

He looked at the screen.

This time he didn't silence it.

"I'll be right back," he said.

He stepped outside into the sunlight, voice low as he answered.

Elle pretended to organize the inspection notes but found herself watching the reflection of him in the front window instead.

His posture wasn't tense.

But it wasn't casual either.

The call was short.

When he stepped back inside, something in his expression had shifted, not dramatically. Just enough.

"Everything okay?" she asked gently.

He exhaled.

"It's my mom," he said.

The words landed heavier than "family."

"She's been dealing with some health issues," he continued. "Nothing urgent today. But it's not nothing either."

Elle stepped closer.

"Do you need to go?" she asked softly.

"Maybe," he admitted. "Soon."

There it was.

Another adjustment.

Another shift.

Not catastrophic. Just real.

"You should," she said without hesitation. "She's your mom."

He searched her face briefly, as if bracing for frustration.

Instead, he found steadiness.

"We'll manage here," she added. "One step at a time."

He nodded slowly.

Outside, the festival banner down the street lifted in the afternoon breeze, sunlight catching its edges.

Inside, Elle walked toward the future prayer wall and laid her palm gently against the unfinished drywall.

Soon this would hold prayers. Names. Requests. Gratitude. Fear.

Three inches of wall would move.

Schedules would shift.

Doors would open in different timing than expected.

But this place would still gather people.

And where two or three gathered,

He would be there.

Elle closed her eyes briefly.

"Build it right," she whispered.

Behind her, Eli picked up his measuring tape again.

Not frustrated. Not hurried. Just steady.

And the cafe, like their lives, adjusted.

* * *

The morning he left Elle arrived at the cafe just after seven to find a handwritten note tucked under the door.

Not a text. Not a voicemail.

A note.

She unfolded it standing on the sidewalk, the morning air cool against her face.

Had to head out early. Mom needs me. Shouldn't be more than a few days. I've left the inspection corrections mapped out on the counter, Luke can handle the wall framing while I'm gone, I'll call him this morning. Don't let Grace touch the electrical. I'll be back before you know it. - Eli

She read it twice.

Then she pressed it flat against her chest for a moment, the way she pressed things that mattered.

He had gone to take care of his mother.

Of course he had.

She stood in the doorway of the unfinished cafe and felt two things at once: the particular warmth of knowing exactly who this man was, and the particular quiet of a space that had grown accustomed to the sound of his work.

She stepped inside.

The morning light moved across the primed walls in long, even streaks. No drill. No steady footsteps from the back. Just the soft creak of the building settling into the day without him.

She set her coffee down on the counter and found the sheet he had left.

He had mapped every step.

Not just the wall framing. The grab bar placement. The sink modification. The re-inspection scheduling window. Each item annotated in his clear, unhurried handwriting, with the specific measurements, the order of operations, the name and number of the sub-contractor he trusted.

He had thought of everything.

Because that was how he built.

With care when nobody was watching.

She ran her finger along the edge of the page and swallowed against the tightness in her throat.

She picked up her phone.

Elle: *Safe travels. Take all the time you need. We've got this here. Your mom is lucky to have you.*

She set the phone down. Then picked it up again.

Elle: *The note was very you, by the way.*

Three dots appeared almost immediately.

Eli: *Seemed more reliable than a voicemail.*

She laughed, the sound filling the empty morning.

Eli: *Tell Grace not to touch the electrical.*

Elle: *She already has opinions about it.*

Eli: *I know.*

Eli: *I'll be back Thursday.*

She looked at the word Thursday for a long moment.

Four days.

She noticed the shape of what four days without him felt like before she had even lived them, the way you noticed the weight of something only when you tried to set it down.

She set her phone on the counter.

Breathed in.

It's okay, she told herself quietly. Family first. That's always right.

And it was right. She knew it was right. She believed it completely.

She also knew, with the quiet certainty of someone who had spent months learning to be honest with herself, that the cafe would be slightly less itself for four days. That the mornings would be good and the work would continue and she would be fine.

And that Thursday couldn't come quite fast enough.

She bowed her head briefly.

"Jesus, be with him on the road. Be with his mom. Give him what he needs to give her. And bring him back steady."

A breath.

"And thank You," she added, almost under her breath, "for sending me a man who goes when his mother needs him."

She lifted her head.

Picked up his work sheet.

And got to work.

***

Thursday arrived the way good things did, quietly, and right on time.

She heard his truck before she saw it. The familiar sound of it pulling into the gravel lot behind the building, the engine settling into silence.

Then footsteps. Unhurried. Sure.

The bell above the door.

She looked up from the counter where she had been reviewing the re-inspection checklist.

He stood in the doorway.

Rain-damp jacket. The same steadiness in his posture that always arrived before he did.

He looked at the cafe. At the framing work Luke had completed along the restroom wall. At the new grab bar placement. At the fresh drywall where three inches had been carefully reclaimed.

Then at her.

"Looks right," he said.

She smiled. "Welcome back."

He stepped inside fully, set his tool bag down, and looked around once more with the slow, attentive survey of a man taking stock of what had been built in his absence and finding it good.

"How's your mom?" Elle asked.

"Steadier," he said. "Needed a few things handled around the house. Groceries. A doctor's appointment she'd been putting off." A pause. "She just needed someone to show up."

Elle nodded.

"You're good at that," she said quietly.

He looked at her.

Something moved in his expression. Not surprise. Something deeper. The look of a man who had spent years being steady for job sites and buildings and strangers' projects and was only now beginning to understand what it meant to be steady for someone who saw him.

"Trying to be," he said.

The morning light filled the cafe around them.

The wall was three inches wider.

The door was open.

And the man who built things to last had come back.

CHAPTER TWENTY-FIVE

What God Is Building

September in Willow Creek carried a quiet kind of promise.

The morning opened cool and crisp, the kind of air that made you wrap your hands around a warm mug a little longer before starting the day. But by midmorning, the sun would stretch wide across Main Street and warm everything it touched.

Elle unlocked The Overflow Cafe just after eight and pushed both front doors open wide.

Let it breathe.

A soft breeze moved through the space, stirring the drop cloths laid carefully across the floor and carrying with it the faint scent of nearby evergreens. She set a small speaker on the counter and tapped play.

Soft instrumental worship filled the room, gentle, unobtrusive, present.

Today wasn't just another workday.

It felt like a gathering.

* * *

Grace arrived first, as usual, carrying two iced coffees and an energy that always entered the room before she did.

"Okay," she announced, stepping carefully over a paint tray. "This is officially my favorite Saturday project ever."

Elle laughed. "You say that every time you drink coffee."

"I stand by my motivations," Grace replied.

They moved together easily, setting out rollers and brushes, opening paint cans, laughing as they draped old sheets over the future seating area. The color Elle had chosen was warm and welcoming, a soft cream with the faintest honey undertone. Not stark. Not trendy. Timeless.

A place people would exhale the moment they stepped inside.

Luke arrived next, carrying a ladder over one shoulder like it weighed nothing.

"Where do you want me?" he asked.

Grace blinked. "Wow. Straight to work. No dramatic entrance?"

He shrugged lightly. "Figured we're building something here."

She handed him a roller without another word, but her smile lingered longer than necessary.

Paisley and Mara followed soon after, arms full of supplies, laughter trailing behind them as they stepped inside and took in the transformation.

The cafe was no longer just studs and plans.

It was becoming.

Paint trays lined the floor. Drop cloths stretched wall to wall. Sunlight streamed through open windows, carrying with it the sound of the town waking up.

And everywhere, movement.

* * *

"Before we start on that wall," Elle said gently after a while, stepping toward the front section near the windows, "I want to show you something."

Everyone gathered near the wide framed section she had outlined earlier in pencil.

"This," she said softly, touching the center of it, "is going to be our declaration wall."

They waited.

"Not just decor," she continued. "Not just quotes. A place where we keep track of what God is doing. Prayers answered. Stories. Scripture. Reminders of His goodness."

Grace's eyes softened immediately.

"Like a living testimony," Mara said quietly.

Elle nodded. "Exactly."

She stepped back, letting them see it not as drywall, but as something sacred.

"I want people to walk in and remember who He is," she said. "What He's done. What He's still doing."

No one spoke for a moment.

Then Luke picked up a brush and dipped it into paint.

"Let's build it right," he said simply.

And they began.

* * *

By late morning, the cafe hummed with life.

Paint rolled smoothly across walls. Laughter echoed softly between the open windows. Someone had turned the music up just enough to hear gentle harmonies beneath conversation.

Elle stepped onto a small ladder near the front counter to reach the upper trim. As she worked, she noticed Caleb standing near a shelf along the side wall, running his hand slowly over something propped against it.

The old bread board.

It had been leaning there since she'd brought it from storage, solid wood, worn smooth from decades of use. A piece of the original Daily Bread Bakery. Too meaningful to throw away. Too sacred to repurpose casually.

Caleb lifted it carefully, studying the surface.

"Is this from the bakery that used to be here?" he asked.

Elle climbed down and walked over. "Yeah," she said softly. "Daily Bread Bakery. It was here for years."

He traced a shallow groove in the wood where countless loaves had been shaped. "Feels like history," he said.

"It is," she replied. "I couldn't leave it behind."

He was quiet for a moment, then looked at her. "Would you trust me with it for a few hours?" he asked gently.

She blinked. "What do you mean?"

"I think it could become something really special for this place," he said. "Something that carries both stories forward."

Elle looked down at the board again. It mattered to her. More than she'd realized.

But something in Caleb's tone, steady, respectful, careful, felt right.

"You'd take good care of it?" she asked softly.

"Always," he said.

She exhaled slowly, then nodded. "Okay."

He wrapped it carefully in a cloth he'd brought and lifted it like it was something fragile, something sacred.

"I'll bring it back soon," he promised.

She watched him carry it out, a strange sense of anticipation settling gently in her chest.

* * *

The afternoon warmed, sunlight spilling across freshly painted walls and catching the soft cream tones as they dried.

Around two, another figure appeared at the open doorway.

Tall. Thoughtful. Sketchbook tucked under one arm.

"Hi," he said simply. "Micah."

Elle wiped her hands on a cloth and walked over with a smile. "You must be the designer Caleb told me about."

He nodded and stepped inside, not rushing, just observing. Taking in the declaration wall. The open layout. The light. He had the quality of someone who needed to understand a space before he could speak to it.

"It feels inviting," he said finally.

Elle smiled. "That's the goal."

He pulled a small notebook from his pocket and flipped it open. "I've been sketching some typography ideas. Nothing final. Just direction." He showed her simple lettering concepts. Warm. Flowing. Not corporate. Not trendy. Something that felt like it belonged.

"I don't want it to feel branded," he said quietly. "I want it to feel like an invitation."

The words landed perfectly.

"Yes," Elle said softly. "Exactly."

She introduced him to the others easily, and he moved around the space with the quiet attentiveness that had already become recognizable in him. He didn't say much. But what he said mattered.

* * *

Caleb returned just before sunset.

He stepped inside carrying something wrapped in the same cloth as before.

Conversation softened instinctively.

He set the wrapped bundle gently on the front counter.

"I finished it," he said.

Elle stepped closer, heart already aware that this mattered.

He unwrapped the cloth slowly.

The old bread board lay revealed.

Restored.

Sanded smooth.

Still bearing its history but now transformed.

And engraved across the center in simple, beautiful lettering:

Give us this day our daily bread. Matthew 6:11

No one spoke.

Elle reached out slowly, fingers tracing the engraved words.

Daily Bread.

Provision. Dependence. Grace.

Past and present woven together.

Her eyes filled before she could stop them.

"It started as Daily Bread," Caleb said quietly. "Felt right that it wouldn't lose its roots."

Elle traced the letters slowly. *Daily bread.*

Not the building's name. The prayer underneath it. The acknowledgment that every cup, every morning someone walked through this door, would be an act of dependence. Not on her vision or her savings or her supplier relationships or even her community. On Him.

She thought of the verse she had found months ago, sitting on the floor of this space before it was anything. The Bible falling open to John.

I am the bread of life. Whoever comes to me will never go hungry.

Daily Bread had held that metaphor for seventy years.

She understood now that it had not been an accident.

It had been a promise kept open, waiting for someone to walk through the door and finally understand what it was offering.

Micah stepped closer, studying the engraving with quiet appreciation. "This belongs here," he said simply.

Elle nodded, unable to speak for a moment.

"It's perfect," she whispered.

* * *

As evening settled, golden light filled the cafe through the open windows.

Paint dried. Ladders leaned quietly against walls.

Friends gathered their things one by one, laughter lingering as they stepped out into the cooling air.

"Same time next weekend?" Paisley called lightly.

"Absolutely," Grace answered before anyone else could.

Luke lingered just long enough to help Grace carry supplies to her car, their easy conversation trailing into the parking lot.

Eventually, only Elle and Eli remained.

The cafe felt different again.

Closer. Warmer. Alive.

She stood in the center of the room, turning slowly as she took it all in, the declaration wall, the fresh paint, the engraved bread board resting carefully on the counter.

"It's starting to look like what I saw in my heart," she said softly.

Eli leaned lightly against the doorway, watching her rather than the room.

"It already does," he replied.

She looked at him then.

Not dramatic. Not overwhelming.

Just a quiet, steady recognition of what was being built, around them and between them.

Outside, the evening air cooled again, carrying the first faint whisper of fall.

Inside, the cafe held warmth.

And something deeper than construction.

Something being built by hands, yes,

but led by grace.

The Ones Who First Taught Us

The afternoon light in late September felt different than summer.

Softer.

Lower.

Like it lingered intentionally.

Elle stood alone inside The Overflow Cafe, a soft instrumental version of "Goodness of God" playing quietly from her phone. The doors were open, letting in the steady hum of Main Street and the gentle breeze that carried the first hints of fall.

The paint had dried into a warm cream glow. The declaration wall stood framed, waiting for its first testimony. The engraved bread board rested on a shelf behind the counter, visible, meaningful, grounding.

She stepped back and took it all in.

Not just walls and shelves.

History. Legacy. Calling.

The bell above the door didn't ring, the doors were open, but she felt the shift in the air before she heard his voice.

"Looks different every time I come by."

She turned.

Ben stood just inside the threshold; hands folded loosely in front of him.

For a second, she didn't see the widower.

She saw her youth pastor.

The man who used to stand at the front of the church basement with a Bible in one hand and a stack of pizza boxes in the other. The man who told a room full of teenagers that Jesus was real and worth following.

"Hi, Ben," she said softly.

He nodded, offering a small smile. "Afternoon, Elle."

He stepped further inside, looking around slowly.

"I remember when this was Daily Bread," he said. "Marqua loved it here."

Elle's heart tightened gently.

Marqua.

Her fourth-grade Sunday school teacher.

The woman who sat cross-legged on a tiny chair and taught her about David and Goliath. Who helped her memorize Psalm 23. Who told her that Jesus knew her name.

"She used to bring cinnamon rolls to class," Elle said quietly, a small smile touching her lips.

Ben looked at her, surprised. "She did."

"She'd say, 'We learn better when we're fed,'" Elle added.

His smile softened.

"She always believed that."

Silence settled, but it wasn't empty. It was full of memory.

Elle moved around the counter slowly, not rushing him.

"You know," she said gently, "you two are the reason I know what Psalm 23 means."

Ben looked up at her.

"Marqua made us write it in glitter pen on construction paper," she continued. "And you told us that even when we walk through dark valleys, we don't walk alone."

His throat worked slightly as he swallowed.

"She loved teaching," he said quietly.

"She loved Jesus," Elle replied.

He nodded.

"She did."

His gaze moved toward the shelf where the bread board rested.

"Feels strange," he said after a moment. "I always thought I'd go first."

The words were simple. Honest. No drama in them.

"Marqua used to joke I worked too hard," he continued softly. "Said I'd wear myself out before she ever would." A faint breath of a laugh escaped him. "Turns out, I was stronger than I knew."

Elle felt the weight of those words.

"I wasn't supposed to be the one left," he said.

And there it was.

Not anger at God.

Not bitterness.

Just a man who had loved deeply and was learning how to live with the silence.

She stepped closer, close enough that he didn't feel alone in the open space.

"The house feels different?" she asked gently.

He nodded.

"Church too," he admitted. "I keep reaching for her hand during worship." He paused. "Funny how your body remembers before your heart can catch up."

Tears stung Elle's eyes.

Not just because he was hurting.

But because she remembered sitting between them in youth group, feeling safe, feeling known, feeling pointed toward Jesus.

"You both shaped my faith," she said quietly.

Ben looked at her.

"I wouldn't be opening this place if you hadn't taught me who Jesus is," she continued. "Marqua taught me He's near. You taught me He's steady."

His eyes filled.

"Elle," he breathed softly.

"It's because of you," she said, voice trembling slightly but steady in conviction, "that I know He's still near now."

The room felt holy in that moment.

Not because of what it looked like.

But because of what it held.

Ben's shoulders sagged slightly, not in defeat, but in release.

"I wasn't planning to come in," he admitted. "I was walking by and saw the doors open." He looked around. "Felt like she would've wanted me to step inside."

"She would have," Elle said.

He exhaled slowly.

"I just... miss her," he whispered.

The honesty of it landed heavy and pure.

"I know," she said gently.

There was no fixing grief.

No solving it.

Only carrying it together.

"Would you let me pray for you?" she asked quietly.

He nodded immediately. "I'd like that."

She reached out, resting her hand over his, the same hands that had once opened Bibles and pointed her toward truth.

"Jesus," she began softly, "thank You for Marqua. Thank You for the way she loved You, and for the way she loved all of us."

Ben closed his eyes.

"Thank You for the faith she planted in children who didn't even understand how deeply it would matter one day."

Her voice grew steadier.

"Be close to Ben in the quiet moments. In the spaces where her chair sits empty. In the mornings that feel too still. Remind him that the same Savior he taught about is holding him now."

She paused.

"And thank You for the legacy they built together, in marriages, in teenagers, in little fourth-grade classrooms." Her voice softened. "Let that legacy continue to overflow."

"Amen," Ben whispered.

They stood there a moment longer.

Not rushed.

Just two believers holding space for grief and grace at the same time.

When he opened his eyes, something had shifted.

Not gone. Not erased.

But lighter.

Like he wasn't carrying it alone in that moment.

"She'd like this place," he said quietly.

Elle smiled gently. "I hope so."

He looked around again, at the declaration wall, at the bread board engraved with Give us this day our daily bread, at the sunlight filling the room.

"She always said God meets people in ordinary places," he said. "Maybe this will be one of them."

"It already is," Elle replied softly.

He nodded, a faint, quiet hope settling across his features.

As he stepped back out into the afternoon light, his shoulders weren't as heavy.

Still grieving.

But steadier.

Elle watched him walk down the sidewalk, remembering a younger version of herself walking into church, unsure, eager, learning.

They had pointed her to Jesus.

And now, somehow, Jesus had brought her back to steady them.

She turned back inside.

The cafe felt different again.

Not just a dream. Not just a project.

A continuation.

A place where faith would keep being planted.

She walked over to the declaration wall and laid her hand against the frame.

"Let this place honor them," she whispered. "And glorify You."

The breeze moved softly through the open doors.

And for a moment, it felt like heaven was closer than usual.

CHAPTER TWENTY-SEVEN

Final Preparations

By midmorning, The Overflow Cafe held laughter again.

Grace burst in wearing a Willow Creek College hoodie and carrying a tote bag full of children's books like she was delivering literature to the nations.

"Okay," she announced. "The reading corner is happening today."

Elle laughed. "Good morning to you too."

Grace kissed her cheek. "I have class in an hour, but I needed to bring these before student teaching because the kindergarteners are counting on me spiritually."

Elle raised an eyebrow. "The kindergarteners?"

Grace nodded solemnly. "Yes. They don't know it yet, but they're going to grow up loving Jesus and books and coffee."

Elle snorted. "Coffee might be a stretch."

Grace waved a hand. "Okay, how about hot chocolate?"

As Grace arranged books on the shelves, Luke walked in, still in his firehouse uniform, jacket unzipped, hair slightly damp from cold air and urgency.

He looked tired.

But his smile appeared the second he saw Grace.

"Morning," he said casually, like his heart didn't do anything different at the sight of her.

Grace straightened and tried to look normal.

She failed.

"Hi," she said, suddenly too bright.

Luke's eyes flicked to the tiny chairs in the children's corner. "These are... small."

Grace nodded. "Yes. Because children are small."

Luke blinked. "Right."

Grace narrowed her eyes. "Do you not know what children are?"

Luke raised both hands. "I fight fires, Grace. I don't fight toddlers."

Grace laughed, and the sound softened something in Luke's tired face.

Elle watched from behind the counter, heart warm.

Luke moved toward the counter and leaned in, lowering his voice. "You got more of that honey blend?"

Elle nodded. "Caleb dropped off another bag. Want a cup?"

Luke sighed like a man being saved. "Yes."

As Elle brewed, Luke glanced around the cafe, quieter now.

"This place is going to be good for people," he said, almost under his breath.

Elle's chest tightened. "I hope so."

Luke shook his head once. "No. It will. Town needs somewhere that feels... safe."

Grace overheard and pointed at him dramatically. "Say it louder so the Lord can hear."

Luke grinned. "I think He heard me the first time."

Grace's smile softened into something proud and tender.

* * *

In the early afternoon, Paisley arrived straight from the children's hospital.

Elle knew before Paisley even spoke.

Her face carried that particular expression, softened, thoughtful, emotionally present in a way that meant she'd been holding someone's fear in her hands.

Paisley set her bag down gently and exhaled.

"Long day?" Elle asked quietly.

Paisley nodded once.

Then she smiled like she was trying. "But God is faithful."

Elle walked around the counter and hugged her.

Paisley held on for a second longer than usual.

When she pulled back, her eyes were bright.

"There was a little boy today," Paisley whispered. "Six years old. Scared. He kept asking if he was going to die."

Elle's throat tightened.

Paisley blinked quickly, forcing her voice steady. "I sat with him. Told him the truth, that doctors are helping him. That he's not alone. That Jesus is with him."

Elle reached for her hand.

Paisley squeezed it.

"And then," Paisley continued, "his mom asked me if I could pray. In the hospital room. With all the machines."

Her voice softened. "And I did."

Elle's eyes stung.

Paisley let out a shaky laugh. "I didn't feel brave. I felt... small."

Elle shook her head gently. "That's usually when God uses us most."

Paisley exhaled slowly.

They sat together for a long moment at the end of the counter, the afternoon light shifting warmly around them.

Elle thought about the prayer basket near the wall. About the notes accumulating there. About a six-year-old boy in a hospital room with machines beeping and a nurse who had stayed and prayed.

"You brought Jesus into that room," Elle said softly.

Paisley looked at her.

"That's the whole thing," Elle continued. "That's the Overflow."

Paisley pressed her lips together against emotion. "It doesn't feel like enough sometimes."

"It's never about enough," Elle said. "It's about showing up."

Paisley nodded slowly, something settling in her expression. "Yeah."

Then, as if she needed something tangible to do, she looked toward the milk bottles lined neatly in the cooler.

"Is that the dairy guy's delivery?" she asked, suddenly lighter.

Elle smiled. "Owen. Yes."

As if summoned by his name, the bell chimed and Owen stepped in with another crate of milk.

He paused when he saw Paisley.

Paisley paused too.

Owen's expression softened slightly, like he noticed the tiredness in her eyes and didn't try to fix it. Just acknowledged it.

"Hey," he said quietly.

Paisley smiled. "Hey."

Owen set the crate down gently. "How's the hospital today?"

Paisley blinked, surprised he knew.

Owen shrugged slightly, voice calm. "My niece was there a lot when she was little. I recognize that look."

Paisley's throat tightened.

For a second, she didn't make a joke. She didn't fill the space. She simply nodded.

"Yeah," she whispered. "It was one of those days."

Owen held her gaze for a beat, steady and kind. Then he said, softly, "You did good work."

Paisley's eyes shimmered.

She laughed suddenly, too bright, trying to keep emotion from spilling over. "Okay, farmer man, don't go making me cry in a coffee shop that isn't even open yet."

Owen's mouth twitched. "Noted."

Then he nodded to Elle. "I'll bring cream next time too. For the kids' hot chocolate."

Elle smiled. "We'll be ready."

As Owen left, Paisley watched him for just a second longer than necessary.

Then she looked at Elle and whispered, "He's... nice."

Elle smiled innocently. "He is."

Paisley narrowed her eyes. "Don't do that."

Elle laughed. "I didn't do anything."

Paisley pointed at her. "You did something."

* * *

Later, Micah arrived with a roll of printed mockups and a pencil behind his ear, looking like someone who saw the world in shapes and meaning.

He spread designs across the community table while Caleb poured coffee like it was a sacred ritual.

Micah tapped the logo gently. "This is strong. It feels inviting."

Elle's eyes softened. "That's what we want."

Micah nodded. "Then we add one line beneath it."

He wrote quickly in neat script:

Come in. Rest. Be filled.

Elle's breath caught.

Caleb glanced at it and smiled. "That's... actually perfect."

Janelle, walking in at that moment, read it and whispered, "That's ministry."

Micah looked up, slightly embarrassed by the attention. "It's... just words."

Elle shook her head gently. "Sometimes words are doorways."

Micah's expression softened, thoughtful. "Yeah," he said quietly. "Sometimes they are."

* * *

As the afternoon stretched toward evening, the cafe held more moments like that.

A teenager wandered in hesitantly and asked if there would be "somewhere people can talk if they don't want to go home yet."

Grace immediately began designing a quiet corner in her mind.

A young couple stopped by with a stack of hymnals they'd found at a garage sale and offered them "for the shelf, if you want."

Elle accepted them like treasure.

An older woman left a note on the counter that simply read: My son is far from God. Please pray.

Elle added it to the prayer basket with reverence.

Each moment was small.

But together, they formed something undeniable. The town was already leaning in. Already trusting this space. Already believing it might hold something good.

* * *

Elle was still smiling when she turned back to the counter and found Eli standing near the doorway.

He'd come in quietly, no bell, just steady presence, and was watching the whole room with that particular attentiveness he brought to spaces. Not evaluating. Receiving.

He leaned slightly toward Elle and murmured, "People are pairing off in here."

Elle's cheeks warmed. She whispered back, "Stop."

His gaze held hers, warm, steady, quietly charged. He didn't say anything else.

But the way he looked at her felt like a gentle reminder:

He'd been gone. And now he was here again.

And she was aware of him in a way she hadn't fully been before.

The last of the afternoon light moved across the walls. The prayer basket on the counter held its first notes. The reading corner waited. The menu designs lay spread across the community table.

Tomorrow, The Overflow Cafe would open its doors for the first time.

Elle set down her cloth and looked around at everything that had been built over the past months. The counter framing. The shelves. The declaration wall. The bread board with its engraved words. The Bible beneath the threshold that no one could see but everyone who stepped through the door would stand upon.

Her throat tightened.

Eli moved to stand beside her, close but unhurried. He looked at the room too.

A long, quiet moment passed between them.

"You ready?" he asked.

Elle exhaled slowly. Fully.

"I've been ready my whole life," she said. "I just didn't know what I was getting ready for."

Eli looked at her then. Something in his expression moved the way it moved when she said things that reached him.

"Yeah," he said. "I think I understand that."

She believed him.

He locked up while she gathered her bag, and they walked out into the cool evening together, the string lights glowing warmly through the front windows behind them.

Elle didn't look back.

She didn't need to.

Tomorrow the doors would open.

And whatever came after that, she already knew:

It was going to overflow.

CHAPTER TWENTY-EIGHT

The Overflow Opens

The sun hadn't fully risen when Elle stepped onto the walking path.

Morning in Willow Creek carried a quiet that felt less like silence and more like anticipation. A pale ribbon of gold stretched across the horizon, and the crisp fall air brushed gently against her cheeks as she walked.

Her music. Her headphones and the steady rhythm of her steps and the whisper of leaves overhead.

This was where it had begun.

Where she had first prayed for courage to come home. Where she had wrestled with leaving the city. Where she had asked God if obedience would truly be worth it.

Now she stood at the overlook, hands resting lightly on the railing as the river below caught the first light of morning.

"Thank You," she whispered. The words came easily. Fully.

"For every step that led here. For every delay. Every door You opened. Every person You brought into my life to build this with me."

She closed her eyes.

"Let this place be Yours. Every laugh. Every tear. Every conversation. Every prayer whispered over a cup of coffee. Let people walk in heavy and walk out lighter."

A small pause.

Then softer still:

"And... thank You for him."

Her cheeks warmed slightly even alone.

She didn't elaborate. She didn't need to. God knew.

Elle exhaled slowly and turned toward town, her steps light with peace.

Today, The Overflow Cafe would open.

* * *

The lights glowed warm when Elle unlocked the door and stepped inside.

She paused just past the threshold, as she always did, glancing down toward the place beneath the doorway where the Bible rested unseen but foundational.

Her hand pressed gently against the frame.

"Still Yours," she whispered.

Inside, everything waited.

Tables polished. Chairs arranged.

Micah's hand-lettered sign, Come in. Rest. Be filled., hung above the counter like an invitation from heaven itself.

Elle moved slowly through the space, straightening a pillow, adjusting a chair, breathing it all in.

The bell chimed softly.

Janelle stepped inside first.

She carried a small woven basket filled with prayer cards, pens, and a few slim devotionals tied with twine. Her presence, as always, felt like calm entering a room.

"Good morning," she said warmly.

Elle smiled, instantly comforted. "Good morning."

Janelle set the basket gently on the community table and began arranging the cards with quiet intention. "I thought we could place these here," she said softly. "For anyone who wants prayer... or a moment with the Word."

Elle's throat tightened. "That's perfect."

Janelle glanced around the cafe, eyes gentle. "This place already feels... sacred."

Elle swallowed. "I was praying it would."

Janelle reached out and squeezed her hand. "It is."

The door chimed again.

Grace burst in next, already emotional. "I'm not crying," she declared immediately. "I'm just... spiritually hydrated."

Elle laughed and hugged her tight.

Luke arrived carrying two pastry boxes and a quiet pride he didn't try to hide. "Fuel for the saints," he said.

Paisley followed with two nurses from the children's hospital, talking fast and smiling wide. "Everyone needs to see this place," she insisted.

Owen stepped in soon after with fresh milk deliveries, dressed in a clean button-down that made Paisley do a double take she hoped no one noticed.

Caleb arrived with bags of roasted beans and a grin that matched Elle's own nerves. Micah came beside him with the final printed menus and a small wooden stand for the counter.

Mara slipped in quietly.

She paused just inside the doorway, her gaze lowering instinctively toward the threshold. Though she couldn't see the Bible beneath, something in her expression softened as if she could feel it there.

Then she looked up at Elle.

Tears shimmered in her eyes.

Elle stepped forward and squeezed her hand. "We're here," she whispered.

Mara nodded. "We are."

The cafe slowly filled with people from across Willow Creek, neighbors, church families, curious passersby. Not a chaotic crowd. A gathering. Warm and expectant.

* * *

Janelle moved gently among them, placing prayer cards near the wall, greeting people with quiet warmth.

When a young mother entered with tired eyes and a toddler on her hip, Janelle offered a soft smile and guided her toward a cozy chair. "If you need a moment," she said gently, "this is a good place to find one."

The woman's shoulders relaxed immediately.

Janelle settled into the chair beside her a few minutes later. Not with a clipboard or a program or an agenda. Just with her full attention and a willingness to listen.

The young mother's name was Sara. She had moved to Willow Creek eight months ago from a city two hours south, following her husband's job transfer. She didn't know anyone. Her toddler's name was Noah. She hadn't slept properly in six days.

Janelle listened to all of it.

She didn't offer solutions. She didn't redirect to resources. She simply received Sara's story with the grace of a woman who understood that being heard was itself a form of healing.

When Sara finished, she looked slightly surprised at herself, as if she hadn't meant to say so much.

"I'm sorry," Sara said. "You came to an opening. I just..."

"You came to the right place," Janelle said simply.

Sara's eyes filled.

"Would it be okay if I prayed with you?" Janelle asked.

Sara nodded quickly, like she'd been waiting for someone to offer.

Janelle reached out one hand, Noah still on Sara's hip between them, and prayed quietly. No performance. No attention drawn. Just steady compassion and the name of Jesus spoken over a woman who needed to be reminded she was not invisible.

Elle noticed from across the room.

She turned away before the tears could fall in front of everyone.

Yes.

This was exactly why Janelle belonged here.

* * *

Pastor Nathan eventually raised a hand near the doorway.

"Before we open fully," he said warmly, "Elle would like to share something."

The room quieted.

Elle stepped forward, heart full but steady.

"There's a Bible beneath this doorway," she said softly. "Placed here before anything else. Before paint. Before furniture. Before coffee."

Several people blinked back tears already.

"We wanted every person who walks in here to step over the Word of God," she continued. "So, this place would always be grounded in Him."

Silence settled, reverent and full.

Pastor Nathan placed his hand on the doorframe.

"Lord," he prayed, voice calm and strong, "bless every step that crosses this threshold. Let this be a place of peace, healing, truth, and joy. Fill it with Your presence always."

Soft amens rose throughout the room.

Elle exhaled slowly.

Then someone whispered, "Elle...will you sing?"

She hesitated only a moment.

Then nodded.

Caleb handed her a small acoustic guitar, and she stepped toward the center of the cafe. Her fingers settled naturally on the strings.

She didn't perform.

She worshiped.

"You're my firm foundation...

Her voice filled the room, gentle, steady, reverent.

Conversation stopped completely.

Janelle closed her eyes; hands folded loosely in front of her.

Mara pressed a hand to her heart.

Paisley blinked rapidly.

Grace leaned into Luke's shoulder without realizing it.

And Eli...

He stood near the back, having slipped in quietly. He hadn't announced himself. He didn't need to.

He simply watched her.

Listened.

Felt.

As Elle sang, something settled fully in his chest.

This woman.

This calling.

This place God was building through her.

He knew.

When the final note faded, the quiet lingered like a blessing.

Pastor Nathan smiled softly. "Well," he said, voice thick with emotion. "Let's open a cafe."

Laughter broke gently through the room.

And just like that, The Overflow Cafe opened.

* * *

The day unfolded like a living prayer.

Coffee poured. Milk steamed. Laughter rose. Prayer cards filled the basket.

Frank Alderman sat by the window with his hands wrapped around a mug of The Returning Blend, the same quiet smile on his face as the morning he had walked in with a photograph and a scripture and the memory of his mother's Saturday cinnamon rolls. He didn't stay long. He just sat and watched the room fill with life, and when he finally set his empty mug down and rose to leave, he paused at the door and looked back at Elle behind the counter.

He nodded once.

She understood completely.

Teenagers gathered at the community table, talking freely in a way that felt safe.

Grace read to two neighborhood kids in the corner while Luke pretended not to listen and clearly did.

Elle stepped back behind the counter at one point and simply watched.

This wasn't just opening day.

This was ministry.

Living. Breathing. Beautiful.

She glanced across the room.

Eli stood near the espresso machine, helping Caleb adjust a setting. He laughed at something Luke said, then looked up.

Their eyes met.

And held.

Across the hum of conversation and warmth and community, they felt it.

Not sudden. Not overwhelming.

Just certain.

* * *

By evening, the crowd thinned.

Goodbyes stretched into promises to return. Chairs slid back into place. The lights dimmed softly as dusk settled outside.

Eventually, the door closed.

Silence returned.

Elle stood behind the counter, hands resting lightly on the wood. She exhaled slowly.

"We did it," she whispered.

Eli turned the sign to Closed and walked toward her. "God did," he said gently.

She smiled. "Yeah. He did."

String lights glowed overhead. Peace settled around them.

"I kept thinking about this place while I was gone," he said quietly. "About what it would feel like when it opened."

Elle tilted her head. "And?"

He looked around slowly. Then back at her. "It feels like home," he said.

Her throat tightened.

A pause.

Then softer:

"I don't want to build anything in this life... without you in it."

The words landed gently.

She stepped around the counter.

Now only a breath separated them.

His hand lifted slowly, brushing a strand of hair from her face.

Tender. Reverent.

He leaned in.

The kiss was soft. Unhurried. Warm. Not a spark that startled, but a flame that had been patiently waiting for its moment.

Her hand rested lightly against his chest.

The world didn't spin.

Instead, peace. Rightness. Home.

When they pulled back, neither spoke.

They didn't need to.

String lights glowed softly.

The cafe stood warm and quiet around them.

And beneath their feet, unseen but steady, the Word of God remained their foundation.

God had built something beautiful here.

A place. A community.

And now, a love story grounded in Him.

CHAPTER TWENTY-NINE

After the Doors Open

The morning after the kiss felt different.

Not awkward. Not overwhelming. Just...aware.

Elle unlocked the door to The Overflow Cafe as the first pale light of day stretched across Willow Creek. The air was cool and clean, and the quiet hum of early morning felt like a soft continuation of everything God had done the day before.

She stepped inside and paused, just past the threshold.

Her eyes lowered instinctively toward the place beneath the doorway where the Bible rested unseen.

"Still Yours," she whispered.

Then she lifted her gaze, and saw him.

Eli stood near the counter with two mugs already poured, as if he'd been there long enough to settle but not long enough to interrupt the sacredness of the morning.

He looked up when she noticed him. "Good morning," he said.

Her heart warmed immediately. "Good morning."

She stepped inside fully, closing the door gently behind her. The cafe felt peaceful in the early quiet, sunlight just beginning to filter through the front windows, touching the tables and chairs with soft gold.

Eli held out one of the mugs. "The Returning blend."

She accepted it, their fingers brushing briefly. Neither pulled away too quickly.

A small pause lingered.

Then he smiled, steady, calm, certain.

"You sleep at all?"

Elle laughed softly. "Eventually."

"Me too."

They stood there for a moment, both holding warm mugs, both aware of what had shifted between them without needing to rush it.

"Last night..." Eli began, then paused.

Elle met his gaze, giving him space to finish.

"It mattered," he said simply.

Her throat tightened. "It did."

A quiet breath passed between them.

Then Eli spoke again, voice gentle but grounded.

"I want to do this right. God first. Always."

Elle nodded without hesitation. "Always."

No grand declarations. No dramatic promises. Just intention. Just peace.

And somehow, that felt even more solid than fireworks.

They shared a small smile, one that carried warmth, hope, and a quiet understanding that something real had begun.

* * *

By Tuesday morning, the cafe buzzed with a gentle rhythm of regulars already forming.

A young man named Trevor began coming in each morning with a worn notebook and tired eyes. On Thursday, he struck up a conversation with Luke while waiting for his coffee, something about being between jobs, trying not to sound desperate about it.

Luke listened. Asked a few questions. Then pulled out his phone, texted the mechanic over at the firehouse, and slid a number across the counter to Trevor.

Trevor left that afternoon looking a little lighter than he'd arrived.

* * *

On Wednesday, a folded card appeared on the prayer wall.

Simple. Written in careful handwriting.

My daughter's surgery went well. Thank you for praying. – A grateful mom

Elle stood holding the card for a moment longer than necessary, emotion rising gently in her chest.

Janelle stepped beside her, reading it silently. Then she smiled that soft, grounded smile of hers. "He's already moving here," she said quietly.

Elle nodded, blinking back tears. "Yes, He is."

They pinned the card to a small section of the wall now labeled:

Praises

It didn't take long for more to follow.

* * *

By Friday morning, a small group of young moms had begun gathering at the large community table near the windows.

It started accidentally.

One exhausted mother with a stroller. Another with a toddler and dark circles under her eyes. A third who simply needed somewhere to sit where no one expected perfection.

They introduced themselves slowly. Shared coffee. Shared stories. Shared the weight of motherhood and the beauty of it too.

Paisley joined them on her day off, offering laughter and understanding from her work at the hospital. Janelle brought a small stack of devotionals and set them gently in the center of the table.

No one led officially. They just gathered.

One morning, Elle overheard quiet prayer rising from that table, soft voices asking God for patience, strength, and wisdom for their children and themselves.

She stepped back behind the counter, emotion swelling.

This was what she had prayed for. A place where people didn't have to pretend they had it all together. A place where they could grow, together.

* * *

Saturday afternoon brought a different kind of moment.

Elle almost missed it.

She had been behind the counter for the better part of two hours, making drinks, laughing with Grace, watching the gentle rhythm of people coming and going. The cafe had developed a Saturday afternoon quality she was already beginning to love, unhurried, warm, the light falling just right through the front windows.

Then she noticed him.

A man in his early thirties, sitting alone in the corner near the prayer wall.

He had been there a while. Long enough that his coffee had gone from steaming to still. Long enough that he had read nothing, looked at his phone once and put it away, and simply sat with his hands wrapped around the mug like he was trying to absorb warmth through his palms.

His eyes kept returning to the prayer wall. To the handwritten cards. To the word at the top:

Praises.

Elle watched him for another few minutes, praying quietly under her breath, asking God for wisdom on whether to approach.

The answer came simply.

Go.

She came around the counter with a fresh mug and walked toward him slowly, the way you walked toward something fragile.

"Can I warm that up for you?" she asked.

He blinked like he'd forgotten where he was. "Oh. Yeah. Thank you."

She refilled his cup. Then, gently: "First time here?"

He nodded. His jaw worked slightly. "Yeah."

She didn't push. She set the carafe on a nearby table and took a breath, asking God again.

Then the man spoke first.

"I walked past your sign," he said, eyes still on the prayer wall. "Three times today. Kept coming back." He paused. "The words. Come in. Rest. Be filled." He exhaled. "I don't know. Something made me stop."

Elle pulled out the chair across from him and sat.

"We meant it," she said softly.

He looked at her then, for the first time directly. His eyes were tired in a way that didn't come from bad sleep.

"I haven't been to church in years," he said. "I don't even know if I believe anymore. I used to." A pause. "I grew up in it. And then some things happened and I just... stopped."

Elle didn't offer a counter-argument. She didn't cite a verse. She simply said, "What happened?"

And he told her.

It wasn't a long story, but it was a real one. A father who left. A church that felt more like performance than presence. A season of grief where he had prayed and heard nothing.

"I didn't stop believing because I wanted to," he said. "I stopped because it hurt too much to keep hoping and feel like nothing was there."

Elle's chest ached with recognition.

She thought about the bridge. About the night she had knelt on her apartment floor. About every unanswered prayer that had felt like silence and had turned out, in time, to be preparation.

"I understand that," she said. "More than you might think."

He looked at her. Really looked.

"What changed?" he asked.

Elle considered the question carefully, the way it deserved.

"I stopped looking for God to show up the way I expected," she said slowly. "And started paying attention to where He actually was."

The man was quiet.

"I think He's been trying to get your attention," Elle said gently. "Three times past a sign is usually not an accident."

Something shifted in his expression.

Not dramatic. Not sudden. The way things shifted when a door that had been locked for a long time felt the right key.

"I don't know how to start again," he said. His voice cracked slightly on the last word.

Elle leaned forward, arms resting on the table between them.

"You don't have to have it figured out," she said. "You just have to be willing to take one step. That's it. One step."

He swallowed hard. "What's the step?"

"Tell Him," she said. "Just say it out loud. That you want to find your way back."

The man looked at the prayer wall again.

Then he nodded, very slowly. "Okay."

Elle said softly, "Can I pray with you?"

He nodded again, eyes bright now with something she recognized as the particular vulnerability of a person who has decided to stop running.

His name was Aaron, she learned.

And there, in the quiet corner of a small-town cafe on a Saturday afternoon, with soft worship playing in the background and the scent of honey and roasted coffee in the air, Aaron bowed his head and whispered a simple prayer.

Not rehearsed. Not polished.

Just true.

"God, I don't know if You're listening. But I'm asking. I want to find my way back. I think I need You. I'm not sure how this works anymore, but... I'm here."

A pause.

"Help me find You again."

When he lifted his face, tears had broken the surface of his eyes and were tracking slowly down both cheeks.

He looked almost surprised by them.

"Thank you," he said hoarsely.

Elle shook her head gently. "Thank Him."

From across the room, Eli watched quietly, understanding the sacredness of what was happening without needing to step in. He had seen enough built and enough broken to know when God was doing the work only He could do.

Later, when Aaron rose to leave, he paused at the doorway.

His hand rested briefly on the frame.

He looked back at Elle with an expression that was quiet and unguarded and new.

Then he stepped out into the afternoon.

Differently than he had walked in.

* * *

Amid all the movement and meaning, another quiet story continued to unfold.

Grace stood behind the counter one early morning attempting latte art that looked suspiciously like abstract clouds when Luke walked in straight from a night shift.

He looked tired. But when he saw her, his expression softened immediately.

"You're up early," she said.

He shrugged. "Shift ended. Figured caffeine was a good life choice."

She handed him a mug before he could ask. He blinked. "You already made this?"

She shrugged casually. "I saw you walk by the window."

Luke smiled into the cup before taking a sip. "Perfect," he said.

Grace tried not to look pleased. Failed.

"You're good with kids," Luke added after a moment. "Heard from Pastor Nathan you finish student teaching soon."

Grace's face lit. "Kindergarten."

Luke nodded like that made complete sense. "They're lucky."

The sincerity in his voice caught her off guard. "Thanks," she said softly.

He held her gaze for a beat longer than necessary. Then cleared his throat and took another sip of coffee.

Across the cafe, Elle pretended not to notice.

She noticed everything.

* * *

One evening, after the last customers left and the chairs were reset, Elle stepped outside into the cool night air. The cafe lights glowed warmly behind her.

Eli joined her a moment later.

They stood side by side on the sidewalk, looking through the window at the space that had already begun changing lives.

"It's happening," she said softly.

He nodded. "Yeah. It is."

A comfortable silence settled between them.

Then Eli spoke, voice quiet but steady. "I meant what I said last night. About doing this right."

Elle looked up at him. "I know."

"I'm not in a rush," he continued. "But I'm also not pretending this is casual."

Her heart warmed deeply. "Me neither."

He nodded once, satisfied. "Good."

They stood there a moment longer, not needing to fill the space.

Inside the cafe, the prayer wall held new notes. The community table sat ready for tomorrow's gathering. The coffee bar gleamed softly under the lights.

Outside, the town of Willow Creek settled into evening.

And as Elle stood beside the man God had quietly woven into her story, she felt something settle gently in her spirit:

The Overflow Cafe was doing exactly what it was meant to do.

Hearts were healing. Lives were connecting. Faith was growing.

And the love story unfolding between them was only just beginning.

* * *

The cafe was clean and still.

Chairs reset. Cups rinsed. The string lights casting their gentle warmth across the prayer wall, the testimonies layered there now like a quilt made of people's most honest moments.

Elle stood at the counter, tracing the rim of a mug with her thumb. The cross etched into the clay, rough and grounding. She had held it through a hundred difficult mornings.

Eli came in from the back where he'd been checking the sink pressure. His jacket was over one arm. He was almost at the door when he noticed her expression.

He stopped.

"Hey," he said. Not alarmed. Just present.

She looked at him for a long moment.

"I want to tell you something," she said quietly.

He set his jacket down on the counter.

No hesitation. No checking the time.

Just: "Okay."

She exhaled.

"Before I came home," she said, turning the mug slowly in her hands, "there was someone. His name was Daniel. We were together for almost two years."

Eli didn't move. Didn't fill the silence.

"He wasn't a bad person," she said carefully. "He just couldn't hold what I was. And instead of accepting that, I started making myself smaller." She swallowed. "Quieter. I stopped saying what I thought. Stopped talking about Jesus the way I actually think about Jesus, like He's in everything. I thought if I took up less space, I'd be easier to keep."

She set the mug down.

"And he left anyway."

The cafe held the words.

Eli was quiet for a moment. Then he asked, gently: "Did you lose yourself?"

Elle looked at him.

"Yes," she said. "For a long time."

He nodded once. Slowly.

Then: "I know," he said. "I've been watching you find yourself back."

Her throat tightened.

"The bridge," she said softly. "The cafe. All of it."

"All of it," he confirmed.

He picked up her mug from the counter and turned it in his hands, feeling the cross the same way she did. Then he set it back down and looked at her directly.

"I want you to know," he said, "that I'm not interested in the smaller version. I never was."

Elle blinked fast.

"I want all of it," he said. "The Jesus talk at seven in the morning. The strong opinions about counter spacing. The way you pray like it's breathing." His voice was steady. "All of it is what I want."

She laughed, a small, unsteady sound.

He smiled, quiet and certain.

They stood there in the warmth of the cafe, its walls holding prayers, its floor holding the Word.

She felt the last tension in her chest, the one she had been carrying since a different apartment floor in a different life - finally, fully, set down.

"Thank you," she whispered.

"Thank you for telling me," he said.

She picked up the mug with the cross.

Held it.

Felt the weight of it, and for the first time in a long time, felt held back.

CHAPTER THIRTY

The Ripple Effect

By the time the first frost dusted the edges of Willow Creek, The Overflow Cafe had become more than a place people visited.

It had become a place people returned to.

Not just for coffee, though Caleb's honey-finished blend had earned a loyal following and more than one dramatic declaration of, "This is the only thing getting me through Monday."

Not just for the cozy chairs, though the front window corner had become a sacred seat for grief and journaling and quiet prayers whispered between sips.

But for something harder to describe.

A feeling.

A breath.

A moment to rest.

A place where, somehow, the weight of life didn't feel quite as crushing.

Elle noticed it in the way people stepped inside.

They didn't just walk through the door.

They exhaled.

As if their shoulders knew before their minds did: You're safe here.

That morning, Elle stood behind the counter watching the cafe wake up.

The string lights still glowed softly overhead, warm against the gray morning outside. A soft instrumental worship song played low, barely noticeable but present like a heartbeat.

Janelle arranged fresh prayer cards in the basket near the wall with steady hands.

Grace was perched on a stool at the end of the counter, studying flashcards for an upcoming test and occasionally muttering, "Why do children need to know so many shapes?"

Luke had stopped in five minutes earlier, still in his firehouse jacket, and now stood near the pastry case debating aloud whether cinnamon rolls were "breakfast or dessert."

"They're ministry," Grace told him without looking up.

Luke grinned. "That's what I've been saying."

Grace rolled her eyes. "No you haven't."

Luke took a sip of coffee and said with full sincerity, "Grace, I'm a first responder. I know what healing looks like."

Grace finally looked up, laughing. "Okay, dramatic."

Elle smiled to herself.

Across the room, Paisley breezed in wearing scrubs, cheeks pink from the cold air, eyes bright from her shift. Owen followed a few minutes behind carrying a crate of milk like it weighed nothing, his breath visible in soft puffs as he stepped inside.

Paisley tried not to notice him.

She noticed him.

She greeted him like she greeted everyone, big, warm, confident, but her voice softened just slightly. Owen's calm kindness met her energy without flinching, like he'd been built for steady love.

And somewhere between the hum of the espresso machine and the quiet laughter at the community table, Elle felt the truth settle again:

God was moving. Not in flashy ways. In faithful ones.

* * *

The first testimony came before Elle could even finish wiping down the counter.

Trevor walked in, cheeks flushed from the cold, wearing a clean work jacket with a logo stitched over the chest. He looked different than he had that first week, lighter, stronger.

He approached the counter like he was walking toward something holy.

Elle smiled. "Good morning."

Trevor grinned. "I brought proof."

"Proof?" she asked.

He tapped the logo on his jacket. "I'm officially employed."

Elle's heart swelled. "Trevor..."

He shook his head quickly, eyes bright. "No. Listen. That first conversation h ere... it changed something. Luke introduced me, yeah. But also..." He swallowed, emotion rising. "I felt like God hadn't forgotten me anymore."

Elle blinked fast.

Trevor reached into his pocket and pulled out a folded prayer card, worn at the edges like it had been handled a lot.

"This was my first prayer request," he said, voice thick. "I wrote it here. I didn't even know what I was doing. I just... needed help."

He handed it to her.

Elle unfolded it carefully.

I need work. I'm scared I won't be able to provide. God, please open a door.

Elle looked up, eyes shining.

Trevor nodded, swallowing. "He did."

Janelle stepped closer quietly, reading the card. Her smile was soft and reverent. "Praise God," she whispered.

Trevor exhaled, relief and gratitude in one breath. "Yeah."

Then he walked to the prayer wall and pinned his old request beneath the section labeled Praises, writing one final line beneath it:

ANSWERED. GOD PROVIDED.

When he turned back, he looked at Elle like she'd helped build more than a cafe.

"You don't know what this place means," he said quietly.

Elle swallowed hard. "Maybe I do," she whispered.

* * *

Later that morning, Janelle came to the counter holding a stack of prayer cards.

Her eyes were glossy.

Elle immediately stepped around the counter. "Janelle?"

Janelle shook her head, smiling like she was both overwhelmed and grateful. "Come look."

Elle followed her to the wall.

The Praises section had grown. Not just a little. It was overflowing.

Cards layered over one another. Handwriting from every generation.

My marriage is healing.

My son came home.

Cancer is in remission.

We got the house.

My anxiety is quiet today. Thank You, Jesus.

My daughter is sleeping through the night. Praise God.

I had the courage to forgive.

I felt God for the first time in years.

Elle stared, hand covering her mouth.

"I didn't realize..." she whispered.

Janelle's voice was soft. "People are bringing their real lives here, Elle."

Elle blinked hard. "This was all Him."

Janelle nodded, her expression tender. "Yes."

They stood there for a moment longer, two women simply witnessing the faithfulness of God written in pen and tears and gratitude.

Then Janelle reached into the basket and pulled out one more card.

"This one came in yesterday," she said quietly. "I thought you should see it."

Elle took it.

The handwriting was shaky.

I almost didn't make it another day. But I walked in here and felt hope. Thank you.

Elle's vision blurred.

She pressed the card gently to her chest.

She thought about the bridge.

About standing over the river and asking God for weary people. About praying that someone who was exhausted and empty and couldn't see a reason to keep going might walk through a door in Willow Creek and feel something shift.

She had prayed that prayer not knowing what it would look like.

Now she was holding it.

"Jesus," she whispered.

Janelle placed a hand on her shoulder. "He's doing what you prayed He would."

Elle nodded, tears slipping down her cheeks. "He is."

* * *

At the community table, the young moms group had grown too.

It was no longer just three women awkwardly introducing themselves over lukewarm coffee and tired smiles. Now it was eight.

Strollers lined the wall like a small parade of motherhood. Diaper bags hung from chair backs. Little hands gripped warm cocoa cups. Cheerios appeared mysteriously in places no one could explain.

And in the middle of it all, laughter.

Real laughter. The kind that came from people who had been lonely for too long and finally found a place to breathe.

Elle walked past with a tray of muffins and heard one of the moms say softly, "I didn't have any friends in town."

Another mom nodded, voice quiet. "Me either. I cried in my car the first time I came here."

Grace leaned in, eyes wide. "Wait, you cried in your car too?"

All the women laughed, and the sound carried warmth across the cafe.

Paisley, sitting with them for a moment between shifts, nodded seriously. "Ladies, the car-crying season is real."

They laughed again, but then the conversation softened.

Janelle's voice rose gently, guiding without leading, offering Scripture like a warm blanket.

"Jesus doesn't shame tired hearts," she said. "He invites them."

One mom wiped her eyes. "I just want to be a good mom."

Grace reached across the table without thinking and squeezed her hand. "You are. And you're not alone."

Elle stepped back quietly, letting the moment stay theirs.

This was community. This was the church beyond Sunday. This was what she had longed for in the city and never found.

And now it was happening in a little cafe in Willow Creek.

* * *

That afternoon, Aaron returned.

Elle recognized him immediately, not because his face was unforgettable, but because the peace in his eyes was.

He walked in slower this time. Not hesitant. Like someone who belonged.

He approached the counter, holding a small notebook. "Hi," he said quietly. "Elle?"

Elle smiled. "Hi, Aaron."

He swallowed. "I started going to The Gathering Place."

Elle's heart lifted. "You did?"

He nodded, eyes shining. "I sat in the back. I didn't want to be seen."

Elle nodded gently. "That's okay."

Aaron's voice softened. "But I heard worship and...it felt like coming home. I didn't know I missed God that much."

Elle blinked quickly, emotion rising again.

Aaron pulled a folded paper from his notebook. "I wrote something," he said. "I don't know who it's for, but...I think it's for here."

He handed it to her.

Elle opened it slowly.

Thank You for meeting me at my lowest. Thank You for saving me. Help me live like I've been rescued.

Elle's throat tightened completely.

"Can I put it on the wall?" she asked softly.

Aaron nodded. "Please."

As he pinned it beneath Praises, he turned back with a faint smile. "I brought someone with me," he said.

Elle glanced toward the doorway.

A younger man stood there, hands shoved deep in his pockets, eyes wary.

Aaron nodded toward him. "My brother."

Elle's heart squeezed.

The ripple effect. Already.

"Tell him he's welcome," Elle whispered.

Aaron's shoulders eased as if he'd been holding his breath. "Okay."

And Elle watched as Aaron walked back toward the doorway, not as a man who had once wandered in desperate, but as someone now bringing others toward hope.

* * *

Near the end of the day, Luke stood at the counter finishing his coffee while Grace stacked children's books in the corner.

Luke watched her for a moment, quieter than usual.

"You're going to be a good teacher," he said.

Grace froze slightly, then kept stacking. "You say that like you know."

Luke shrugged. "I do know."

Grace finally turned, brows lifted. "Based on what?"

Luke looked slightly uncomfortable, like compliments weren't his natural language. "Based on how you talk to kids," he said. "Based on how you notice people. Based on how you show up."

Grace's smile softened into something more tender.

"Well," she said, voice quieter now, "you show up too."

Luke's gaze held hers for a beat longer than necessary.

Then he cleared his throat and pointed awkwardly at the reading corner. "Those chairs are...still small."

Grace laughed, grateful for the release. "Yes, Luke. Kids are still small."

Luke smiled into his cup.

And Elle watched from behind the counter thinking:

Oh, this story is going to be beautiful.

* * *

That night, after the last customer left and the chairs were reset, Elle stepped outside into the cold air.

Eli followed a moment later, hands in his jacket pockets, breath visible as he stood beside her.

They looked through the window at the cafe, warm lights, prayer wall covered in testimony, community table ready for tomorrow.

"It's bigger than I imagined," Elle whispered.

Eli nodded, gaze steady. "Yeah."

He looked at the floor just inside the doorway.

The threshold.

He had knelt there in April, boards lifted, the old wood resisting the pry bar the way old things resisted being opened. He had worked carefully, the way his father had taught him to work with things that had been standing a long time. You didn't tear into them. You listened first.

He had placed the Bible with both hands.

He had nailed everything back down over it, one board at a time, and the whole time he had understood with a clarity that didn't require words that this was not a construction decision. It was a declaration. He was saying: whatever goes up from here goes up over this. The Word first. Everything else after.

He had built that way his whole career without always knowing why. His father had modeled it without naming it. You built on what would hold. You didn't cut corners on the foundation because the foundation was the thing nobody saw and the thing everything rested on.

Standing here now, looking through the window at the answered prayers on the wall and the mugs with the cross etched into the clay and the table where Trevor had pinned *ANSWERED. GOD PROVIDED* beside his original card, Eli understood something with the same quiet clarity.

Asking her would be the same.

Not the ring. Not the words. The intention underneath them. The decision, made in full knowledge of what it cost and what it required, to build something on the right foundation. To say: whatever goes up from here goes up over this. Over faith. Over the Word. Over the deliberate choice to make something that was meant to last.

He had spent years moving from town to town carrying his father's tools and his father's faith and a wound he had told himself was about Sarah but had really been about whether he could trust his own judgment again. Whether he could read a structure correctly. Whether what looked load-bearing actually was.

He knew now.

He had known for a while.

He had just needed to stand on it long enough to be sure.

A pause.

Then he turned slightly toward her. "Can I ask you something?"

Elle looked up. "Yes."

Eli's voice was calm, steady, but there was something intentional underneath it.

"Will you meet me here Sunday morning?" he asked. "Before we open."

Elle's heart shifted. Not panic. Not fear. A soft knowing.

"After church?" she asked.

He nodded. "Yeah."

Elle held his gaze, searching his face. Something in his eyes was warm and sure.

"Okay," she whispered. "I will."

Eli exhaled slowly, like he'd been holding that question carefully.

Then he nodded once, voice quiet. "Good."

They stood side by side, the cold air around them and warmth behind them.

And Elle felt it again, the truth written into every answered prayer card on the wall:

God was faithful. He was moving. He was building.

The cafe had become a lighthouse in Willow Creek.

And something else was coming.

Something she could feel in her bones.

Not rushed. Not forced. Just steady, like every good thing God ever built.

CHAPTER THIRTY-ONE

Foundation

Sunday in Willow Creek never hurried.

It arrived gently, crisply, like the town itself exhaled into rest.

Elle sat in the sanctuary of The Gathering Place with Grace on one side and Janelle on the other, the air filled with quiet conversation and the soft tuning of instruments on stage. Strings of warm lights framed the platform, and the worship team moved with calm purpose, not performance. The room felt like expectancy, like people had come ready to lay down what they carried and pick up what God was offering.

Elle rested her hands in her lap and breathed.

This place still amazed her. Not because it was perfect. But because it was real.

Grace leaned over and whispered, "If I cry today, no one mention it."

Elle smiled. "You cry every Sunday."

Grace nodded solemnly. "Yes. I'm consistent."

Janelle's quiet laugh rose beside them.

As the house lights dimmed and the first chord rang out, the room stilled.

Then worship rose.

Not loud at first, just steady, like a river building strength. A familiar song began, simple and presence-heavy, the kind that didn't ask for big emotion but invited honesty. Hands lifted slowly around the room. Voices joined, some strong, some trembling, some barely audible.

Elle closed her eyes.

She sang softly, not as a worship leader, not as someone trying to be heard, just as a daughter of God grateful to be home.

The lyrics washed over her like balm.

She thought about The Overflow Cafe.

The prayer cards.

The answered testimonies.

The young moms laughing through tears.

Aaron bringing his brother.

Trevor's job.

Frank's quiet nod from the window seat.

She thought about the quiet miracle of community.

And then her mind drifted, inevitably, toward Eli.

She opened her eyes.

Across the sanctuary, near the sound booth, he stood with Luke, focused, steady, hands loosely at his sides, worshiping with the same quiet sincerity he brought to everything.

Eli's gaze lifted for a moment.

Their eyes met. Just a second. But it held warmth, an unspoken steadiness that made her chest soften.

His expression didn't change dramatically. It didn't need to.

It simply said: I'm here.

Elle turned her attention back to worship as the song built, the room lifting in one voice.

And for a moment, it felt like heaven had leaned close.

* * *

After worship, Pastor Nathan stepped to the front with his Bible open, eyes scanning the room with the calm strength of someone who loved his people deeply.

"Good morning," he said warmly. A chorus of greetings returned. He smiled. "I've been thinking a lot this week about foundations."

Elle's heart gave a small, quiet leap.

Pastor Nathan continued, voice steady. "Not the kind we pour for buildings, though some of you have been doing a lot of that lately." A few people chuckled. "I mean the kind we build our lives on."

He turned a page.

"Jesus tells a story about two men who built houses. One built on sand. One built on rock. The storm came for both."

The room quieted.

"The storm didn't prove who God loved," Pastor Nathan said, his voice gentle but firm. "It proved what they were standing on."

Elle felt the words settle into her spirit like something meant for her.

Pastor Nathan's gaze softened. "Some of you have walked through storms you never expected. Some of you have rebuilt after loss. Some of you are building something new and holy, and it has required more patience and trust than you thought you had."

Elle swallowed.

Beside her, Janelle nodded slowly, eyes already shining.

Pastor Nathan continued, "And let me say this clearly: delays do not mean denial. They often mean reinforcement."

A quiet murmur of agreement moved through the room.

"God is not just interested in what you build," he said. "He's interested in who you become while you're building it."

Elle blinked quickly.

Grace leaned over and whispered, "Okay. That one hurt in a holy way."

Elle smiled through the tightness in her throat.

Pastor Nathan lifted his hand slightly. "So if you're in a season where you're building, keep building. Keep obeying. Keep praying. Keep showing up. The storm will come, but your foundation will hold if it's Christ."

Then he smiled again, softer. "And if you've been praying for provision, for community, for restoration, look around. God is moving in Willow Creek."

People nodded. Some wiped tears quietly.

Elle sat still, breathing.

It felt like the message had wrapped itself around the story of the last few months and tied it into a bow that said: God was faithful. God is faithful. God will keep being faithful.

As service ended, Pastor Nathan prayed one final blessing over the congregation, and worship rose again, one song, bright and hopeful, voices lifted like joy was something you could breathe in.

Elle sang with her whole heart. Not because life was perfect. Because God was.

* * *

Outside, the crisp air held the scent of leaves and Sunday morning coffee drifting from downtown.

People lingered in the parking lot, laughing, chatting, making the same plans they made every Sunday now.

"Overflow after this?" someone called.

"Always," another person replied.

Grace slipped her arm through Elle's. "Okay," she said, eyes shining. "I know this is normal now, but it still feels like a miracle."

Elle smiled. "It is."

Janelle walked beside them, calm and glowing. "It's a miracle we get to participate in."

Elle nodded, heart full.

She spotted Eli a few yards ahead, talking briefly with Luke near the edge of the lot. Luke clapped Eli's shoulder with a grin, then peeled away toward the crowd like he'd just been dismissed from a mission he'd been trying not to smile about.

Eli turned.

His gaze found Elle immediately.

There was something different in his expression today, still steady, still calm, but intentional. Like his heart had already chosen its words.

He walked toward her, closing the distance with quiet certainty.

"Hey," he said softly.

Elle smiled. "Hey."

Eli's eyes flicked to Grace and Janelle, then back to Elle. "Can I steal you for a minute?"

Grace's face lit up like a fireworks show. Janelle's smile softened, knowing and gentle.

Grace squeezed Elle's hand once and whispered, "I will be normal."

Elle whispered back, "You will not."

Grace grinned. "Correct."

Janelle touched Elle's shoulder lightly. "Go," she said softly. "We'll meet you there."

Elle nodded, breath steady.

Eli extended his hand.

Elle placed hers in it.

Warm. Steady.

The moment felt like walking into something God had already written.

* * *

The walk to The Overflow Cafe was short, but it felt like crossing a threshold inside her own heart.

They walked slowly.

Elle was aware of his hand in hers, the easy weight of it, the way they had arrived at this without ceremony or announcement, the way most of the best things in her life lately had arrived, not through striving, but through staying.

The street was Sunday-quiet around them. A family passed going the other direction, kids running ahead, a dad carrying a baby on his hip, a mom talking animatedly with her hands. They smiled at Elle and Eli as they passed.

Neither of them spoke for a moment.

Then Eli said, voice low and easy, "Do you remember the first time I walked into the bakery?"

Elle smiled. "You were very professional."

"I was trying to be."

"I could tell."

He looked at her sideways, a quiet warmth there. "I'd heard the worship music from the sidewalk. Before I even opened the door. I stood there for a second, just listening."

Elle blinked.

She hadn't known that.

"I thought," he continued, "whoever is in there, they're not performing that. That's just who they are."

Her throat tightened.

"And then I walked in and it was you," he said. Simply. Like it was the most natural conclusion in the world.

Elle was quiet for a moment, watching the sidewalk ahead of them. She thought of Psalm 23, the one she had read on the worst night of her year, the one that had sent her home. She thought of the key on the nightstand beside her Bible. She thought of kneeling on those old floors and asking God to use the space for something more than coffee.

She had not imagined this when she prayed that prayer.

She should have. God's answers had a way of being more specific than the prayers.

"I'm glad you stayed," she said softly. "In Willow Creek. I'm glad you didn't keep moving."

Eli was quiet for a beat.

"So am I," he said.

Not more than that.

It didn't need to be more than that.

The Overflow Cafe came into view at the end of the block, sunlight catching the windows.

Elle felt something settle in her chest. The peace that had been growing for months, steady and unhurried, the kind that didn't depend on circumstances but rested somewhere deeper than them.

Still Yours, she thought, looking at the building.

Then she looked at the man beside her.

Still Yours.

As they reached the cafe, sunlight caught the windows and made the string lights inside glow faintly even in daytime.

Eli paused near the entrance. "Before we go in," he said quietly.

Elle looked at him.

His expression was calm, but his eyes held depth, something tender and resolved.

"You remember the first day we placed the Bible beneath this doorway?" he asked.

Elle's heart softened instantly. "I do."

Eli nodded slowly. "That stayed with me."

He rested his free hand lightly on the doorframe, gaze lowered for a moment like he was honoring something unseen beneath their feet.

"You built this place on the Word of God," he said. "Before anything else was visible. Before anyone could see what it would become."

Elle's throat tightened.

Eli looked back at her, voice gentle but steady. "And watching you...I realized you didn't just build a cafe that way."

He swallowed. "You built your life that way."

Elle blinked quickly.

Eli's voice lowered. "I prayed for a woman who loved Jesus more than she loved me. I prayed for a woman who would make me want to be more faithful, not just more romantic." A faint smile flickered. "Someone who would remind me that the best love stories start with God."

Elle's eyes filled.

Eli breathed in slowly, holding her gaze. "And then God brought me you."

The world around them faded. Not because it disappeared. But because this moment had become holy.

Eli's hand squeezed hers gently.

"I don't want to build anything in this life without you," he said, voice thick now, the steadiness still there but softened by emotion. "Not a cafe. Not a home. Not a future. Not ministry. Not ordinary mornings."

Elle's tears slipped free.

Eli released her hand slowly, just long enough to reach into his jacket pocket.

Elle's breath caught.

He pulled out a small velvet box.

For a heartbeat, everything inside her went still.

Eli lowered himself to one knee right there, at the entrance of The Overflow Cafe, above the hidden Bible beneath the threshold.

Gasps rose behind them.

Someone whispered, "Oh my goodness."

Grace made a sound that could only be described as a holy squeal.

Eli looked up at Elle, eyes shining, voice steady even through the emotion.

"Elle," he said softly, "will you marry me?"

Elle's hand flew to her mouth.

Tears blurred the edges of everything.

The cafe. The sidewalk. The people gathering behind them. The church family. The friends.

All she could see clearly was him.

The man God had brought into her life with patience and purpose. The man who had waited for God's timing. The man who had shown up, steady and faithful, again and again. The man kneeling before her not with flashy words, but with a foundation.

Elle inhaled, trembling.

Then she laughed through tears, the kind of laugh that came from joy so full it had nowhere else to go.

"Yes," she whispered.

Eli's eyes closed briefly like he was thanking God before he even moved.

"Yes," Elle said again, stronger now, voice shaking with laughter and tears. "Yes, Eli. A thousand times yes."

The town erupted.

Grace screamed, "YESSSS!" like she was at a revival and a concert at the same time.

Paisley burst into tears immediately. "I'm crying! I said I wouldn't cry!"

Janelle covered her mouth, eyes shining, whispering, "Thank You, Jesus."

Luke grinned so wide it made his whole face look younger, shaking his head like he couldn't believe he got to witness something this good.

Owen clapped quietly, smiling in that steady, grounded way that somehow made the joy feel even more real.

Caleb whooped. Micah smiled like an artist watching a masterpiece land exactly where it should.

And Mara stood with one hand pressed to her chest, tears slipping down her cheeks, her smile soft and full of hope. As if this moment didn't just celebrate Elle. It reminded her: God still writes beautiful endings.

And at the edge of the crowd, hands folded, eyes shining, stood Ben.

He had walked over from the parking lot without anyone quite noticing, drawn by the gathering the way he had always been drawn toward wherever his people were.

He looked like a man who had just watched something Marqua would have loved.

His eyes were full.

His shoulders were straight.

And the expression on his face was one Elle had seen only once before, in the cafe, the day she had prayed over him and spoken her faith teacher's name aloud.

The expression of a man who was not as alone as he had been.

* * *

Eli rose to his feet, hands gentle as he opened the box and slid the ring onto Elle's finger.

It fit perfectly. Of course it did.

He cupped her face with both hands then, reverent and full of love, and pressed his forehead to hers for a moment.

"Thank You," he whispered.

Elle nodded, unable to speak around her tears.

Then Eli pulled her into his arms.

Elle held on, laughing and crying into his shoulder, feeling the steadiness she had come to trust wrap around her like home.

Applause broke out again, and someone behind them shouted, "Open the cafe! We need celebratory lattes!"

Grace yelled, "YES! ENGAGEMENT LATTES FOR EVERYONE!"

Luke muttered, "I support this ministry."

Paisley laughed through tears. "I'm writing a prayer request that says 'Help me stop crying' and pinning it to the wall right now."

Janelle sniffed and said softly, "Don't you dare stop crying. This is holy."

Elle pulled back from Eli just enough to see his face again.

His eyes were bright. Steady. Full.

"I love you," he said quietly, simple, sure, without fanfare.

Elle's breath caught.

Then she smiled through tears. "I love you too."

Not louder than it needed to be. Not for the crowd.

For him. For God. For this moment.

Eli took her hand, ring catching sunlight, and together they stepped over the threshold into The Overflow Cafe.

* * *

Inside, the lights glowed warmly.

The prayer wall held testimonies.

The community table sat ready for laughter and tears and Scripture and life.

Elle looked around at the people filling the space, friends she'd prayed for without knowing their names, neighbors carrying hope, a church family that felt like an embrace.

Then she looked at Eli beside her, their hands linked, their future unfolding.

Joy rose in her chest so strong it felt like worship.

"Jesus," she whispered, voice barely audible, "You did this."

The cafe held the warmth of it all around them: coffee poured, laughter rising, tears falling freely, prayer cards pinned to a wall that had once been covered in ink and hope and then painted over and then filled again, always filled again.

Eli's thumb moved lightly across her ring.

Elle looked down at it once.

Light caught the stone.

She closed her eyes, and in the brief quiet before the celebration swept them back in, she thought of the bridge. The river. The downstream turn. The cold railing under her palms and the words she had wept into the morning air:

I want to be known. And I am asking You to make that feel possible again.

He had.

She squeezed Eli's hand.

He squeezed back.

And beneath their feet, unseen but unwavering, the Word of God remained the foundation.

Epilogue

E pilogue

One Week Later

The ring still surprised her.

Not in an anxious way. In the way of something so new it had not yet settled into ordinary. She kept noticing it at unexpected moments. The weight of it against the mug handle. The faint catch of morning light when she reached past the espresso machine. The way her hand looked different now. Not smaller or larger. Just marked.

She was getting used to it.

She was in no hurry to finish getting used to it.

* * *

The Overflow Cafe smelled like espresso and Clara's honey rolls and something Elle had stopped trying to name. The name didn't matter as much as the fact of it. The fact being: the place felt like what it was built to be.

Every morning when she unlocked the door and stepped inside, that was the first thing she felt. Not pride. Not relief. Something older and quieter than either.

Rightness.

The kind that came from obedience rather than achievement. The kind you couldn't manufacture or hustle toward. You could only receive it, and she was learning to do that without flinching.

* * *

He came through the front door at seven forty, tool bag over one shoulder, jacket on against the October air. Not staying. Just stopping.

That was new. The stopping.

He had a renovation starting on the east side of town, a Victorian on Birch Street that needed its bones read before anyone touched anything. He had been talking about it all week the way he talked about buildings he respected. With the attentiveness of a man who understood that old things deserved to be listened to before they were changed.

Elle had his coffee ready before he reached the counter.

He accepted it with the quiet that had always been his language and looked at her the way he had been looking at her all week, like something had settled in him that he had not known was unsettled until it finally came to rest.

"New project today," she said.

"Victorian on Birch." He wrapped both hands around the cup. "Good bones."

"Of course it does," she said. "You would not have taken it otherwise."

The corner of his mouth lifted. He looked around the cafe, the way he always did when he arrived somewhere, slow and attentive, taking honest stock.

"You good here?" he asked.

She looked at the room. At the prayer wall and the community table and the door still swinging from the last customer through it.

"Yeah," she said. "We're good here."

He held her gaze a moment. Then nodded once, the way he nodded when something was exactly what it was supposed to be and picked up his tool bag.

"I'll be back by close," he said.

"I know," she said.

She watched him push through the door into the morning.

She had never once in her life thought she would feel this way about a man walking out a door. Like the leaving was safe because the coming back was certain.

She turned back to the counter.

There was work to do.

* * *

Grace arrived at seven fifty-three, apron already tied, moving through the morning with her characteristic brightness. She restocked the prayer cards. She reorganized the pastry case in a way that was technically correct and completely unsolicited. She made two customers laugh before their orders were ready.

Elle watched her from behind the counter.

Grace was herself, fully and completely, the way she always was. And also, just behind her eyes, there was something she was carrying. Something she had not set down and had not named out loud, at least not to Elle.

Elle recognized that. She had worn it herself, in a different season.

The weight of a question you were still learning to trust God with.

She didn't ask. Grace would say it when she was ready.

She simply refilled her sister's water without being asked and let the morning continue.

* * *

By midmorning the rush had softened into the rhythm Elle was learning to love best. Frank in his window seat, hands around his mug, the quiet satisfaction of a man returned to a place that had always mattered to him. The prayer wall full. The community table holding two women she didn't know yet but would.

Elle stood behind the counter and looked at all of it.

At the door that kept opening.

At the people who kept coming through it.

At all of it, held up by something no one could see but everyone who walked in could somehow feel.

You never thought about foundations.

You only knew them by what they held.

Elle picked up the mug with the cross etched into the clay and wrapped both hands around it and let the warmth move through her palms.

Still Yours, she thought.

Always.

Also, by Jess Merkt

The Willow Creek Romance Series continues with
Walking Through Fire
Coming in Summer of 2026